WON'T BACK DOWN

WAYWARD SONS
BOOK 1

HARPER JACKSON

TAKE THE LEAP PUBLISHING

PROLOGUE
SAWYER

"Is it safe?"

The voice came from under a blanket in the back seat. I looked out through the windshield of my ancient clunker of a truck and scanned the beach. Practically every student from Sutter's Ferry High School was here, drinking and dancing around a massive bonfire. This was the annual unofficial summer kickoff for us locals on Hatterwick Island. I was pretty sure my passenger was going to hate every minute of this party, but that was her call, not mine.

"Yeah, no grownups waiting to rat you out to your parents. You can come out."

A slim figure popped up in my rearview mirror, caramel hair mussed from the blanket, cheeks flushed, and hazel eyes sparkling with excitement. Willa Hollingsworth scrambled awkwardly into the front seat, and I absolutely did not notice the long, tanned legs beneath her cutoffs, or the swimsuit top peeking out from under her Oxford shirt. She was my best friend's little sister, for God's sake.

Jace might just rip me a new one for helping her sneak out tonight.

"Before you head out there, let's go over the rules."

One slim brow arched in an expression that was the sole betrayal of her privileged upbringing. "Rules?"

"Yeah, rules." I smiled as her eyes darted away to the beach before she pulled them back to me. I could practically feel the anticipation coming off her, but there were nerves, too. In all likelihood, she'd spend a good part of the night cuddled up with someone's dog. "You're probably the last girl on the island who needs to hear this, but I have to say it anyway."

She folded her hands primly in her lap and waited patiently, those long-lashed eyes fixed on mine. They were a mix of gold and green with streaks of gray. A guy could get lost in those eyes. In the worlds behind them...

"I'm listening."

Damn it, where was I? Oh, right.

I ticked off the points on my fingers. "Don't take drinks from anyone. Pull the can straight from the cooler yourself. Guard whatever you drink and don't leave it unattended. Don't go anywhere with randos. Don't leave without me, Jace, or one of the other Wayward Sons. If anybody makes you feel uncomfortable, find one of the four of us. If you want to go home, no matter how early, you come find me. I've got no problem leaving whenever you're ready."

That was too true. I wasn't going to come tonight at all. Given what I lived with, hanging out with a bunch of drunk classmates was hardly my idea of a good time. But I never could say no to Willa.

"Understood." The corners of her mouth tipped up in a shy smile that made my heart do a little shimmy in my chest. "Thank you for helping me escape the tower, Sawyer."

I wished I could do that for her more often. I'd never understood why Willa's parents kept her on such a short leash. They let Jace do whatever he wanted, more or less. Was it because she was a girl? Because she was two years younger? Or was it because she wasn't quite like everyone else, and they were afraid she'd tarnish the Hollingsworth name somehow? Being shy and uncomfortable in the public eye was nothing to be ashamed of—unless you were a Hollingsworth, I guess. But how was she ever going to get comfortable with it if they never let her go anywhere and do anything?

"Anytime, Wren."

I grinned when her cute little nose wrinkled at the nick-name. I'd been calling her that since we were kids, because she'd always been one to hide in the corner of a room full of people, the way a wren would roost in the corner of a porch.

Rolling her eyes at me, she slid out of the truck. She wasn't a kid anymore, and she wanted to be part of things, just like everyone else.

I followed a minute later, close enough to keep an eye out, but not so close anyone would think we were here together. Not that I had a problem being seen with her, but the island's princess showing up with the son of the town drunk would have made for gossip that might get back to her parents. They had enough of a problem with Jace's friendship with me—no sense kicking that beehive.

Willa didn't stride straight into the crowd the way her brother would have. She reached the sand and skirted the edges of the group, darting forward and back like a sandpiper in the surf, probably looking for her friends.

"Jace is gonna kick your ass for bringing her," Ford announced, making his way toward me with Bree, a girl who'd been as much his shadow as his partner in crime since elementary school.

"She's got just as much right to celebrate the end of school as the rest of us," Bree argued.

"I know that, and you know that, but with all these people here? No way this isn't getting back to her parents."

"I'll talk to Jace." And I needed to do that before he spotted his sister, but I wanted to make sure she was okay first. She might just get so overwhelmed by all the people that she'd want to leave in the next ten minutes. It wouldn't be the first time.

"Surprised to see you out tonight," Ford continued. "You said you weren't coming."

Not wanting to admit that Willa was the only reason I'd changed my mind, I shrugged. "It's the start of our last summer before you and Jace head to the mainland for college. Shame to waste any of it."

I didn't know what I'd do without the other Wayward Sons. These guys were brothers to me in all but blood. A family we'd all chosen when our own had fallen short. Well, except for Ford, who'd won the parent lottery. His moms had unofficially adopted us all. But this would be the first time we'd split up for any real length of time, and that was just one of the changes barreling down on us that I didn't know how to handle. Ford and Jace were headed for lives that would take them away from here, and Rios and I would stay. Rios to protect his sisters from their hot-headed father. Me to look after my own dad, to make sure he didn't drown in the bottle he'd fallen into years ago, when he lost my mother and baby sister in childbirth. And Rios and I would look after Willa, too, in Jace's absence—as best we could, from our positions in what their parents considered the gutter.

"Then let's get to it, my man." Ford swung an arm around my shoulders and steered me toward some coolers.

I couldn't keep my eye on Willa without being obvious about it, but nobody else had a chaperone hovering, and I needed to find Jace anyway. Willa just wanted to be a normal high school girl for the night, and there wasn't a guy on the island who'd lay a hand on her with all four us here. She'd be fine without me going all mother hen on her.

I scooped up a Coke and wandered toward a group of girls

on the far side of the bonfire. Chances were, Jace would be at the center of them, holding court. It might've been easy to hate him for that, but for the fact that he was just such a damned good guy. He didn't lord his position in the high school hierarchy over anybody, and not once, since we became friends in the first grade, had he ever made me feel like less. That wasn't something I could say about most of our classmates.

Turned out, he wasn't holding court alone. Rios sat on a picnic table, guitar in hand, singing and smoldering at Cara Conroy, the junior he'd had his eye on since midterms. She sat at his feet, clearly eating up all that Latino swagger and the smooth baritone of his voice. I did him a solid by not bursting into laughter. Who was I to interrupt his fun?

Instead, I came up beside Jace, keeping my voice low. "Need to talk to you about something."

"What's up?"

"Willa's here."

His head snapped toward me. "What?"

"She wanted to come."

"This is no place—"

"She's fine." I pointed to where I'd spotted her down by the shoreline, predictably playing with someone's dog. Rios's younger sister, Gabi, and another of their friends, Gwen Busby, were with her. "It's not about drinking or hooking up. You know that, man. She just wants to be like everybody else. And there won't be much of that once you leave for school."

Jace's shoulders came down a notch. I knew he worried about what would happen when he wasn't there to run interference with their parents. "Alright. Fine. You'll keep an eye on her?"

"Of course. The party isn't gonna go on all that long, anyway. A storm's rolling in." Now that I wasn't focused exclusively on Willa, I could feel the electricity in the air and see the boil of clouds in the distance to the east, a stark contrast to the sunset wash of sky behind us.

"Weather guys said that was going to miss us."

"They're wrong." I knew it with the certainty of a fifth-generation fisherman who'd grown up as much on the water as on the island.

Jace searched out his sister again. "Hope they're right, for her sake."

We both watched her for a minute as she romped in the surf with the dog. Assured that she wasn't in danger of an anxiety attack, and that she seemed content, I finally let myself relax a bit. For all I hadn't wanted to be here, it was hard to resist the energy. This was a party, after all, and I was here with the guys who were brothers to me in all but blood.

As twilight gave way to dark, groups began to cluster tighter, and couples started peeling off to find a patch of sand away from the firelight to make out. It wasn't the general air of horniness in the air that had me seeking Willa again, though my brain helpfully offered a flash of those lean, tanned legs. I hadn't seen her for a bit, and I wanted to check in, make sure she was still okay, and that no guys had decided to try their luck with the shy little island princess. Not that I had any kind of claim. I was just looking out for her. Making sure nobody took advantage.

You keep telling yourself that, Malone.

All this noticing I'd been doing of Willa, as definitely *not* a sister, was a problem. That might be the only good thing about Jace leaving in two months: he wouldn't be around to notice and call me on it. Not that I'd dare do anything about it. Shit, Willa deserved so much better than the likes of me. But I needed to get a handle on things and find some way to shove her firmly back into the sister column. Even though she hadn't truly been there for more years than I was willing to admit.

Friends. We were friends. That was all we'd ever be. And that was fine. I was damned lucky to have her as that. A girl like her would've been well within her rights not to give me the time of day, let alone all the shy smiles and deep, quiet conversations we'd shared over the years.

The rumble of thunder had been moving steadily closer over the past hour or so. The air held an electric edge that told me things were gonna get rained out in short order. As if underscoring the point, a bolt of lightning split the sky, lighting up the beach like a beacon. It was enough to get everybody's attention.

From somewhere closer to the fire, I heard Jace call out, "Storm's coming in! Let's get all this wrapped up." Taking charge, as usual. And because he was still a Sutter by blood, folks listened.

He'd trusted me to keep tabs on his sister, so as people began gathering up their gear, I wove through, cursing the lack of light that kept me from seeing faces clearly until I was practically on top of people. Still, as kids began to stream back toward vehicles, I hadn't found her.

Spotting Gabi, I grabbed her arm. "Where's Willa?"

Her eyes widened. "I don't know. I haven't seen her in a while."

She promised she wouldn't leave without one of us.

"What about Gwen? Could she be with her?"

"Maybe. I haven't seen her in a bit either. She said she was going to get food."

I didn't have time to track Gwen down on the off chance she knew where Willa had gone off to.

Where the hell was she?

Starting to get really concerned, I tried to put myself in her head, to imagine where she might have gone. I didn't see the dog she'd been playing with earlier. If she'd gotten overwhelmed, she might have stepped away. While she'd promised not to leave the beach, if she'd taken a walk farther down the sand, she probably thought that didn't count.

Following instinct, I headed north, toward the section of the island that her grandparents owned. It was the largest uninhabited stretch of Hatterwick. She knew that area like the back of her hand. If she'd wanted to get away, that would've felt safe. But would she have headed up the beach or into the woods?

Without a flashlight, searching the woods was a recipe for a sprained ankle. I'd explore the beach for a stretch. If I didn't find her, I'd head back to the truck to grab a light. Breaking into a jog, I headed north along the shoreline. Worst-case scenario, we got caught in the rain. We wouldn't melt. I'd get her home safe, either way.

But when I hadn't found her in any reasonable range of the party, worry rolled in with the tide that was steadily rising. The wind had kicked up, and the storm was all but on top of us now.

"Willa!" I bellowed her name, over and over.

What trouble could she have gotten into on her own? She was too smart to go into the water on this side of the island. She well knew about all the riptides. And she'd hardly risk a swim when an obvious storm was coming.

Maybe I was wrong. Maybe she'd gotten overwhelmed and hadn't been able to force herself to navigate the crowd to find me. Maybe she'd taken herself home. The island was only three miles across at its widest point, and she was no stranger to walking. I should go back, see if she'd found one of the guys. At least grab a flashlight from my truck.

I was just on the verge of turning around when I heard a soft sound beneath the gale winds. What was that?

"Willa?"

I spun in a circle, hunting for the source. And despite all my certainty, I looked toward the water.

In the next flash of lightning, I spotted something white amid the frothing waves.

A slim, pale arm.

Terror turned my insides to ice. "Willa!"

I was already running toward the ocean when I saw that arm disappear beneath the surface.

CHAPTER 1
WILLA

Years later...

"Willa!"

I glanced up from the grant application on my laptop to find one of my oldest friends stepping straight over the long, low planters that edged the perimeter of the outdoor patio space at Panadería de la Isla.

"Gabi!" I shoved up from the table so fast that my massive pit bull, Roy, came to his feet in alarm. He settled on his haunches as I launched myself at her. "I wasn't expecting you until next week!"

"Got in on the latest ferry. I was able to come back a little early. I'm just on my way to the clinic to sign the last of my hiring paperwork."

Pulling back, I beamed at her. "Welcome back to Hatterwick, Dr. Carrera."

Gabi grinned, but I couldn't help but notice it didn't quite reach her eyes. "I do like the sound of that."

"Do you have a few minutes?" I gestured at the empty seat across from mine. "Time for a coffee?" Maybe I could suss out what was going on with her.

"No time for coffee, but I'll sit for a few." She moved toward the table. "This cutie must be Roy. Is he good with pets?"

"He looks terrifying, but he's really a big teddy bear." My hand automatically dropped to scratch just behind his ears, and Roy leaned his bulk against me.

Gabi let him sniff her hand and waited for a nuzzle before she likewise gave him a good ear scritch. "I gotta know. Why Roy?"

"He's black and scowlly, but secretly has a heart of gold, like a certain AFC Richmond player in *Ted Lasso*."

"Ahhh, Roy Kent. I got it."

We took our seats, and I closed the lid of my laptop. "So, when do you start?"

"Three weeks. That'll give me time to find a place and get settled in. For now, I'm gonna be staying with Caroline and Hoyt and the kids."

"I'm sure Aubrey will be beside herself that you're going to be here for her birthday."

"That definitely factored in when I was trying to make arrangements. It's not every day my favorite niece turns seven."

The faint shadow in her eyes faded as she spoke with the unrestrained warmth of someone who loved and valued her family. I loved and valued her family, too. They were so incredibly different from mine, and I was grateful they considered me one of their own. But I always felt a little twinge at the obvious signs of genuine affection. It made me aware of how very alone I was.

Beneath the table, Roy laid his heavy head on my knee.

Okay, never alone with this guy.

I stroked his silky ears, feeling some of the knots loosen. At least, insofar as they ever did when I was out in public. "Have you heard from Rios or any of the other Wayward Sons?"

Gabi shook her head. "Not recently. What about you? Any word from Jace or the others?"

Our brothers and their friends were all deployed hither and yon with the Navy. Unlike Gabi's relationship with Rios, my connection to my own brother was strained, for reasons that really couldn't be addressed when he was thousands of miles away. I'd made my peace with that a long time ago. What I hadn't made peace with was the long stretch of silence from Sawyer.

"No. Nothing." I didn't know if he was on a mission somewhere with poor communication or what, and I was starting to worry. He didn't usually go this long without responding to emails or texts.

He didn't owe me anything. I wasn't exactly family. And while we were friends, things had never been the same as they were Before. And why should they be? I certainly wasn't that same girl. In a very real way, she'd died that night when my heart had stopped.

But if not for him, I wouldn't be sitting here right now.

Shaking off the thought, I determined to focus on my friend. We chatted a few more minutes, catching up since the last phone call we'd managed as her residency in New Orleans was winding down. I wondered if something had happened there that had precipitated her early trip back home, but before I could ask, she shoved back from the table.

"I've gotta get going. Don't wanna keep the new boss waiting."

"No problem. I need to pack up and go check on my grandfather." Not a lie. But I also wanted to get out of here, because now that she was leaving, I was all too aware of the other patrons who'd filled up the surrounding tables while we'd talked. The familiar pressure of being in a crowd was building behind my breastbone.

Gabi's dark eyes shone with sympathy. "How's he doing?"

"He's struggled a lot since Grandma died six months ago."

"I haven't seen you to say it properly, but I'm really sorry for your loss."

"Thanks for that." I accepted the hug she gave, grateful she was finally back on-island.

"Let's get together before Aubrey's birthday party. I want to have a real catch up."

The idea of that sounded fantastic. It had been so many years since we'd been able to hang out without an expiration date. "Absolutely. Text me when you're free."

I left a cash tip on the table and packed up my laptop. Roy immediately rose to his feet. A few other customers cast him a wary glance. Not that he'd made a sound or was focused anywhere but on me. We were no strangers to judgment. It was a big part of why I'd spent so much time training him. I knew he'd face prejudice wherever we went. It was that prejudice that had landed him on the kill list at a shelter on the mainland for a crime no more serious than being a black dog and belonging to a breed that had been terribly maligned by the media. I'd just barely gotten to him in time.

"Time to go, boy."

I picked up his lead, and we hurried down the street to where I'd parked. Not until Roy was loaded into the backseat of my Jeep, his harness clipped to the seatbelt, did I take a full breath. These days of forcing myself to work in public spaces were one of the ways I continued to challenge my social anxiety. I was so much better than I used to be. I'd had to be, in order to support myself since I returned to Hatterwick on my own at eighteen. But it was still hard. That was a big part of why Roy went everywhere with me. He was as much emotional support animal as pet. We'd saved each other. And, okay, the fact that he was massive and kind of terrifying meant most people kept their distance. I was perfectly fine with that.

My shoulders, which had hitched up around my ears by the time I got him loaded into the Jeep, relaxed as we passed the village limits and followed the coastal road north. My grandfather lived as far from Sutter's Ferry as it was possible to get on the island. Sutter House—because, yeah, mine was the founding family many, many generations back on my mom's side—had been built on the highest point, just beyond the maritime forest that occupied the center swath of the island for about eight miles. There was one road cutting through the trees from the Atlantic side to Pamlico Sound. That was a necessary concession my grandparents had made to emergency management a few decades back, when they'd gifted some of the acreage to the island to make a park, which was one of the draws for tourists here on Hatterwick. But the last five or so miles were still privately owned. Developers had been after that acreage for years, but my grandparents had refused to sell—something I was eternally grateful for, as this was my favorite part of the island.

So were the wild horses that still roamed the grasslands and marshes. As I came over a hill, crossing onto Sutter land, I spotted a chestnut mare wheeling away from the edge of the road to race back into the interdune marsh beyond the road. Thought to be descended from the same Spanish horses that spawned the herds on neighboring Corolla and Shackleford Banks further north, the wild horses had always captured my imagination and my heart. They were free in a way I never had been, and I both admired and envied that, spending hours of my childhood, and countless more since I'd returned, tracking and observing them. The herd had shrunk over the years as their habitat had dwindled—something I hoped to do something about, eventually. But Granddaddy hadn't exactly been in the right headspace to talk about conservation efforts. He hadn't been in the right headspace for much of anything since Grandma died. I couldn't blame him for that.

I was grateful I'd managed to reconnect with both of them before she'd passed. I'd cut ties with absolutely everyone in my family, save Jace, when I returned to Hatterwick at eighteen. I hadn't known who I could trust and hadn't been willing to risk ending up under anyone's thumb ever again. It had taken years for them to win my trust. During those years I'd been able to prove to myself that I could stand on my own two feet, without the Hollingsworth name I'd been raised to prize. But I wished I'd had longer with Grandma than the year I'd gotten before a heart attack took her. I'd been too damaged to open up any sooner, though. Hell, I was still damaged in ways literally no one else knew. But that was my burden to bear.

Signs of neglect were everywhere when I pulled up to the house. It was still grand. Three stories, with gabled roofs, lots of windows, and shingled siding. It was one of the few historic structures on the island that hadn't been fully destroyed by one hurricane or another. But those shingles needed a fresh coat of paint, and the foundation plantings around the base were over-grown. I was really going to have to brow-beat Granddaddy into taking on some help. At his age, he couldn't keep up with all this on his own, and I could only do so much.

I let Roy out of the car, and he bounded toward the door, tail already swishing. Noting the wilting potted plants along the walk to the kitchen door, I added watering them to my list. But that could wait. As soon as I had the door open, Roy bolted inside.

"Go find Granddaddy."

The kitchen held a sour smell that I traced to a partly filled bowl of what had probably been cereal. Judging from the pile of dishes, it had been there for a few days. Evidence of multiple partly eaten meals told me I'd need to be having a conversation with him about proper nutrition. Maybe I'd just start coming out here for meals every day.

A sharp bark interrupted my mental list.

"Roy?"

He barked again, more urgently this time, followed by a whine.

Something's wrong.

I hurried through the house, pulling up short when I saw age-spotted legs in worn plaid slippers sticking out from around a corner.

"Granddaddy?" I whispered it once, then said it again as I rushed forward.

He was sprawled on the floor, propped partly against a wall. It looked as if he'd staggered against it and simply slid down.

I knew without touching him that he was gone. No one could have that pallor and live.

Grief rose in my throat, huge and hot, too hard to speak around as Roy whined and nudged Granddaddy's shoulder. His body slumped over like a puppet with cut strings.

The wash of fear was instant and visceral, stealing my breath.

Danger. Not safe. Run.

My vision blurred, flashing white, then black, then white again.

On a cry, I staggered back and—

There was something wet on my face. Groaning, I lifted my hands, fending off... a tongue? Roy. He nosed my face, whining.

What the hell?

Blinking, I stared up at the ceiling, absently registering that one of the bulbs in the hall chandelier was out. I was on the floor. How the hell had I gotten here? Had I blacked out?

Cautiously, I sat up, but the room didn't spin.

Then reality slammed into me like a storm surge as I saw the body again.

Granddaddy was dead, and I was truly alone in the world.

CHAPTER 2
SAWYER

From the forward rail of the ferry, I watched Hatterwick Island creep ever closer as the engines rumbled beneath my feet. The bottom of the chain of islands making up North Carolina's Outer Banks, there was nothing imposing about its sweep of sandy beaches or the sole village of Sutter's Ferry that occupied the southern tip, but my heart sped up, nonetheless. When I'd joined the Navy all those years ago, I'd had no idea I'd be coming home so infrequently. Since the island wasn't exactly quick and easy to get to, short spans of leave had often been spent with my brothers in other locations. But beyond that, a lot of it had to do with the fact that I had no real home to come back to.

The house where I'd lived with my dad had been a rental. I'd let it go after he'd died and I'd enlisted. There'd been no memories I wanted to hang onto there. While I was rich in found family, visiting Rios's sister or Ford's moms still wasn't the same as having a true home waiting for me, and I'd been the guy to turn down leave in the name of taking the jobs others didn't want—a move which had helped me climb the ranks. I'd needed to make something of myself.

For all the good that did me now.

I was coming home with little more to my name than I'd left with. At least my bank account was healthier, so taking things one day at a time for a while wasn't a problem. I had time to figure out what came next.

For today, that was a birthday party.

Would Willa be there?

Though we corresponded regularly through texts and emails, it had been nearly two years since I'd seen her. She'd been on a rare off-island trip the last time I'd been home for a visit, and I'd been simultaneously relieved and disappointed. She was the friend I'd always expected her to be. Nothing more, nothing less.

But things had never been the same between us. I blamed myself for the fact that she'd nearly drowned. Never mind that it had been my hands, my breath, that had brought her back. If not for me, she wouldn't have been out in that storm to begin with. If not for me, she'd never have been dragged away from Hatterwick and had to endure... whatever she'd endured that had put those shadows in her eyes that she never spoke of.

That guilt made it hard to face her. So did the fact that, every time I saw her, I wanted to grab on and never let go. I'd had her life literally in my hands, and I felt responsible for her. Even now. As if I could somehow stand between her and anything or anyone that sought to hurt her. All of which was fucked up, considering the peripheral place I held in her life. But I was here in lieu of her brother as a favor to Jace. I was the one of us who had the flexibility just now, and it wasn't as if I'd say no to my oldest friend. Given that she'd just lost the last of the family she acknowledged, I'd have come anyway. Probably. But coming back to Hatterwick, I'd finally have to confront all those complicated feelings about Willa—the ones her brother knew nothing about—and find a way to live with them.

The ferry captain announced our impending arrival, so I

returned to my truck to wait for my turn to disembark. Twenty minutes later, I rolled off the ferry and onto the island. It felt different coming back this time, knowing there was no ticking time clock dictating my return to service for Uncle Sam. Like maybe I could actually relax and settle and *be* here. Maybe coming back to Hatterwick wasn't such a bad idea after all.

The drive to Caroline and Hoyt's place took less than ten minutes. At thirteen miles long and only three miles across at its widest point, it didn't take long to get anywhere on the island. The multiple vehicles piled in the driveway told me I hadn't missed the party entirely. Wedging my truck in at the end of the line, I climbed out, immediately catching the sounds of revelry from around back. I circled the renovated shingle-style house, now painted a bright, happy turquoise.

The birthday girl spotted me first.

"Uncle Sawyer! Uncle Sawyer!" Aubrey bolted toward me, running as fast as her little legs could carry her, her wild, dark curls trailing like a banner behind her. Before I could warn her not to, she'd hurled herself at me.

Shifting at the last second, I caught her with my good arm, managing to hold in the wince as I scooped her up and onto my hip. "You're getting so big!"

"I'm seven today!"

"I know. Why do you think I'm here?"

Willa was on the far side of the yard. I zeroed in on her like a heat-seeking missile. But there were at least a half-dozen people between me and her, and I had no right to ignore them all to rush to her, even if that was a thing we did.

Which it wasn't.

I spotted Aubrey's mother, Caroline, on the verge of water-works, and headed to her first. "Nope. No way. I know you're doing the preggo thing again, but no crying." I set Aubrey down and pulled the woman, who was the closest thing I had to a sister, in for a tight hug. "Congratulations."

"Thanks for that." She squeezed me tight, tight, before pulling back to study my face. "It's good to see you. We didn't know you had leave, so we weren't expecting you. But there's plenty of food for everybody."

I was gonna have to come clean about that. But for the moment, I'd keep things easy. "It wasn't exactly planned. But it's good to be home."

Bree Cartwright stepped up. "Got a pint with your name on it down at the Brewhouse, if you've got time to stop by while you're here."

It never got less weird seeing her without Ford. But they'd had some falling out when we'd enlisted and hadn't ever patched things up. I was just grateful that her ire hadn't spilled over onto the rest of the Wayward Sons, given she ran the best bar on the island.

"I'll make time. Thanks." I gave her a hug, too, before moving on to shake her grandfather Ed's hand.

Then I came to Willa. Like everyone else, she was dressed for a summer beach party, her sun-streaked hair pulled back into a loose braid that trailed over one shoulder. I noted the signs of strain around her changeable hazel eyes, though her mouth curved into a soft smile I wanted to think was just for me.

"Hey, Wren. I'm sorry about your grandparents." It was a paltry thing to offer, but I had nothing else.

"Thanks."

We stared at each other for a long moment before I gave in to the urge to hug her. The embrace was awkward and didn't last long. Because we'd stopped being hugging friends a long time ago.

"I kept my promise."

Willa angled her head. "Which promise was that?"

I offered a rueful half-smile. "Not to die." She'd issued that edict before I'd boarded the ferry to leave for basic training, right after the last real hug we'd shared.

Her face remained a neutral mask, but I thought I saw relief in her eyes. "I'm grateful for that. What are you doing here?"

Her tone was mild, but I heard the underlying rebuke and knew I'd have to explain myself.

Rocking back on my heels, I shoved my hands into my pockets to keep myself from reaching for her again. "Well, the whole not dying was sort of a near thing."

Amid a chorus of gasps, Willa flinched and stepped toward me before she seemed to catch herself.

"I just finished a two-month stint at Walter Reed, healing up from some injuries. I've been officially honorably discharged for medical reasons. I won't be going back."

She seemed to struggle to hang on to her careful neutrality. "So you're done with the Navy?"

I winced. "Well, the Navy's done with me, anyway." I'd get used to it. Eventually.

"What will you do now?"

That's the sixty-four-thousand-dollar question.

"Come home. I haven't figured anything out yet, but this was my first stop when coming back on-island." I forced a smile that I hoped looked more genuine than it felt. "I couldn't miss Aubrey's big seventh!"

"Yeah!" Aubrey pumped her little fist. "Let's eat!"

As the rest of the assembled guests queued up, Willa didn't move. "Why didn't you tell me?" Her soft voice may as well have been a shout for all that I felt her betrayal.

"I didn't want to worry you." It was the truth, if not the whole of it.

"And you didn't think your silence would make me worry?"

I opened my mouth to protest, but she had a point. One I hadn't considered between surgeries and agonizing PT. "Fair point. I'm sorry."

A behemoth black dog materialized like a ghost at Willa's

side, leaning into her hip. Her hand dropped to his ruff, and something in her posture relaxed incrementally.

"Clearly, this is Roy."

"Yep, this is my baby."

I'd heard about the dog, but this was the first time I'd met him. He was a massive bastard, who could easily take a chunk out of anybody who so much as looked at his mama wrong. His big golden eyes studied me and seemed to say the jury was still out.

Moved along by the rest of the guests, I turned my attention toward filling my plate. I ended up at a table with Bree and Ed. Because she'd been toward the end of the line, Willa seemed to have nowhere left to sit other than next to me. Knowing she'd likely prefer to be at the outside edge, away from the bulk of the guests, I'd chosen the end of the bench closer to the house. It was the kind of concession I'd always made for her, and she glanced at me with something that might have been gratitude before taking her seat.

"It's a hell of a thing, celebrating life one day and mourning death in the same week," Ed muttered.

I blinked and looked at Willa. "Your grandfather's funeral? I didn't realize it hadn't happened yet." Jace hadn't mentioned that. Then again, Jace hadn't known a whole hell of a lot when he'd messaged me.

"Granddaddy wanted to be cremated. That took time. We're having a dual memorial for both him and Grandma in a few days, per their wishes." She cut a piece of burger and fed it to Roy. "I put it off a bit, hoping Jace would be able to come home. But he's out of contact on a mission right now, as usual, so here we are."

No. He'd sent me instead.

Temper flashed that he wasn't here for her when she needed him. Again.

I knew he had his duties, and that their relationship was

strained, but this was fucking ridiculous. He was the only family she had left that she acknowledged, and a funeral likely meant she'd have to face the ones she no longer claimed.

"Are your parents coming?"

Willa stiffened as if I'd hit her with an electric shock. Roy immediately shoved his enormous head under her arm in comfort. "Presumably. They've been informed by my grandparents' attorney. I haven't communicated with them directly."

They'd been fully estranged since she'd turned eighteen, but I hadn't been sure if the recent deaths had changed that. Evidently not. I knew something had happened with her parents during her time off-island. I'd known it that summer I'd joined the Navy, though she'd never talked about it, and I'd left anyway, telling myself that she'd be fine.

She wasn't fine. And I knew the prospect of dealing with them again, on even a limited basis, would have her wound up in knots that even a sailor would be challenged to untie.

"Okay. Where and when?"

She frowned at me. "What?"

"Jace may not be here, but I am. I'm not letting you face them alone."

I didn't want to let her face anything alone ever again. Not if I could help it.

CHAPTER 3
WILLA

"A re we gonna talk about it?"

I hung my purse on a hook in the entryway of the little cottage I shared with Bree and shot my roommate a look. "Are we going to talk about what?"

"Oh, I don't know. The gigantic elephant in the room. Like the fact that Sawyer is back on-island—to stay, apparently—and the first thing he did was seek you out."

If only.

I rolled my eyes. "The first thing he did was come to Aubrey's birthday party. That had nothing to do with me."

"Except his eyes stayed glued to you the entire time, and I'm pretty sure there were points at which he was eye banging you."

My mouth fell open. "He was not!" Sawyer didn't think of me like that. Not that I really had any idea what that would look like. I wasn't exactly adept at reading social cues at the best of times. "Besides, who would do that at a kid's birthday party?"

"A guy who hasn't seen the object of his attraction in two years."

My foolish heart leapt at that. But I absolutely *couldn't* let myself believe any of this. Because believing would give me hope, and that was the last thing I needed. Of course, I'd always been a little bit in love with Sawyer. It was practically in the little sister handbook that I'd fall for at least one of Jace's friends. Sawyer had always been sweet and patient with me, naturally accommodating my social anxiety in a way that never made me feel like the freak I'd so often been accused of being. He'd treated me like a person, not some annoying little sister tagging along, so, naturally, it had been him. And then he'd become my very real hero, risking his life to save mine.

I'd never had an opportunity to even contemplate whether there could be something more between us because, back then, I'd been too young for him, and he was absolutely the kind of noble guy who'd have rules about what was and was not appropriate with his best friend's baby sister. Then my parents had dragged me away, and by the time I'd fought my way home at eighteen, I'd been so damaged, my only focus had been on getting through one day and then the next. There were still days I couldn't look past what was right in front of me.

"Nothing to say to that?" Bree prompted.

"I didn't realize you'd asked a question."

This time, she was the one who rolled her eyes. "How are you feeling about all of this? I know you two are friends. I also know that's not all he is to you."

I still cursed the pitcher of strawberry daiquiris that had loosened my tongue enough to tell her that about five years ago. Having a girlfriend to confide in had seemed like a good idea at the time, and Bree had her own secrets around the Wayward Sons.

"I don't have any idea how to feel. Furious that he was hurt and didn't tell me. Relieved that he's out of the Navy, so he isn't likely to get hurt again." Worrying about him and the rest of them had become standard operating procedure for all of us.

That was what it meant to have family in the military. But it was more with Sawyer, because everything had always been more with him. For me, anyway.

"He's finally home. You should talk to him. Do something about this torch you've been carrying all this time."

Feeling backed into a corner, I dropped onto the sofa next to Roy. "Because that worked out so well for you?"

The moment the words were out of my mouth, I regretted them, even before I saw Bree's flinch. "I'm sorry. I shouldn't have said that."

Bree twitched her shoulders as if she could just shrug off the unpardonable attack I'd made. "We're not talking about me. I'm the one who's been on the outside all this time, remember? I've seen how you two look at each other. If your parents hadn't taken you off-island, and he hadn't gone and joined the Navy, I feel like nature would have taken its course long before now. But here we are. He's back, and you're here, and he wants to help you."

Yeah, he did, and I didn't entirely know what to make of that, other than it was just the sort of guy he was.

I was pitifully relieved that he was going with me up to the house tomorrow. I hadn't been able to make myself go back since I'd found my grandfather, and his body was taken away by the funeral home. I hadn't been able to face it or the fact that I was expected to get the whole place ready to open up for the town to come by and pay their respects. Because I was the last Sutter. Literally, since I'd changed my name the moment I legally could. I'd wanted to put as much distance between me and my parents as humanly possible.

And now they'd be coming back to Hatterwick. I couldn't begin to express all the ways that terrified me. But I didn't want to discuss those fears with Bree. I didn't want to discuss them with anybody, because that would require admitting what had happened to me during those two years I was away from Hatterwick. I didn't talk about that. Not ever.

What I really wanted—perhaps foolishly—was Sawyer. The comfort of his arms. It had been so hard not to give in to that urge to burrow in and hold on when he'd hugged me this afternoon, because no matter how far apart we'd been, he still instinctively felt like my safe place. God, I missed real hugs with him. But everything between us was weird and awkward. Nothing had been quite right since I nearly drowned. We were friends. In some ways, we were extremely close. In others, we might as well be strangers.

Of course, a lot of that was on me. I hadn't let him see my dark side since I came back to Hatterwick. He carried enough guilt over what had happened that night. I might not be able to remember what the hell that was, even now, but I knew in my soul it had nothing to do with him. If I did nothing else, that was something I'd finally make crystal clear—that he bore no responsibility and absolutely needed to forgive himself, because I'd never blamed him. God, when I thought of what he'd risked to swim out and get me? That was a debt I could never fully repay.

"I'm just saying... you deserve a shot at happiness. Both of you. Who's to say that isn't with each other?"

I blinked the room back into focus. "I have too many other things to worry about just now. And you need to get to work."

Not that it would take her more than five minutes to walk down to OBX Brewhouse, the bar she'd taken over from her grandfather. Ed hadn't fully retired. He liked being part of the community too much. But Bree was the one responsible for the expansion into a microbrewery, which had become a destination in and of itself on Hatterwick. Her staff ran like a well-oiled machine, so technically she didn't *have* to go in tonight. But I wanted an end to this well-intentioned attempt at interrogation.

She bit back whatever she'd been about to say. "Lock up after I go. I'll see you in the morning."

"I'll probably be up and out before you're awake." Owning a bar, she tended to keep late hours.

"Fair enough." She grabbed her keys. "But I'll see you at some point tomorrow." The implication being that she wasn't letting this whole thing go for more than the night. Fine. I'd take whatever reprieve I could get.

After she'd gone, I did as ordered, throwing the deadbolt. When I turned from the door, I found Roy staring at me.

"What?"

He blinked big, golden eyes as if to say, *You know what.*

"Okay, yes, maybe she has a point. All the reasons Sawyer and I were a bad idea don't really apply anymore. The age difference doesn't matter now, and we're both here again. But come on, Roy. You know me. I don't date. I don't trust people. Not like that. I don't actually believe in happy, healthy, long-term relationships."

He snorted, the traitor.

"Caroline and Hoyt, and Hoyt's parents, are totally the exceptions, not the rule. I know you haven't met my parents, but trust me. In my experience, marriage is just a leash to control women. That's certainly how it worked with my mom and dad. I won't ever let anyone cage me. Not again."

Roy head-butted my leg in solidarity, and I automatically scratched at his ears. "Not that Sawyer would do that. He's probably the only man on earth I trust implicitly not to hurt me. But all of this is a totally moot point because I'm not looking for anyone. And, frankly, I value his friendship too much to fuck it up. Can you even grasp how mortifying it would be to try to pursue him, make any kind of move toward more, only to get rejected or, worse, pitied? No, thank you. I've had enough pity in my lifetime."

At my dog's rumble of insult, I laughed. "Not 'pittie' the *dog.*

I'll never have enough of you." Laying a smacking kiss on his nose, I sobered. "Besides all the rest, I'm fucked up, pal. In ways that Sawyer couldn't begin to comprehend. How can I even consider putting any of that on him? None of it is his to deal with, and that's not a burden I want to lay on anyone. No, I'll value his friendship as I always have. That's all we can ever be."

CHAPTER 4

SAWYER

"Sawyer Malone, you're not sneaking out, are you?"

I froze, my hand inches from the front doorknob, because that was exactly what I'd been trying to do. Well and truly caught, I blanked the guilt from my face and turned. "I wouldn't dream of it, Mimi."

Delilah Washington—otherwise known as Mimi to Ford and all the rest of the Wayward Sons—smiled knowingly from the kitchen doorway, a hand-thrown mug of coffee in her hands. Probably her own work.

"Come get some breakfast!" This disembodied order came from Delilah's wife, Ford's biological mom, Florence Donoghue —aka Mama Flo.

"Yes, ma'am." Changing directions, I accepted my fate and joined the two women in the kitchen.

I hadn't had any intention of crashing at Ford's moms' place last night, but in true island fashion, by the time Aubrey's birthday party had wrapped up yesterday, they'd heard I was back on-island and insisted the guest room was already made up. I was beyond grateful for these women because they'd been mothers to me after my own had passed. But it still felt weird being here without Ford.

Mama Flo stood at the stove, a tall, slim woman with sun- and silver-streaked brown hair and a no-nonsense demeanor that served her well in her occupation as an environmental rights attorney. It was a marked contrast from Mimi's soft curves and flowing hippie skirts, her own natural hair worn in a cap of short curls that accentuated the perfectly proportioned shape of her head and the fine features of her medium brown skin. They were a study of opposites, but somehow they worked. Mama Flo kept Mimi grounded, and Mimi kept her wife from taking anything too seriously.

"Over-easy or scrambled?" Mama Flo demanded.

I briefly wondered if I could get away with just having a cup of coffee, then rejected the idea. She was already staring at me in Mom tone. That probably meant they'd also heard about my injuries and were as displeased as Willa about my keeping them to myself.

"Over-easy, please."

She gestured with her spatula. "Sit."

Contrite, I struggled to keep my shoulders from hunching up toward my ears, both to hide my guilt and because the motion still made my bad shoulder twinge. "Yes'm."

I sat at the kitchen table nestled in the bay window. The view overlooked the ocean at the south end of the island. That window was one of the original historical features of the house, which had once belonged to the lighthouse keeper. The light-house itself had been decommissioned many decades before, and the property fallen into disrepair. Florence and Delilah had bought it for a song and spent the past thirty years reno-vating and restoring it into the home it was today.

Mimi brought me a cup of coffee. "Sleep okay?"

I sipped at the dark brew, which was so much better than the swill I'd grown accustomed to in the Navy. "Mmm. I did, thanks." It wasn't a lie. My body seemed to recognize that I was finally home and had relaxed in a way I hadn't managed for a long time.

Mama Flo cracked three eggs into a waiting skillet. "That shoulder's not paining you too much?"

Yep. They'd definitely heard about my injuries.

"No, ma'am. It's healing well."

Both women gave me long looks that were about ten times more intimidating than any commanding officer I'd encountered during my service. This was one of those occasions when it would've been great if Ford had been here to either rescue me or for me to throw under the bus.

Mimi sniffed. "Well, you're retired now. What are your plans?"

As I didn't have the first clue what my life plans were, I opted to answer for the day. "I'm going up to Sutter House with Willa to help her deal with stuff up there."

They exchanged another look before Mama Flo turned away to plate up the eggs.

What is that about?

Mimi sipped at her coffee. "It's good she's letting you help. She's shot down everyone else."

Willa wasn't one to share her pain with others. Never had been, and that had only gotten more pronounced in the years since she came back to the island.

"You always had a way with her." Mama Flo slid a plate in front of me. "Eat up. I expect there's a lot to do."

Dutifully, I dug into the eggs. "How has Willa been doing, really?"

These two women might not keep quite as close an eye on Willa as they would on one of the Wayward Sons, but they still looked out as much as she'd let them. Mama Flo had been instrumental in getting Willa into the grant writing she did for a living, including hiring her for freelance work from time to time, and Mimi dearly loved gossip, so if there was anything to know, she probably did.

Predictably, she was the one who answered. "She's doing as well as can be expected. It was good and bad that she reconnected with her grandparents. Since she came back to the island, she's done what her mother never did, devoting herself to giving back to Hatterwick, upholding the Sutter family name. Henry and Vivian were so incredibly proud of who she's become. But for her to lose them like this, practically back-to-back..."

It would have left her reeling. Especially with Jace not around for support.

"What about her parents? Have they been back to the island since she moved home? She hasn't mentioned it to me, but I don't know that she would have."

Mama Flo pulled out a chair and sat. "Both of them came back the first year she was here. They clearly thought they'd be able to cow her into doing whatever they wanted, but they severely underestimated her."

I barely held in a growl. "They've been doing that all her life."

"True enough. Anyway, her mother's been back a couple of times, allegedly to check on Henry and Vivian, but Willa wouldn't see her. Since then, they've left her alone, so far as we know."

I scowled down at the remains of my eggs. "Did they really not come back when her grandmother died?"

"No. Vivian was in the hospital on the mainland when she passed, and Henry insisted they weren't having a funeral or memorial at that time. That they wanted to be honored together after he went. So that's what Willa's planning to do."

Mimi leaned against Mama Flo on the bench seat in the window. "Maybe you can use that influence of yours to get her to open up to the idea of taking help from the rest of us. She shouldn't have to handle all this on her own."

"I don't know how much influence I've got, but I'll see what I can do." Shoving back from the table, I took my empty plate to the sink and rinsed it off before loading it into the dishwasher. "Thanks for breakfast. I need to be getting on."

As I headed out to my truck, I made a mental note to find some time to look for a place of my own. I didn't feel right just camping out in their guest room, even though I knew they were completely okay with it and probably would enjoy the chance to mother me a bit. I was afraid that mothering would turn more into smothering, simply because I was the only one of their adopted chicks here at the moment. But that all had to wait. Right now, Willa came first.

The shadows under her eyes, when she answered the door of the little bungalow she shared with Bree, told me she'd spent a restless night. I wondered if that was because of the stress over her parents' impending invasion or if this was more of her norm than I'd realized. Had she kept as much from me in those texts and emails as I'd kept from her?

"Mornin'. Ready to go?"

She reached for her purse. "Yeah."

"Why don't I drive?" Small though it was, it felt like something else I could take off her plate. Plus, it meant more time with her. I didn't really feel like analyzing whether that was for her or for me.

Willa hesitated. "Roy is coming with me."

As if summoned by the sound of his name, the big dog appeared at her side like a ghost. Hell, he'd rival some of the SEALs I'd met for stealth.

"That's fine. A little dog hair never hurt anything."

She retrieved some kind of seatbelt attachment from her Jeep and loaded Roy into the backseat of my truck. As soon as he was secure, she slid into the passenger seat. For a moment, I flashed back to that long ago night when I'd snuck her out hidden under a blanket in the backseat. God, it felt like a million years since then, but I was still every bit as aware of her sharing the space. Instead of the palpable anticipation she'd radiated on her escape that night, with every mile closer to Sutter House, her anxiety ratcheted up. She didn't speak, and I didn't press for conversation, letting her feel what she needed to feel. Nothing about this would be easy for her.

The house was more rundown than I remembered, though still a grand example of the architecture of its period. A big place like this was probably a lot for her aging grandparents to have kept up, even with hired help. After working construction after school for years before I left for the Navy, it was habit to scan the place, looking for needed repairs. The whole thing could do with a fresh paint job and having the myriad of windows washed, and the driveway needed a fresh load of crushed shells to replenish the bare spots. But there was evidence of some recent pruning and shaping of the bushes and landscaping, so it wasn't completely untouched.

Roy didn't bound off to investigate all the interesting scents when he was sprung from the backseat. Instead, he stayed close to Willa's side, clearly attuned to her mood. She strode to the kitchen door with purpose, her shoulders resolute. But there, she hesitated, her hand hovering just over the knob.

"Are you okay?" It was a dumbass question. I could tell she wasn't.

"Not really." She dropped her hand. "I haven't been able to make myself go back inside."

"How come?"

Sucking in a breath, she turned to face me, and her eyes were utterly devastated. "I was the one who found him."

Oh God.

I didn't think, didn't question. I just pulled her straight into my arms, wanting to do something—anything—to take away some of her pain. Unlike yesterday, when we'd had an audience, she burrowed in, pressing her cheek to my chest and wrapping her arms around my waist like I was the only thing keeping her from being lost at sea. I buried my face in her hair, inhaling the vanilla and lavender scent of it as I held on. This was the first truly real hug with genuine connection that we'd shared since I'd left for basic training.

My hand found its way beneath the fall of her hair to gently massage at the tension in her nape. The muscles at the base of her neck were hard as iron. "Is it seeing where his body was? Remembering?"

"That. And I'm terrified this is going to be the last time I ever see this place."

"What do you mean?"

Willa pressed so close, her voice muffled against my chest. "They only had one daughter. Everything's going to my mother, and we all know my dad controls her. So they'll probably end up selling everything to developers and ruining the island. Relocating the horses. I'm afraid they're going to destroy everything I love about this place."

Given who her parents were, those were legitimate fears. Jesus, no wonder she wasn't sleeping. I didn't want to blow smoke up her ass, but maybe I could mitigate some of this. "Are you aware of what was in your grandfather's will? Did he say he's leaving everything to your mom?"

"No. We didn't talk about any of that. We only reconnected in the last couple of years, and that just didn't feel necessary to discuss or really any of my business. I didn't renew my relationship with them because of what I could get out of them."

Of course she hadn't. That wasn't her way.

I eased back just far enough to tip her face up toward mine. God, her skin was soft. "Then you don't actually know what's going to happen, so let's not borrow trouble. Let's just deal with what's in front of us right now."

She sucked in another breath and nodded. "Okay."

Some of the tension bled out of her before she pulled away and opened the kitchen door.

We stepped inside. The air was stale and still. I noted a pile of clean dishes in the rack beside the sink. The flat cap her grandfather had so frequently worn hung on a peg by the door, above an urn holding umbrellas and the carved wooden cane he used when walking the beach. A fine layer of dust seemed to have settled over everything—the only real sign no one had been here in a while.

I trailed Willa as she moved through the room, scanning everything.

"The kitchen needs to be cleaned. Really, everything needs to be aired out and cleaned."

"Why?" When she just looked at me, I rushed to add, "No disrespect to your grandparents, but why does this need doing now instead of later?"

"I'm the last Sutter. Or, at least, the only one who's here. Everybody's going to want to come through and pay their respects. The expectation is that I'll open the house to the community." As she tensed up again, Roy whined and nudged her hand with his big head. She automatically stroked him.

Mindful of the dog, I cupped the slim shoulders she'd piled so much on. "The island has always held immense respect for your grandparents and everything they've done for Hatterwick. I know it's going to be hard on you, dealing with all those people, dealing with your parents. But you're not going to have to do it alone. I promise, all of us are going to be there for you. And maybe it'll be a good thing to hear from the community how much they'll both be missed."

"Maybe. I won't be able to keep Roy with me in the middle of all that. He's exceptionally well trained, but I'm going to be so wound up, I can't be absolutely certain he won't try to defend me, and I won't risk him getting in trouble for that."

It was so absolutely Willa that she was focused on the consequences to the dog.

"Then I'll be your guard dog."

Her brows drew together.

Her long, swoopy bangs had fallen into her eyes, and I couldn't stop myself from brushing them back. "Look, I don't have to know what happened with your parents to know that this is going to be rough. If you don't want them to get anywhere near you, I won't let them. Period. End of story. Consider me your bodyguard for as long as you need me."

"You'd really do that for me?"

Wren, I'll do anything for you. The certainty of it hit me like a Mack truck, but I kept my tone matter-of-fact. "Of course."

The sudden release of tension in her posture told me she believed me. "My parents and I have been fully estranged for years."

I'd suspected as much, though we hadn't talked about it. That confirmed what Mimi and Mama Flo had said at breakfast. "Okay. Then I'll make sure it stays that way."

Because we'd slid well past the realm of friendly comfort, I forced myself to release her. "Now let's finish making a list of everything that needs to get done, and we'll activate the island grapevine to get you the help to do it."

CHAPTER 5

WILLA

I 'd always loved St. Andrew's Episcopal Church. Its soaring vaulted ceilings and carved beams always reminded me of the inside of some massive, inverted ship, a detail that usually brought me comfort. But not today. I could hardly focus on anything the priest was saying about my grandparents' contributions to Hatterwick over their eighty-odd years. Not with my parents sitting in the front pew a mere ten feet away.

They'd been the ones to greet the other mourners and accept condolences in the narthex, as if they'd had anything to do with the planning of this service. But if there was anything my parents were adept at, it was putting on the proper face in public. Unlike me. Even if they hadn't been here, I wouldn't have been able to face the seemingly endless throngs of people streaming into the church. With them here... Well, I was doing good to honor my grandparents by sitting through the service at all.

Thanks to Sawyer's quick thinking, I'd been sequestered away in the back halls of the church, only coming out from the side door normally used by grooms during weddings to take my place moments before the service began. I'd seen my parents in the front row and kept my eyes averted as I'd hurried to my seat alone on the other side of the aisle. But I'd felt their eyes on me, and it made my shoulders itch with a prickle of *not safe*.

Not that they'd do a thing in front of all these people. And not that anyone here could possibly understand all the ways they'd hurt me without ever laying a hand on me. I'd been the disappointment. The weird one. Never able to live up to family expectations. I'd paid for that failing. God, how I'd paid.

I'm never going back. Not ever. Nothing they can say or do can make me. I'm an adult. They have no hold over me anymore.

A big, warm hand settled on my shoulder from the row behind me. I knew without looking that it was Sawyer because the touch settled me, as he'd always settled me. The bands around my chest loosened, and I could breathe again. In silent gratitude, I covered his fingers with mine.

The prospect of facing them felt so different, knowing that he had my back. I wished he was next to me on the hard wooden bench so I could lean into the warmth and strength of him. But that would give people the impression we were more than we were. He wasn't family in that sense, and I didn't want him having to pay for his kindness by facing any kind of inter-rogation about his place by my side. Still, he maintained that link through the rest of the service, keeping me grounded.

Then it was over, and hundreds of feet began shuffling against the worn stone floors toward the exit. Sucking in a deep breath, I worked to button down my grief so I could deal with what came next.

I should've been making a run for it.

"Wilhelmina."

At the sound of my father's voice, I simply froze. A pure prey response. I'd wanted to appear strong, unaffected, yet I could only stand like a terrified rabbit as they approached, too caught up in old patterns to do anything else.

My mother was crying. Appropriate. This was a memorial service for both of her parents. I hadn't seen her when Grandma passed. Granddaddy had shielded me from both of them, though he hadn't known any of the specifics. But it seemed she felt some legitimate grief. No matter how I felt about her, she had loved them in her own way. Her eyes were drenched with tears as she reached for me.

I flinched, taking a full step back, out of reach.

"How can you be so childish as to deny your mother comfort at a time like this?" My father kept his tone low, but I felt the snap of his displeasure, nonetheless.

This wasn't about my mother's grief. This was about how it looked. Never mind that they'd lived off-island for more than a decade. Appearances were always forefront in my father's mind. If he thought the islanders had somehow missed the fact that they hadn't even returned once a year to check on my grandparents, he was sorely mistaken. I was the one who'd come back. I was the one who'd stayed. I was the one who gave a damn about my legacy here.

But my conditioning ran deep, and as my father's icy disapproval radiated over me, the panic returned with a vengeance, tightening like a vise around my chest. It didn't matter that I recognized it. Logic was about as effective at interrupting a panic attack as it was for stopping a runaway train.

Then Sawyer was there, his hand at the small of my back.

"Willa has the right to handle her grief in whatever way she feels is necessary. That does not include being obligated to interact with you."

It took everything I had not to collapse into him, but by damn, I wasn't going to look weak right now.

My father looked down his nose at Sawyer as he always had, though Sawyer was now taller, bigger, and broader than my father by a lot. And in his dress blues, he looked powerful and in control. Sexy. Not that this was the time to notice *that*.

"This doesn't concern you, boy." My father's tone was one of clear dismissal.

Sawyer just moved closer to me, subtly nudging me slightly behind him. "Willa concerns me. She doesn't want to see you, so she doesn't have to."

Unlike my father's voice, Sawyer's wasn't modulated to not be overheard. At his words, multiple sets of eyes turned in our direction.

No, no. No attention. I just want to go.

I fought not to shrink under the focus.

My father took a step toward us, opening his mouth to deliver some scathing comeback.

Sawyer's hands curled into fists, and he stepped fully in front of me. Even beneath the short beard he'd grown, I could see a muscle jumping in his jaw. This time, he did lower his voice to an outright growl that would've done Roy proud. "Please, give me a reason. If you think I won't physically remove you from her presence, think again, old man. I'm not a kid that you can intimidate anymore."

I'd never considered myself a violent person. In general, I believed calmer heads were always the answer. But having this man I'd known all my life threaten bodily harm against the person who'd made my life a living hell apparently appealed to my baser instincts, because the panic that had gripped me by the throat was washed away in a tide of outright lust.

Well... that was... new. Definitely more appealing than many of the ways I'd worked to overcome panic attacks. It was really just too damned bad there'd be no following through and showing him my appreciation, up close and personal.

"Willa, honey, I just want to talk," Mom pleaded. "After all this time, don't you want to reconnect?"

She might not have been at the root of how I was treated, but she hadn't lifted a finger to stop it, so no. I wasn't about to change my mind.

Instead, I laid a hand on Sawyer's arm, feeling the coiled tension. "Let's go."

After several long moments of glowering, Sawyer laid his free hand protectively over mine and turned us both toward the door. I had no idea what my parents thought of his display, nor did I care. It only mattered that I'd gotten through seeing them without falling apart.

Unless someone talked, and they found out where we were really holding the wake, I'd have a reprieve until the reading of the will.

I'd take every minute I could get.

CHAPTER 6

SAWYER

The Sutter's Ferry Community Center was packed. The whole place held a surprising air of revelry, which was a damn sight better than the somber receiving line Willa had imagined that day up at Sutter House. She'd been so wound up about the idea of having all these people tromping through her grandparents' house that I'd convinced her to think outside the box and do something entirely different. Instead of a formal wake, we were having a memorial potluck at the community center, which the Sutters themselves had funded decades before.

Tables were set up along one wall, groaning under the weight of all the death casseroles, mini sandwiches, dessert bars, and other offerings. There was certainly enough food to feed the army of people who were coming through. Poster-sized photos of Willa's grandparents sat on easels marking either end of a massive bulletin board. Everyone in town had been invited to bring and post pictures of Henry and Vivian. Over the past hour and a half, it had filled up.

I hadn't known Henry and Vivian Sutter all that well, but I thought maybe they'd really appreciate this more community-centric version of remembrance. Certainly, it was a lot easier on Willa herself. All we'd had to do was notify Mimi and Mama Flo, and they'd reached out to everyone else to get shit done. There'd been no written invitation. The call had gone out on the island grapevine. Hence, there was very little chance that John and Victoria Hollingsworth would know about it.

I had no idea if they'd headed up to Sutter House expecting... something. They weren't staying up there. According to the rumor mill, they'd booked a room at the boutique hotel in town. But nobody seemed to know exactly where they'd gone to ground after the memorial service. Were they even now walking through the house they assumed they owned, making an inventory of all the heirlooms that had been passed down by the Sutter family for generations? I didn't really give a shit, so long as they stayed well away from Willa.

My gaze cut back to where she was holding court, flanked by Gabi and Bree, who'd made sure she had food and wine as she spoke to the latest in a long, long line of community members who wanted to pay tribute to her grandparents. Because they'd assumed guard duty, I was patrolling the perimeter, still trying to walk off the simmering rage toward her father. John Hollingsworth wasn't the kind of guy to get his hands directly dirty, but oh, how I'd wished he'd taken a swing, so I could've handed him his ass. Even though I knew Willa would've absolutely hated the scene that would've caused. Squaring off with them at the church, I'd seen more of the little girl I'd dubbed Wren. But she hadn't run, hadn't hidden, no matter how much she'd wanted to.

It made me appreciate how fucking hard she'd worked to build a life here, despite everything. She had support. More, perhaps, than I'd given her credit for. And I was glad of it. In her own quiet way, she'd made her own niche in this community. That was how she wanted it. She'd never been someone who wanted to get anything because of her family name—either of them.

As I made my way around the room, I overheard snippets of conversations that made me realize just how much Willa had given back to the island since returning.

"If it wasn't for Willa's grant writing, we never would have been able to expand the library's technology center last year." This came from Marsha McCubbins, who'd been head librarian since we were kids. "Do you know the impact that's had on our job training classes?"

The elderly man beside her folded his hands over the head of a cane. "I don't know how we would have managed without the free school lunch program she helped establish. So many families rely on that now."

"And don't forget the no-kill animal shelter!" a teenager piped up. "We can adopt pets here now, instead of having to go to the mainland."

It seemed her quiet acts of service had made a huge impact. No wonder she had the respect and appreciation of so many here on the island. It made me proud to see the adult she had become—still inherently kind-hearted and wanting to help others, just like the girl I remembered.

But as my gaze strayed back to her, I couldn't help but see that, even surrounded by all these people I knew would help her in a minute, she managed to seem alone, as if there were a force field around her. I hated that. It made me remember Rapunzel in her tower. I seriously had no idea how anyone like her and Jace could come from the parents they had. Watching her navigate all this on her own, I hoped like hell the mission he was on was worth it. Not like he'd known about the death in the family when he'd taken the assignment, but still, it was hard not to resent the fact that he wasn't here.

Then again, if he had been, I might not get to be this close to Willa myself. And that was another one of those details I just wasn't gonna analyze right now.

Plenty of folks were still hovering, clustered in groups and talking as they waited for the chance to pay their respects, but I could see the droop in Willa's shoulders as she began to wilt from all the people, the subtle flinch at the rising noise of competing voices. She needed a little distance, some fresh air and quiet to recalibrate, so I cut through the crowd.

Old Tobin Ruscoe leaned toward Willa, his rheumy eyes warm. "Your grandparents were the backbone of this community, Willa. I remember when that fierce hurricane hit us back in '98. My family didn't have a safe place to ride out the storm. Without hesitation, your grandparents opened the doors of their home, turning Sutter House into a makeshift shelter for anyone in need. They cooked for us, shared stories to keep our spirits up, and made sure every single person felt safe until the storm passed. Their kindness in those terrifying hours is something I'll never forget. They were the reason so many of us stayed through all the hard years and keep calling Hatterwick home."

Easing next to her, I jumped into the conversation. "I remember my dad talking about that storm. Made a hell of a mess."

"Sure did. But we recovered and made things better than ever, because of the Sutters. We're sure gonna miss them."

She folded one of his gnarled hands between both of hers. "Thank you, Mr. Ruscoe. I appreciate you sharing that with me."

I settled a hand on Willa's shoulder and squeezed. "If you'll excuse us for a few minutes, I need to have a word with Willa."

She shot me a look of vague alarm as I deftly steered her around the crowds and toward the back side of the building that faced the fishing docks. "What's wrong?"

"Nothing. You just need a breather. We're getting out of here for a little bit."

The summer sun hung low, glinting off the water as we burst through the doors. I suspected this would go on for at least another hour. Willa kept on walking out to the end of the nearest pier. Pressing both hands to the small of her back, she arched, stretching until her spine cracked.

"Thanks for that. I did need a break."

Because the urge to touch her was so strong, I leaned back against the railing opposite her. "Thought so. How you holding up?"

"Better than I thought I would. This has been good. It was a fantastic idea, Sawyer. You were right. It helps to hear all these stories from everyone, showing how much they loved my grandparents, and how much they meant to the community. They're going to be remembered here, no matter how things end up with the house and the rest of their property."

I saw the moment the prospective fate of their estate settled over her again and threw all my good intentions out the window. "Come here."

When I reached for her, she came easily, needing the comfort I offered. Having her lean on me was one of the best feelings in the world, though I absolutely hated the reason she needed it. My hand found her nape again and began to rub at the knots there.

"No matter what happens, we're gonna get through it, right?"

"Yeah, I know." She sucked in a bracing breath but made no move to leave my embrace. "I'm no stranger to doing hard things. I just have to see them one more time at the reading of the will tomorrow. And then we'll know and can deal with whatever the fallout is. But no matter what, they'll go. The dispensation of the estate is all they care about, and even if it's all theirs, they won't stay. My father always hated it here."

I thought of all the stories I'd heard today about the things that Willa herself had done for the community. She was a gifted grant writer, and she'd put that skill to work for the betterment of the island. I knew those were all things her grandparents would have been aware of and proud of. Of all those in the younger generations, she was the one who'd actually lived up to their legacy, and I wondered if maybe whatever they'd ultimately decided would surprise her.

I certainly hoped so.

Either way, she was right. Tomorrow she'd find out what came next, and I'd be here to support her no matter what.

CHAPTER 7
WILLA

I arrived at Roland O'Shea's law office with only a couple of minutes to spare. Roy hadn't understood why he was being left at home two days in a row. He'd become so much an extension of me, I felt almost naked without him. But nothing and no one made me more anxious than my parents, and the last thing I needed was Roy losing his shit and attacking my father. Dad was absolutely the kind of guy who would demand that a dog that bit him be put down. I wasn't risking my boy just to try to make this easier on myself.

Nothing would make this easy.

With one more bracing breath, I tugged open the door and stepped inside.

Mr. O'Shea's secretary, Nancy, smiled at me from behind the reception desk. "Hey Willa. Everybody's in the conference room. Can I get you a cup of coffee? Tea?"

Adding caffeine on top of my already jittering nerves seemed like a bad idea. "Maybe just some water?"

"Of course. Go on in."

I untangled the fingers I'd instinctively knotted together.

That was something my mother had tried to drill into me growing up.

A Hollingsworth never shows anything but poise and dignity.

I really didn't know why I was here, other than Mr. O'Shea had told me Granddaddy had wanted me present for the reading of the will. I didn't really understand why I couldn't be told, after the fact, what mementos had been bequeathed to me, but I'd do this last thing for my grandparents. If I was lucky, maybe it would be the last time I ever had to interact with my parents.

With a deep breath, I stepped into the room.

Mr. O'Shea glanced up from where he sat at the center of the table. "Ah, Willa. Welcome. Please have a seat."

My father had, predictably, taken the head of the table on the far side of the room. The position of power. Mom was by his right hand. I dropped into the chair closest to the door, mostly because my knees were trembling, and I didn't want them to notice.

"Will your brother be dialing in for this conference?"

I swallowed, wishing Nancy would hurry with the water already. "Due to his current mission parameters, he's entirely out of contact. He's aware Granddaddy has passed but isn't in a position to be extracted. Whatever pertinent details need to be relayed to him will have to wait until he's back in contact."

I refused to acknowledge the possibility that whatever was keeping him away could prospectively stop him from ever being in contact again. I could only handle so much loss at once.

"Understood." Mr. O'Shea straightened the papers in front of him.

I laced my fingers under the table, wishing desperately that Sawyer could've come with me for this. Stupid, maybe, but he was becoming as much of an emotional support as Roy. My brain immediately pictured him with a reflective vest reading *Emotional Support Human*, and I almost giggled. That was the last thing I needed. Laughing at a time like this would just reinforce the idea that I "wasn't quite right." Schooling my features, I glanced toward my parents.

The skin beneath Mom's eyes looked bruised enough that even her skilled hand at makeup couldn't hide it. She'd obviously spent a restless night. Was it because she'd just lost the last of her parents? Because she was estranged from me, and her son was risking life and limb for the military, God knew where? Per usual, Dad was well appointed in a bespoke suit. He looked perfectly well rested, with an unmistakable gleam of avarice in his eyes, as Mr. O'Shea cleared his throat to begin.

"I have a letter here from Henry, to Victoria and John, that he requested be read first."

As Nancy slipped into the room and handed me a bottle of water, I nodded in thanks and twisted off the cap.

The lawyer slid a pair of thick, black-framed reading glasses onto his wide nose. "Victoria and John, let me speak plainly now that I've passed."

I froze, the water bottle halfway to my lips. *Uh-oh.*

Granddaddy had gotten a lot more salty in his last months without Grandma around to curb him. What had he done?

"Victoria, our relationship since you moved off-island has not been the best. I am regretful that both of us passed without rectifying that. But we did have the great privilege of reconnecting with our granddaughter, Willa. She is a joy and a true testament to the Sutter name. I can't say that any of that can be credited to either of you."

I was barely breathing. Despite the fact that Mr. O'Shea was using a fairly inflectionless tone, I heard every word in my grandfather's booming captain's voice, and as such, each one hit with the weight of a fist.

"John, I'm dead now, so I feel safe in saying that I never liked you. I don't like who my daughter became when she married you. And I certainly don't like how you treated either of my grandchildren. They were the greatest gifts you could ever have, yet you squandered them. I don't know the specifics. I don't have to. I saw what Willa was like when she came back to Hatterwick. May you rot in hell for whatever you put her through during those years off-island."

Oh my God. I can't believe he actually said any of this!

All color had drained from my mother's face, and rage clearly simmered beneath my father's even expression.

Mr. O'Shea hesitated, clearly uncomfortable, but he resolutely continued. "I know you will think I'm being unduly harsh and unreasonable, but I promise all of it is relevant as to the dispensation of my estate. You both have profoundly disappointed me as parents. I need you to know that—to understand it—so that when I say that, other than a few provisions for my grandson, John Christopher Hollingsworth, IV; and a trust that has been laid by for the continued betterment of Hatterwick Island; the entirety of the remainder of the Sutter estate, including the land, the house that sits upon it, and the ferry company itself, goes to my granddaughter, Willa Sutter, as she embodies the grit, loyalty, and community spirit at the heart of the Sutter legacy. My spirit will rest easier knowing she will preserve what matters most."

Ears ringing, I stared in abject shock at the lawyer. At least until my father exploded from his chair.

"This is utterly absurd. That's not even her name!"

For all that I wanted to shrink from his anger, I lifted my gaze to his. "Yes, it is. I changed it years ago, because I want nothing to do with you."

Apparently, for the first time in my entire life, I'd shocked him. Not that it lasted long. His hands curled to fists that he pressed to the tabletop as he leaned toward me. There might have been ten feet of wood separating us, but I still felt him looming. "This is ridiculous. You manipulated your grandparents in their old age. Everything rightfully belongs to your mother. We're going to challenge. There is no possible way they could have been in their right minds when they did this."

Mr. O'Shea cleared his throat again. "Actually, they were quite in their right minds. The will was changed years ago. The... letter was a more recent addition. Certainly, you can attempt to contest, but you're going to fail."

Dad's nostrils flared with outrage for long moments before he straightened and snapped his fingers at my mother. "Victoria, we're leaving."

She scrambled to her feet, trailing after him like a dog. A few moments later, I jolted as the building shook from the force of a slamming door.

"Willa, can I get you anything?" Mr. O'Shea's voice was very gentle.

"I..." My head spun, trying to sort out the implications of all of this. "Is this real? Or did he decide to punk my parents as his last act?"

The professional demeanor cracked, and he smiled. "I can assure you this is absolutely real. Your grandparents adored you, and they chose to leave their estate to the person they believed would do right by it. That's absolutely you."

"But I never expected... any of this."

"And that's exactly why. Henry and I had many frank conversations about your parents. I can't say that I agree with his choice to have that letter read, as I don't know what the fallout might be for you, but I absolutely understand and agree that you are the best of the Sutters for generations."

That simple faith—from him, from my grandparents—had tears burning in my eyes.

Mr. O'Shea extended a pocket square toward me. "Now that

your parents are gone, perhaps you'd like to go over the rest of the details?"

Numbly, I took the handkerchief and dabbed my eyes. Then I nodded.

He reached for the folder. "Then let's begin."

CHAPTER 8

SAWYER

Restlessness drove me from the lighthouse on the point out into Sutter's Ferry. Well, restlessness and the lingering threat that Mimi might corner me to ask more questions I didn't have answers for. I didn't like the knowing looks she and Mama Flo kept sharing over the subject of me and Willa. Like there was something there.

I mean, obviously, there was something there. We were friends. We had history. But it wasn't like those looks were making it out to be. It couldn't be.

The reading of the will was today. Obviously, I had no business being there. It wasn't anything to do with me, and Willa hadn't asked me to meet up with her after. But I couldn't forget her grief and fear over what her parents would do with whatever they got, not to mention her stress over even being in the same room with them. I wanted to be there to help repair whatever additional damage they caused.

Because I had no idea how long the meeting would take, I decided to wander the village to see what had changed. Sure, I'd been back to Hatterwick some over the years. But those visits had been brief, and I hadn't wanted to revisit the ghosts on memory lane. Maybe I'd been hiding.

My route took me past the marina. The noisy cry of gulls filled the salty air as they wheeled over the water. At this hour, all the fishing boats were already out on the open ocean. Despite the often backbreaking nature of the work, a faint pull of nostalgia had me smiling. Not that I wanted to go back to commercial fishing as an occupation. I just loved being out on the water. Fishing. The Navy. The one true constant in my life had been the ocean.

Moving on, I made my way into the residential part of town, where a row of modest rental houses had evidently been bought up and gentrified since I'd lived here with my dad. It looked so different that I walked right past the house at first. The eaves that used to sag were straight. The shutters that had once hung forever cattywampus on rusty hinges were neatly fastened against siding now painted a bright, sunshiny yellow. A pair of flowerbeds bursting with blooming butterfly bushes flanked a walkway of stone pavers that led up to the red front door. I might have thought it had been turned into a vacation rental but for a child's bike that lay abandoned on its side in the front yard beside a swing that hung from a tree that hadn't been big enough to support its weight when I'd left.

It had been made into a home.

It hadn't been that when I'd lived here with my dad. Life would've been so much different had my mother and sister lived. It wasn't something I dwelt on. What was the point? When they died and Dad fell into the bottle, I wasn't enough to keep him afloat. He'd never been aggressive or problematic as a drunk. Never hurt anybody. He'd just drowned in his grief and heartbreak for the rest of his life. Which, really, hadn't been all that long, considering. I'd had to grow up fast, and if not for the rest of the Wayward Sons, I didn't know where I'd be. They were my family, and I was feeling the distance from all of them.

Without them, without a place here, a purpose—hell, even a damned job—I felt rootless and unmoored. Being there for Willa had distracted me from that, and maybe that was part of why I was so focused on her.

Right, Malone. Everybody believes that.

She pulled at me, even more than she always had. The past few days of being near her seemed to have rolled back some of the reserve that had built up like dunes between us. I knew none of that had been Jace's intention when he'd asked me to come. If it had been Ford or Rios who'd been available, one of them would have been the stand-in for her brother. I wondered if Jace would've thought twice about asking if he knew the feelings I'd hidden about his sister all these years.

Didn't matter. I was the one who was here, and I was the one who'd stand by her to help through whatever she needed. That sense of purpose wouldn't last forever. I'd have to figure out what the hell to do with my life, sooner or later. Sort out what a sailor without ship actually was.

But it could wait.

I made my way downtown to Panadería de la Isla, which was conveniently located midway between Roland O'Shea's law office and where Willa had parked her Jeep. I wasn't especially hungry, as Mama Flo had made sure I ate before I left the house this morning, but I could go for a coffee.

Marisol Gutierrez smiled at me from behind the counter. "Sawyer, welcome home."

"Thanks, Marisol. Can I get a large dark roast and one of your empanadas for here?"

"Of course. Would you like that heated?"

"Please." Spotting the trays full of big, beautiful cookies, I decided to grab one of those for Willa. Something sweet to take the sting out of whatever was happening in that meeting. "And a couple of the snickerdoodles to go."

Her smile flashed again. "Seeing Willa later?" At my blank look, she explained, "They're her favorite."

"I know. And yes, thanks."

As Marisol bustled behind the counter, I heard someone snort behind me. "As if sugar's enough to buy his way into the good graces of someone like *her*."

My shoulders went stiff. I told myself not to turn around. Whoever was opining about my purchase didn't matter one iota.

Someone else continued, "Oh, you know Willa. Always a bleeding heart for a faithful dog."

Marisol's smile had slipped when she brought me my coffee and food, her heated gaze fixed somewhere over my left shoulder. When she opened her mouth as if to say something, I gave a bare shake of my head. It wasn't worth it to draw attention to these jackasses. It might've been years since I'd been subjected to this kind of bullshit, but it was hardly the first time.

Marisol huffed and finished ringing me up.

I saluted her with my coffee. "Thanks. Have a good one."

Deliberately keeping my back to the bakery at large, I headed out to the patio. Only once I'd found a table outside did I dare to glance in through the window to see who'd been running their mouths.

Marcus Hoffman and Chet Banks. Well on toward their fifties now, they gossiped worse than a bunch of old women. They'd once given Caroline all kinds of grief over Rios's supposed crimes, so this didn't surprise me a bit. It was always the small minded and the miserable who had to make themselves feel better by tearing others down, and as the son of the town drunk, I'd been a popular target growing up. I had kinda thought they'd have moved on to someone else by now. Dad had been dead for more than a decade.

Twitching my shoulders to rid myself of the itch of shame trying to claw its way up my back, I shifted focus down the street toward the law office. It didn't take long. I'd barely brushed the pastry crumbs from my fingers before I saw Willa step out of the office.

I couldn't get a clear read on her from here. Her movements were slow, almost confused. As if she were trapped underwater. I'd tossed my trash and crossed the street before she even turned toward her Jeep. The view up close didn't tell me much more. She looked... shell shocked.

Bracing myself for her answer, I asked one of the world's dumbest questions. "Hey. You okay?"

She turned instinctively toward the sound of my voice, looking up at me, but I didn't think she really saw me. There were no tears. No rage. She didn't have that haunted look I'd come to associate with whatever traumas she kept to herself. She simply appeared thunderstruck.

I glanced around. "Where are your parents?"

"Gone." The single syllable came out quiet. Numb.

Something huge had just happened, and she was in the quiet before the storm of reaction. I needed to get her out of town before it hit.

"Okay. Come on."

When she didn't immediately follow, I grabbed her hand and tugged gently. She fell into vaguely stumbling step beside me. Oh, yeah. Major overwhelm here.

At her Jeep, I held out my free hand. "Keys?"

Wordlessly, she handed them over.

I bundled her into the passenger seat and circled around to climb in myself. This close to her, I could sense the frenetic energy under the surface of the emotions she simply couldn't process. There was far too much input here. I could fix that, at least for a little while.

Quick and efficient, I navigated through the village, working my way off the main thoroughfares that were clogged with summer tourists, until we hit the coastal road that ran north, toward Sutter land. I drove by instinct as much as habit, leaving signs of civilization behind until, at last, we were parked near the dunes that marked the edge of the marshes beyond the woods. This had been our place when we were young. Where we'd hang out and talk and watch for the band of horses that brought her so much joy.

Too late, I second guessed my choice. If the worst had come to pass, seeing them might break her in ways I wasn't prepared to handle. I hoped I wasn't making a mistake bringing her here.

Before I could do anything else, she'd climbed out and moved toward the edge of the woods, where the thick, low branches of a live oak stretched gnarled, twisted arms and made a convenient hiding spot to sit unobserved. Unerringly, she climbed into one of the crooks. I followed suit, wedging myself a little less easily into the opposite curve of the branch than I had when I'd been younger. She stared out at the marsh, and I waited. Eventually, the frantic energy I sensed pumping off her began to calm, the panic she hadn't acknowledged waning. I'd done at least one thing right in bringing her here.

"They left me everything."

I jerked to look at her, not a hundred percent certain I'd heard her right over the whisper of wind and the distant roar of the surf. "They what?"

"They left me everything. There's some stuff that's been earmarked for Jace, and a trust to go toward the betterment of the island. But the ferry company, the land, the house, the assets—they left them all to me."

Something in me unclenched. I hadn't dared hope for this for her, but after all the stories I'd heard at the memorial, I wasn't surprised.

She finally looked at me, those hazel eyes almost luminous. "What were they thinking?"

"That you were the best of the Sutters, and that you'd do right by all of it."

Willa huffed a laugh. "That's what Mr. O'Shea said, too."

I nudged her foot with mine. "See? Majority rules."

With a helpless shrug, she scooped a hand through the hair the wind had determinedly tugged from her braid. "But I don't know anything about how to run a ferry company or how to do any of this stuff. There are going to be all these people counting on me and looking to me for leadership. I'm not prepared for any of that."

Ah. And here was the sticking point for the overwhelm.

Leaning toward her, I offered the bag with the cookies I'd bought. "Here."

Her brows drew together. "What's this?"

"Fortification."

She opened it, her expression lightening as she pulled out a cookie. "You got me snickerdoodles?"

"You used to say they helped everything."

A smile fluttered at the corners of her mouth. "So I did. Here, you have one, too."

She handed me the cookie, then pulled out the other.

I took a bite and leaned back against the tree. "So, shit's got to go through probate, right? There's time to figure out the rest. The ferry company has been running perfectly fine on its own. Your grandparents have people in place who've been running the day-to-day of it for a long time. There's no reason to change the setup just because you're going to be the CEO or president or whatever the hell."

A little of the tension seemed to bleed out of her shoulders. "I suppose you're right on that. I've got time."

We sat a while in silence as that sank in.

"What do you want to do? I remember growing up how much you loved their house. Do you plan to move up there?"

"I hardly know. I mean, I've been living with Bree for years now. She doesn't need the money for rent necessarily. I guess I could. I don't know. That's... Nothing went the way I thought."

Understatement of the century. "I bet your parents were pretty pissed."

Her laugh this time held a harsh edge. "Oh, my parents. Yeah. So my grandfather decided since he was dead, he was absolutely going to tell them exactly what he thought of them, in no uncertain terms, before announcing they weren't getting a penny."

"Seriously?"

I listened as she reeled off what she could remember of the letter the lawyer had been required to read aloud. Then I whistled. "Damn. I mean, most of us have wanted to say the same, but never had the opportunity. So I say, good on Granddaddy Henry. Your parents needed to hear all that."

Willa shook her head. "I don't know that they did. It's not going to change anything. We're not going to suddenly not be estranged. And now it's infuriated my father. He insists he's going to contest the will. Mr. O'Shea says that there's no way to contest it—that it's solid—so if they want to waste their time and money on attorneys, then okay. Apparently, that's not going to change anything for me."

I hoped Roland O'Shea was as good an attorney as he thought he was and that he'd run interference, so whatever legal tactics her parents employed wouldn't touch her.

"I still say that it's nice for somebody to have called them out for being shits as parents." I could think of a laundry list of other infractions from growing up. Things I wished I could have done something more about back then. I was so fucking grateful she was no longer in a position where she had to be protected from her parents.

"You're your own woman, Wren. And you're going to do amazing things with every single asset you inherited. I have faith in you."

She shot me a rueful smile that finally looked a little more like the woman I knew. "Well, that makes one of us."

CHAPTER 9

WILLA

In the two days since the reading of my grandfather's will, I'd sequestered myself up at Sutter House. I wasn't staying here. Not yet, anyway. But I'd been taking the time to give the whole house a thorough clean from top to bottom. Help would've been available at only a word, but I needed the space to process the implications of the legacy I'd been gifted. Banishing dust and grime provided visible progress over something I actually felt in control of. Soon enough I'd have to start making a list of all the things that needed doing, but right now I was content to bask in the ocean breeze floating through all the open windows as it blended with the scents of lemon polish, rosemary, and the Vivaldi that played on the little Bluetooth speaker I'd been carting from room to room. Roy napped in a spot of sunshine in front of a window, paws twitching as he chased seagulls in his dreams.

It felt good to tend to the house. To feel I had the right to, though I hadn't yet fully grasped that all this was mine. Mr. O'Shea had notified the ferry company staff, and I'd be meeting with them later to allay any fears that I intended to make any major changes. I'd need to meet with my grandparents' accountant to go over the books, both private and business. All things that rather terrified me. I wanted to honor the gift I'd been given. Granddaddy wouldn't have done this if he thought I wasn't up to the task. So I'd get myself there. Somehow.

The sound of tires crunching on the crushed-shell drive pulled my attention out front. Roy rose from his nap, instantly on alert as he trotted toward the door.

It was Sawyer, probably. He was the one most likely to seek me out up here. I was trying not to think too hard about what that might mean because I hadn't forgotten what Bree had said about him that first night he'd been back. I simply accepted that he'd been a fixture in my everyday, pitching in without my asking since he'd returned to Hatterwick. That was all I had the capacity for just now, so I'd let it ride.

But when I stepped out front, it was Roland O'Shea stepping out of his stately sedan. Even before he shoved up his sunglasses, I registered the tension in his frame and around his mouth.

My hands fisted around the microfiber cloth I'd been dusting with. "What is it?"

"Can we go inside and sit down?"

Talons of anxiety dug into my ribs. Roy leaned against my hip in comfort.

"Of course, please come in." My voice came out admirably level and controlled considering the chaos inside me.

He followed me into the kitchen.

"Can I offer you coffee or tea?"

"No, no. Have a seat. Please."

Every instinct was shouting at me to run from whatever news he brought, but I lowered myself into a chair, digging my fingers into Roy's ruff.

Mr. O'Shea cleared his throat. "I will be brief and to the point, because time is going to be of the essence."

"Time for what?"

He took a moment to fold his hands on the table. "Your grandfather assumed, rightly so, that your parents were going to fight the terms of the will, and so he left funds earmarked for the purpose of hiring a private detective to follow their movements for a span of time after the reading."

Well, that was a level of paranoia I hadn't expected from Granddaddy.

"I don't understand. We already knew they were planning to challenge."

"Yes, we did. I didn't think that there were any grounds on which they could legally challenge. I may be wrong."

Those talons dug in deeper, dragging lower to skewer my gut. My fingers automatically tightened on Roy's ruff, but he didn't protest, simply leaned harder against me.

"Okay, what does this mean? What are they doing?"

"They're not challenging the competency of your grandparents in writing of the will. They're challenging *your* competency."

His words barreled into me like a freight train.

This was my worst nightmare. In a flash, everything I'd experienced off-island came flooding back. The hospital. The drugs. The locks.

I didn't realize I'd started hyperventilating until Mr. O'Shea gently forced my head between my knees. Roy whined, nosing and licking at my face.

Five things I can see. Roy. Flip flops. Chair leg. Frayed hem of my cutoffs. Mr. O'Shea's dress shoes.

Four things I can feel. Roy's tongue. Roy's fur. The hard seat of the chair. Cotton of my shorts.

Three things I can hear. Roy's panting. Violin from the speaker. Gulls.

Two things I can smell. Lemon. Rosemary.

A glass was thrust into my line of vision, and slowly I

straightened, wrapping both hands around it. Carefully, I lifted it to my lips.

One thing I can taste. Water.

I drew in a ragged breath, and then another, until the leading edge of terror waned. As if I hadn't just had a panic attack in front of my attorney, I squared my shoulders. "I'm an adult. How can they do that?"

"I don't know for sure whether they could pull it off, but I was given to understand that there are some circumstances in your past that make this a more viable possibility than it might otherwise be." He was hedging in a way that made it impossible to know what he knew. He wasn't offering any information on that front, and I sure as hell wasn't offering up the reality of what I'd been through. Not yet. Not unless it became absolutely necessary.

Hold it together, girl.

"Okay, so what do we do?"

He spread his hands in apology. "Honestly, I don't know yet. Some of it will depend on the specifics of what they file. But I wanted you to be aware of what was coming so that you could prepare."

How could I possibly prepare for this? This was everything I'd cut myself off from my parents to prevent.

I shook my head. "How can they possibly have any grounds to say what I'm like as an adult?"

"It'll depend on the judge. I'll continue to look for precedent and some way to combat this, but I didn't want to move forward without both your awareness and permission. We're going to be ready for whatever they're bringing."

Did they train that confidence in law school, or was he really that certain? He was here, delivering this news in person, where we wouldn't be overheard. Surely, that meant he had his doubts. Or maybe it was simply a sign of his discretion and awareness of client confidentiality.

"Thank you, I understand." Except I really didn't.

I'd slid from panic into numbness because this was all too much to process at once. I needed to speak to someone I trusted about all of this. Another attorney. Someone who knew at least the broad strokes of what had happened to me while I was off-island.

Somehow, I managed to get O'Shea out the door. Then I systematically went through the entire house, shutting all the windows and locking up before loading Roy into the Jeep and driving to the opposite end of the island.

The lighthouse rose like the beacon it once had been. I sent up a prayer that it would give me hope, as it had to countless sailors on stormy seas in the past.

Delilah answered the door, massive feather earrings dangling from her ears. Her lovely dark eyes went wide at the sight of me.

"Is Florence here?"

"Yes, absolutely. Come in, child." Her warm arm slid around me, ushering me inside, and I managed not to flinch at the touch.

Florence emerged from her home office, a pair of reading glasses perched on her long nose. At the sight of me, she pulled off the glasses and straightened into battle posture. I must've looked pretty bad.

The back door slammed. "Hey, I thought I saw—Wren, what's wrong?"

Sawyer closed the distance to where I stood in a blink, stopping just short of touching me.

I couldn't look at him or give into the urge to throw myself into his arms, or I'd never get through this. Instead, I kept my focus on Florence. "I need your advice as an attorney. I know that this is not going to be your area of expertise, but you are the only one that I trust."

She offered a decisive nod. "Okay, do you want to talk privately?"

I thought about it. I wasn't keen to share even the barest details of my own private hell with anyone, but I trusted everyone in this room. "No."

"Then let's move this into the kitchen, and I'll make you some tea." Delilah steered me in that direction, and the rest of them followed.

As Delilah clattered around, putting a kettle on to boil and filling a tea ball with loose leaves, I told them what Mr. O'Shea had told me.

"That's ridiculous!" Sawyer burst out. "How could they possibly challenge your competency? You are one of the most stable, sane people I know."

I'd never told him this. Never wanted to tell him, because I didn't want to change how he looked at me. But if this went forward, he'd find out, eventually. Better to get it over with now, before my foolish heart managed to convince me there could be anything more between us but friendship.

I wrapped my hands around the warm mug Delilah passed me. "Because I was institutionalized for two years."

He stared at me, brows drawn together in confusion. "What?"

"That's where I went when they dragged me off-island. After I got out of the hospital, they had me committed and kept me there for two years."

With a rush of profanity, Sawyer shot to his feet so fast, his chair clattered to the floor. His fury was palpable. I both appreciated his instant defense and was overwhelmed by it. This was as much rage over what was done to me as rage at his own impotence to stop it. Not that he'd have been able to do anything about it if he had known back then.

"Sawyer!" Florence's voice snapped out. "Reel it in. She doesn't need that right now."

He stopped his restless stalking of the kitchen, hands curled to fists, and worked on stuffing his rage back down. "Tell me one thing. Did Jace know?"

Ah, so that was also underneath this reaction. Needing to know if his oldest friend would've betrayed me like that.

"No. Not until after I turned eighteen and managed to contact him. He's the reason I got out. And that's the only reason I didn't cut him off with everyone else."

A little of the tension in him eased, and he righted the chair, sitting back down. "Sorry."

I clutched the mug a little tighter as I turned my attention back to Florence. "What I want to know is if they can really do this."

The older woman dragged a hand down her face. "Well, as you know, this is not my area, but to my knowledge, yes, they can try."

My breath wheezed out as that sucker punch hit me again.

"But there is a way out. Potentially," she added.

Maybe I'd get the hope I'd come seeking after all. "Great. What is it?"

"Well, the reason they have the right to challenge is because they are your next of kin."

"Even though we've been estranged for a decade?"

"Even though."

"So, what's the answer?"

Florence carefully folded her hands as she seemed to search for the right words. "If you had a different next of kin, that would solve the issue."

"How am I going to get a different next of kin? I can't change my family. Do we need to try to get Jace back? I mean, he's out of contact until God knows when."

"That is one option, though not the only one."

I gave a humorless laugh. "Are you planning to adopt me the way you've adopted all the Wayward Sons?"

Delilah laid a hand on my arm. "Oh, child, we would in a heartbeat."

"But since you're too old for that... Well, if you were married, your husband would be your next of kin. That would override any blood ties your parents have."

Stunned, I could only stare for a long minute. "Where the hell am I gonna get one of those? I don't even date. I can't even remember the last time I had a date." Because I didn't trust men enough to get that far.

"I didn't say it would necessarily be easy or truly practical, but getting married in a hurry would save you from all of this."

The absolute absurdity of the suggestion left me speechless.

Before I could open my mouth to ask for more options, Sawyer announced, "I'm in."

I frowned at him. "In what?"

"I'll do it. I'll marry you."

How many shocks could one person take before her head exploded? I couldn't possibly have heard him right. Because this was my childhood crush, the guy I'd been at least halfway in love with from the time I was thirteen, saying he was willing to enter into what amounted to a marriage of convenience in order to save me from my parents.

"You don't know what you're saying."

"I know exactly what I'm saying. I couldn't do anything to stop them from the bullshit they put you through when we were young." He covered my hand with his. "Let me do this for you now, Wren."

Conviction was written all over his face. He truly meant this. And though I suspected this was largely driven by an extra heaping of misplaced guilt, I was... actually considering it. There was no one else on offer. Not even any other candidates I could scare up in the next week or ten days before my parents made their filing. And I did trust Sawyer. Implicitly. He'd do whatever was necessary to protect me.

But if I did this... if I married him... who was going to protect me from my own heart? Because no question, if I made this choice, we'd have to sell it, and there wasn't a chance in hell that the torch I'd carried for him for years wouldn't fan to full flame.

It didn't really matter. I trusted him a lot more than I trusted my parents, and God knew I'd survived far worse than heartbreak.

"This would only be temporary, until everything else is resolved." Because even under the best of circumstances, I hadn't seen much that made me believe in the institution of marriage.

"Until we're certain you're safe," he corrected.

I couldn't find fault with that.

"I can't believe I'm saying this, but okay. Let's get married."

CHAPTER 10

SAWYER

I didn't ask what story Mama Flo gave to Rex Monaghan for why she needed to borrow his Boston Whaler. I wasn't asking much of anything, because if I stopped to analyze what we were doing, I'd... Well, I sure as shit wouldn't back out. Wren needed me. I was trying not to think about the wisdom of this decision and what the hell Jace was gonna say when he found out. I could think about damage control after the deed was done.

My brain helpfully conjured up an image of Willa's long, tanned limbs splayed out for my feasting.

We're not doing that *deed, you cretin. You don't get to* really *claim her as your wife.*

Not that we'd talked about any of those details, either, since this plan had been hatched yesterday afternoon, but I'd sooner cut off my own arm than take advantage of her vulnerability. This was a business arrangement. I was going to be her live-in bodyguard. I'd have to be to sell this to everyone. But I couldn't deny a deep sense of gratification at the idea of finally having the right to shield her from her asshole father the way I'd always wanted. If that made me the faithful dog Chet Banks and Marcus Hoffman had accused me of being, so be it.

There was no waiting period to acquire a marriage license in North Carolina, and the nearest place we could get one was from the Dare County Register of Deeds in Manteo, which was about sixty nautical miles north of Hatterwick, on Roanoke Island. Hence the Boston Whaler. We'd needed the speed. Conditions were favorable today, with the wind at our backs and a blue sky full of cotton candy clouds. We were already an hour into the two-hour trip, and Willa hadn't said a word from where she sat beside me in the cabin.

I kept casting glances at her to gauge whether she'd hit the point of freaking out or wanting to call the whole thing off. Mirrored sunglasses hid those changeable eyes from my view. She seemed... not exactly relaxed, but not as if she was dreading what was coming. I wondered if the reality of it had even sunk in yet. She'd had to handle so much the past few weeks. Especially in the past few days. I wouldn't be surprised if it hadn't processed. That she hadn't asked for more details herself spoke volumes. But when Mimi insisted she'd take care of booking things for the wedding, we let her. What else were we going to do?

Mama Flo spoke up from the seats behind us, raising her voice loud enough to be heard over the engine and wind. "Okay, you two, we need to discuss some things while we're all in private, as the four of us will be the only ones who know the truth of what we're doing today."

I glanced over my shoulder from where I stood at the helm. "Such as?"

"There will probably be a challenge to the marriage because it's new, and we need to discuss how you two can make it believable that you've been engaged and in a long-distance relationship for years, if that becomes necessary."

"We've been friends for years. We wrote to each other

during my entire career in the navy. Letters, emails, texts. We had phone calls. There's history. Who's to say it didn't turn more intimate than it actually did?"

My brain conjured up an image of Willa's hair spread out over my pillow.

Not a good enough reason to use the word 'intimate,' dumbass.

But it did make me think about what it would have been like if she really had been waiting for me at home all this time. No question, I'd have come back a lot more often. As often as I could've managed. She'd have been absolutely worth whatever headaches making the journey would've brought. I might even have elected to retire sooner by choice if she'd been mine, because I wouldn't have wanted to be that far away from her.

Willa swiveled in her seat. "All of that is true, but what if we're expected to produce some kind of documentation about all of this? We've talked about intimate things, but none of it is the ooey gooey and mushy or the kind of interactions you'd expect from two people in love and in a long-distance relationship. If they subpoena our email or text records, nothing in that correspondence is going to sound like more than friends."

Intimate. There's that word again.

I cleared my throat and tried to focus on the matter at hand instead of picturing her naked. "I know a guy who can help with backdating and creating an electronic trail, if needed." Dax owed me for saving his ass a few years back, and he had a real soft spot for damsels in distress. He'd help.

She tipped up her sunglasses and stared at me.

I shrugged. "I know a lot of people who can do a lot of things." And I'd call in every single favor anyone owed me to keep her safe. This was my chance to finally do what I'd wanted to do for her all my life. And, yeah, maybe it was temporary—how things would officially end, and when, were more details we hadn't discussed—but the threat wasn't going to pass quickly. Her dad was absolutely the type who'd circle like a shark, waiting for the faintest hint of blood in the water. People had to believe this marriage was legit, and that meant we had to make it for more than a few months. I staunchly ignored the part of myself that was grateful for that because it meant I got to spend more time close to her, even if it would be a marriage in name only.

"I don't know if a judge would grant a subpoena for your personal correspondence, but it probably wouldn't be a bad thing to lay the groundwork there," Mama Flo said.

"You also need to lay the other groundwork for the questions people will ask as soon as they find out," Mimi added.

"Like what?" Willa asked.

"Like, how did he propose? How long has this been going on? Why didn't you tell anyone? You've lived on Hatterwick almost all your life, sugar. You know how everybody is."

I glanced at Willa again, checking her reaction. Her face was screwed up in a wince.

"I know you hate having people up in your business, Wren—"

"But they're not wrong. We'll decide on a story. If I know what I'm supposed to say, I should be fine."

"We'll stick to the truth as much as possible. That makes for fewer details we have to remember."

Truth: I've been willing to do anything for you pretty much from the time you first took my hand when you were four and looked up at me with those big, trusting eyes.

Willa probably didn't need to know that.

"There's also the matter of when and how you're planning to get the news out," Mimi continued. "I had some ideas on that front."

Willa glanced at me, and I didn't need to see her eyes to catch the trepidation now. "Can't we just sort of drop it in the island grapevine? It'll spread like wildfire."

"You could, but you want to be seen, honey. Out and about

and happy. Y'all are eloping because you just couldn't wait any longer, and you want everybody to know."

"You mean some kind of party."

I didn't blame Willa for the flat tone. She'd been massively over-peopled already in the past week.

"Just a little one. Friends and family. The ones who matter. You won't have to do a thing but show up. I'll take care of the rest," Mimi assured us.

I reached out to lay a hand on Willa's shoulder and squeezed. Much as she had at the memorial service, she reached up to curl her fingers around mine.

"Okay. I'll do the thing. Even peopling isn't worse than dealing with my parents."

The rest of the trip was taken up by talking about more minutiae of the plan. I wasn't sure if we ought to be worried by exactly how much thought and preparation these two women had managed to put into this in less than twenty-four hours. Either way, I was grateful they were on our side.

Once we reached the marina at Manteo, a car was waiting to take the four of us to the Register of Deeds. We didn't look much like a wedding party. We'd dressed for a morning on the water, though we'd each brought garment bags with more dressy attire for the actual ceremony. There'd be a bathroom or something where we'd change at the courthouse. But even in beach clothes, Willa was gorgeous. And for a little while, she'd be mine. At least on paper. That made me an incredibly lucky bastard, because I definitely didn't deserve her.

As it was late morning in the middle of the week, there was no line. It took less than fifteen minutes to present our documentation and get the paperwork to sign. Easy sailing. Not until her pen hovered over the dotted line did Willa hesitate. Maybe all the discussion of the details was finally making this real for her. Or maybe standing here in this official setting, signing very real legal documents to perpetrate a lie in the name of protection, was activating her conscience.

I wrapped an arm around her shoulders and, under the guise of pressing a kiss to her temple, murmured, "It's all gonna be okay."

She relaxed into me with a sigh, then signed her name with a flourish.

The clerk did whatever she had to do, and we paid the fee. Then the marriage license was in my hand.

We'd officially declared our intent to marry. Me, the wrong-side-of-the-island son of the town drunk and the legitimate island princess who'd soon be taking the helm of her family's little empire.

This was really happening.

Mimi clapped in delight. "Okay, you two, let's go get married."

CHAPTER 11

WILLA

I fully expected to go from the registrar's office to whatever civic building housed the justice of the peace, but the car that was waiting for us—yet another thing that Florence and Delilah had orchestrated—took us out of the town proper.

"Where are we going?"

Squished in the backseat between Delilah and the door, I felt her give an excited bounce. "You'll see."

Probably it would have been beneficial to ask more questions about everything these two had managed to set into motion since yesterday, but at this point, I was just along for the ride. If I stopped and thought too hard about it, I was going to barrel straight into overwhelm, and in truth, we didn't have time for that. I trusted these women to have taken care of the details. God, it was such a blessing to know that I could.

Fifteen minutes later, we were weaving through a residential area full of old-growth trees that dappled the street with shade. The car pulled to a stop in front of a two-story shingled house that reminded me so much of Sutter House that I wondered if it dated to the same period. A porch sporting an assortment of comfortable wicker chairs and benches wrapped all the way around the house. There were magnificent views on all sides, both of the sound and the lush green gardens that looked like a cover spread for *Southern Living*.

As we slid out of the car, a woman in a broad-brimmed straw hat and Bermuda shorts came walking around the side. She lifted her hand in a wave. "Flo! Delilah! Is this our happy couple?"

"Sure is," Delilah crowed. "Aren't they cute?"

Um.

Sawyer's hand found mine, and gratitude swamped me that he always just seemed to *know* what I needed.

Florence took on a serious air. "May I present to you the bride, Willa Sutter, and the groom, Sawyer Malone? Kids, meet the Honorable Judge Agatha D'Angelo."

In her lime green T-shirt, tropical patterned shorts, and Birkenstocks, this woman didn't look anything like I imagined a judge. Her explosion of gray hair was gathered back into a ponytail that was thicker than mine, and her blue eyes were warm as they fixed on us. "Welcome, both of you. I'm so delighted to have you. Willa, I knew your grandparents. Lovely people. I'm so sorry for your loss."

Stunned, I couldn't do much more than take the hand she offered. "I... thank you. For the condolences and for doing this."

Judge D'Angelo rubbed her hands together with unmistakable glee. "I never get to do weddings. It'll be a delightful change of pace from being the local hard-ass. Come on inside and change."

Dimly, I wondered if she'd be officiating in her gardening gear. Not that it mattered to me either way. I hadn't spent much time imagining my wedding day. After the example my parents had set, I never really expected to marry. Certainly, I never wanted the big society wedding my mom would've insisted upon, so this mid-week affair at a private home, where no one but a couple of witnesses were invited, was fine. And it wasn't like this was a real marriage anyway, where we were going to be together for the next fifty years and look back at pictures with nostalgia.

Sawyer and I were shown to separate rooms. It didn't take me long to don the breezy white V-neck midi dress. In no universe did it qualify as a wedding dress, but there hadn't been time for me to find a real one. And even if it had been a real wedding, why would I waste that kind of money on something that I'd never wear again? For that amount, I'd rather feed the entire Sutter's Ferry Animal Shelter for a month or more. The dress hit the kind of dressy casual note I hoped we'd both manage for today's ceremony. Plus, it was the only white one I owned.

My hair was going to take longer to sort out. The wind on the two-hour boat ride up to Roanoke Island had whipped it into a snarl. I was working a wide-toothed comb through the tangles when a knock came on the door.

"Come in."

Florence slipped inside. "I thought you might want a little help with your hair."

"Oh, I... yes, actually." With a little laugh, I gave up on the tangles. "I should've braided it before we got on the boat."

"You've had a few things on your mind." She took the comb and nudged me onto an ottoman.

"I kind of didn't expect this from you, being the mom of a boy."

The hands in my hair slowed a bit. "I always kind of wanted a girl, too. It just wasn't in the cards. So thank you for letting me fuss."

We were silent for a few minutes as she gently worked the tangles free.

"Are you ready for this?" And it was Mama Flo asking, not the stiff attorney.

"Does it matter if I am?"

"I suppose not." She cupped my cheek in her palm and looked at me with more softness and genuine affection than I'd ever seen from my own mother. "You've had to face so many things you weren't ready for."

Uncomfortable with the moment of vulnerability stretching between us, I twitched my shoulders. "Isn't that life?"

"To some extent. Yours has been made harder than many by the very people who were meant to look out for you. I won't belabor the point. Just know that everything we're doing here is to defend you from that."

I gently squeezed her wrist. "I know."

"Sawyer was a good boy, and he's grown into an even better man."

"I know that, too." And he was, perhaps, the only reason I hadn't absolutely lost my shit.

Apparently seeing whatever she needed to see in my face, she went back to my hair. Once the tangles had been dispensed with, she managed some kind of quick, loose, beachy look, with the sides twisted and held back with bobby pins. Then she affixed a little crown of sand lilies she'd gotten from who knew where and declared me ready.

I pulled her in for a hug. "Thank you for being here for me."

"Anytime."

We made our way out to the back of the house, which opened into a courtyard exploding with blooms. Live oaks and behemoth magnolias provided dappled afternoon shade over stone pathways, accented with seashells and framed by over-flowing garden beds, where foxgloves, lilies, and delphiniums swayed gently in the breeze. At the garden's edge, a massive arbor drowning in climbing jasmine and morning glories framed a path that led down to the glittering sound beyond. Beside it stood our officiant. Judge D'Angelo had changed into a linen suit and done something to tame her mane of hair into a more sedate Gibson tuck. Beside her stood Sawyer.

I stopped at the sight of him. The sleeves of his untucked Oxford cloth button down were rolled, revealing muscled forearms, but his dark slacks were creased with military precision. The mix of casual and dressy was just exactly right for this garden wedding.

He broke off in the middle of a sentence as he spotted me, his gray eyes honing in with a focus that froze me in place. Without finishing whatever he'd been saying, he strode over, stopping on the step below me, which put us almost on eye-level, though he was still taller.

"You look beautiful."

He didn't have to say it. More, he didn't have to mean it. But I believed him as he stared down at me with an intensity I wasn't entirely sure how to read. My heart kicked into high gear because this was the man I was about to *marry*. For real. Even though it was just for show. My inner thirteen-year-old was swooning because this was *Sawyer*. My Sawyer. Who'd been there for me so many times. Who'd saved my life. Who was saving my life again in a wholly different way.

"Thanks. So do you."

The corner of his mouth quirked up.

"You're going to need these, baby." Delilah thrust a mammoth bouquet of blue hydrangeas and white lilies into my hands.

I stared down at the neatly beribboned bouquet. "How?"

"I'm an artist. I can do flowers. Just because this wedding got put together fast, doesn't mean it can't be beautiful." She squeezed me in a hug. "Now, let's get this show on the road."

We were herded over beneath the arch and positioned until Delilah was satisfied we were properly framed, a process that seemed to amuse the judge immensely. Then, at last, we were beginning.

"Do you have the rings?"

Sawyer's face blanked in uncharacteristic panic. "Oh, hell, I forgot—"

"I didn't." I reached into the pocket of my dress—its number one selling point—and produced a pair of simple gold bands. "These were my grandparents'. We may end up having to get yours resized, but I thought..."

"No, they're perfect."

"Okay then, let's begin."

We pocketed our respective rings, then Sawyer took both my hands in his. As I faced him, I felt a burble of hysterical laughter catch in my chest. This was absolutely *insane*.

He must've seen the rising overwhelm because he squeezed my hands, gently stroking his thumbs over the pulse points in my wrists. I focused on that soft brush of his skin against mine, over and over, through the simple, traditional vows I barely registered repeating. That touch was almost drugging, giving the proceedings a dreamlike quality as we slid rings onto each other's fingers and finished saying the words that would bind us together.

"I now pronounce you husband and wife. You may kiss the bride."

That dreamlike state popped like a bubble, and suddenly time was moving normally again, with no insulation from the vague hint of panic.

We hadn't discussed this. Maybe he hadn't thought it was necessary to talk about because it was a wedding. Of course this was part of it. But somehow I hadn't remembered and—

He bent and pressed his lips to mine, and my mind went utterly blank. There was nothing salacious in the kiss. It was respectful, almost chaste. But that brush of his lips against mine rocked me to my marrow. I'd thought of having his mouth on mine a million times since he saved me from drowning, and now here it was. Our first kiss.

I swayed toward him, instinctively rising to meet him as all the denied desires I'd bottled for years fizzed up and boiled over. His hand slid beneath my hair to cup my nape, his fingers settling over the little tattoo he didn't even know I had, and the touch set me on fire. It felt possessive and comforting, and I wanted to feel it everywhere.

Then the kiss was over.

Sawyer pulled back, leaving me wanting and aching in places I had no business expecting him to soothe, considering this marriage was essentially a favor.

But as I numbly turned toward Delilah's demand for more pictures, a little voice echoed in my head.

But he's your very real husband.

CHAPTER 12
SAWYER

With the ease and familiarity of a lifetime around boats, I eased the Boston Whaler back into its slip and cut the engine. Mama Flo had already looped the stern line around a piling as I leapt to the dock to tie off the bow. We were officially back on Hatterwick.

Everybody gathered their stuff, as if something momentous hadn't just happened. I handed Mama Flo and Mimi safely to the dock, then reached to take Willa's hand. She was more than capable of making the transition herself, but I couldn't stop myself from stepping close and wrapping an arm around her waist, plucking her from the boat and hauling her safely into me until her feet touched the worn wood planks.

We stared at each other for a long moment, because we'd done the thing we set out to do and now... now was the after we hadn't talked about.

The wind had snatched a lock of her hair from her braid, plastering it across her cheek. I tucked it behind her ear. "Now what?"

She stood close enough that I felt her chest rise and fall

with a sigh. "Well, at the very least, I need to go tell Bree, because obviously I'm not taking you back to the cottage tonight. That would be weird."

Because it's our wedding night.

And, shit, now I was trying desperately *not* to think about that, because, of course, it wasn't going to be *that* kind of wedding night. My dick wasn't getting the memo because this was my *wife*. She still wore the pretty white dress. Color flushed her cheeks, and her hair was windblown and a little wild. I preferred it this way. Not so hemmed in by perfection. I liked that for Willa, who'd been jailed by rules around appearance and propriety for so much of her life.

"That would be a great place to start spreading the news," Mimi agreed. "Why don't y'all go on by the Brewhouse on the way back?"

"May as well. At least it won't be very busy this time of day." That would certainly be easier on her than any kind of formalized *Surprise! We Eloped!* reception Mimi might dream up.

"Okay. I wouldn't say no to a glass of wine, even if it's not even four o'clock."

"I feel like we can make that happen."

We piled our stuff into Willa's Jeep and made the short drive up to OBX Brewhouse. Mimi and Mama Flo followed in their own car. The sprawling two-story structure was clad in weathered gray shingles, with a wraparound porch dotted with rocking chairs and benches for patrons to wait until their table was ready or enjoy a glass of beer made on-site. The microbrewery had been added during the rebuild, after an arsonist had burned the place nearly to the ground during my last summer on the island before joining the Navy. Awning windows were propped open on three sides, taking advantage of the sea breezes and the view of Pamlico Sound a couple of blocks away. It looked as if it had always been here, exactly like this. Bree had worked hard to ensure the rebuild stayed true to the character of the tavern her grandfather had run his whole life, even as she'd added a new addition to house the stainless-steel kettles and other equipment for the microbrewery that had become a tourist draw in its own right.

As predicted, the parking lot was only partly full when we arrived. Before we got out of the Jeep, Willa shoved her sunglasses up on top of her head and looked at me. "We have to behave like married people."

Where was she going with this? "That's the point of this little exercise, right? To let people know we're married?"

"I mean, yes. I just... We can't go in there as friends."

"We're still friends, Wren."

Her cute little nose screwed up. "I know. But I mean, they're going to expect PDA."

Ah, was that what had her worried? She'd seemed okay with the kiss at the wedding. In fact, she'd seemed into it, something I'd been trying to *not* think about when I'd forced myself to let her go. Maybe it was the public part of PDA that bothered her.

"I won't do anything you aren't comfortable with."

She waved a hand. "I'm not worried about *that*. You'll just have to remember to, you know, touch me."

Oh Wren, wanting to touch you is not something I have to think about. It's keeping my hands off you that's the problem.

But I wasn't about to admit that.

Keeping a perfectly straight face, I nodded. "Understood."

When she still didn't get out of the car, I reached out to take one of the hands she'd knotted together in her lap. "Are you worried Bree's going to be upset?"

"No. Maybe? I don't really know *how* she's going to react, honestly."

"And you're afraid of having that conversation in a public place?"

Her shoulders relaxed. "Yes."

"You've been friends for years. She knows you. She's not going to make some kind of scene, even if she is upset. And I can't think why she would be, even if this is a surprise." Unless she was worried that I'd somehow taken advantage of Willa's vulnerable, grieving state to force her into something she didn't want. But if Bree thought that, she'd take it up with me first, not Willa.

"Okay. Let's do this."

We strode to the main doors, and I opened them for her, placing a hand at the small of her back to steer her through. Then, mindful of the edict Willa had just handed down, I left it there as we moved through the entryway and past the empty hostess stand.

The roar of whoops and hollers and cheers that greeted us as we rounded into the restaurant startled Willa so badly she practically leapt out of her skin, jolting back into me. Instinctively, I wrapped around her, turning to shield her from... whatever the hell was happening.

Over her head, I spotted a banner stretched across the top of the bar. *Congratulations Willa and Sawyer!* There were wedding bells on either side.

"What the actual hell?"

Willa lifted her head from my chest and peered past my shoulder to where a wall of our friends stood. Bree and Ed were behind the bar. Gabi was perched on a stool at the end, grinning from ear to ear. Caroline and Hoyt, Hoyt's folks, the kids. There were a handful of other locals in the rest of the restaurant, but this was effectively most of our found family already gathered right here. And obviously, they knew.

I looked back at Mama Flo and Mimi, who'd followed us inside. Mimi just shrugged, a grin ruining her innocent, *who-me?* expression. Clearly, this was her doing.

Caroline was the first one to hurry over. "Congratulations!

Oh, my God, I'm so excited for you! I *knew it!* I *knew* you two were in love with each other."

Wait, what? Things aren't like that between us.

But as Caroline dragged us deeper into the room, and we accepted more congratulations and handshakes, there was more of the same from literally everybody.

"Always suspected."

"You two make the cutest couple."

"Predicted this all the way back in high school."

Willa and I kept looking at each other until finally she stopped moving. "We thought y'all would be surprised."

I'd never heard a unanimous scoff before.

Caroline propped both fists on her hips. "Honey, the way you two feel about each other has been the worst kept secret on Hatterwick in ages. We totally knew as soon as he was back to stay that something like this was going to happen. I do confess, I did not expect elopement this fast. I'm really proud of you! That's great."

Bree had come out from behind the bar. She was smirking at both of us as she pulled Willa in for a hug. "Nothing between you two, my ass."

Willa just gave a helpless shrug and smile before she snuggled back into me. It was instinct to tighten my arm around her and brush a kiss to her brow.

Gabi clapped her hands. "Let's celebrate. Bree is, of course, in charge of drinks. There are appetizers, and we even got cake." She gestured expansively to a tiered stand loaded with little cupcakes iced in wedding white with what turned out to be our initials piped on top in blue.

Willa took one look at those cupcakes and teared up. "I didn't... We didn't... How did you do all of this?"

Hoyt's grin was secretive. "A little bird told us what you two got up to today."

Now it was Willa who looked back at Mimi, who simply blew her a kiss and said, "You're welcome."

I braced myself to do whatever was needed to extract my bride in case this was all too much, but instead she laughed. "Thank you."

And that was how we found ourselves in the middle of a wedding reception we hadn't planned for the marriage we hadn't known we were entering more than twenty-four hours ago.

Somebody produced a knife, and we were ordered to cut the cake. Together, we sliced right down the middle of one of the cupcakes, which turned out to be Italian cream—Willa's favorite. Mimi wasn't the only one who had her phone out to take photos as we fed bites to each other. I didn't smash cake in Willa's face. She'd have hated that. Instead, I held it out so she could take as big or small a bite as she liked. I ate the entire half she offered me. Her eyes lit with challenge as she did the same, then turned to lick a trace of icing off my thumb.

My dick leapt at the feel of that little tongue against my skin and the expression of impish delight on her face as she did it. I told myself it was just in the name of selling our cover that I reeled her in. "You've got a little something right…"

I licked the icing off the corner of her mouth. And then that mouth was *right there*. No newly wedded man in his right mind *wouldn't* kiss his wife after that. It was strictly performative.

Except she sighed into the kiss, rising against me, wrapping her arms around my shoulders as she kissed me back, and I was lost. She tasted of butter and sweetness and something deeper, richer that had to be simply her. Everything in me craved more of that taste, and I chased it, deepening the kiss, pulling her closer. She opened for me on a little whimper that set my blood aflame.

It was the cheering and whistles that broke through my out-of-control lust. For a moment, I could only wonder why the hell all these people were here, why we weren't alone to follow this madness to its inevitable conclusion.

And then I remembered.

Somehow, I found the strength to pull back. But as I stared down at my wife, with her rosy lips swollen from mine and those eyes so hugely dilated with arousal, all I could think was, *I am in so much trouble.*

CHAPTER 13

SAWYER

The summer sun hadn't yet set by the time I rolled up to Sutter House later that night, but I was already yawning. The sugar high from the cupcakes I'd eaten was wearing off, and everything that had happened in the past few days was catching up to me. After our impromptu wedding reception—I still couldn't get over how enthusiastic everyone had been about this marriage—we'd gone by the lighthouse to collect Sawyer's things, and by the cottage for me to pack a bag with the basics for a few days, along with Roy and all of his accoutrements. He was in full velcro mode after being left at home for so much of the past week. Poor neglected pup.

Sawyer parked beside me as I got out of the Jeep and sprang Roy from his seatbelt. He climbed out, shouldering a duffel bag. "Is it just me, or do you also feel like you've been hit by a semi after all that?"

"Definitely not just you. I still can't believe everything Delilah and Florence managed to organize."

He popped the back hatch and snagged one of my bags. "Let's just be grateful they're using their combined powers for good."

"Seriously." I snagged the other bag, and we trudged toward the porch.

Roy's soft, almost soundless woof drew my attention down to the beach. I gasped. "Look."

Far below, at the edge of the water, the wild horses milled. Waves frothed around their hooves. Sun glinted off the pewter gray coat of the stallion who'd protected this band most of my life. He looked positively regal as he circled around them, which was the reason I'd dubbed him Triton years ago. King of the Sea. Automatically, I did a quick headcount. Twenty-four. This was most of the herd. It felt almost as if they'd come out en masse to give their blessing to this marriage. Which was a ludicrous thought on multiple fronts, since this wasn't real.

I thought back to the reception, to that kiss after the cake. No, that hadn't just been a kiss. That had been full-on making out. In public. And damn, now I really wanted to do more of it in private. With considerably fewer clothes. Because this was our wedding night, damn it. Even if this was supposed to be temporary, why shouldn't we take advantage of this? Clearly, we were both attracted. Weren't we? Or had that whole thing just been a performance on his part to sell our newlywed status?

It hadn't felt like a performance.

But I'd been too caught up in my own arousal to focus on anything but how he'd made me feel.

I knew he'd married me to protect me, probably not in small part out of the guilt I *knew* he still carried over the night I'd drowned. I wanted it to be more than that. Not that all that wasn't huge, and not that I wasn't grateful. But I couldn't bear to put myself out there, only to be reminded of all that and gently rejected if he didn't feel more for me. So I said nothing as I turned toward the door and let us into the house.

Inside, I was immediately struck by the mountain of things that needed doing. "I guess there are a lot of logistics we've got to figure out. I'll need to pack up all my things at the cottage to move up here. And what about your stuff?"

"Right now, this is pretty much it, other than what's still in the truck. I've been on the go for quite a while. Friends packed up the rest of my shit in Naples, and it's waiting to be shipped. I need to contact the Navy and give them the address where to deliver it."

That was going to be here. We were going to share an address. An address was the least of the things I expected us to share, but somehow it felt intimate. A sign of joining lives. Why that felt different from sharing an address with Bree, I couldn't pinpoint beyond the fact that I didn't imagine getting naked with her. And I certainly hadn't just vowed to love, honor, and cherish her.

We moved through the house, toward the staircase that would take us up to the bedrooms. At the corner of the hall, I stopped, blinking as my vision grayed.

"Hey, you okay?" Sawyer's arm came around my shoulders, the touch grounding me.

I shook my head as if that would somehow clear the mental image of feet I could still picture there. I didn't want to bring up that this was where I'd found Granddaddy. No doubt I was having a bit of a trauma response. It would fade in time. "Yeah, I... had too much sugar and not enough substance, I guess."

"A good night's sleep will help."

What were those like? I hadn't had one in years.

Sawyer stuck close as we made our way upstairs to the primary bedroom.

I stepped inside the space, noting the way the wood trim gleamed in the setting sun that streamed in through the west-facing window. The room itself was massive, with heavy wood furniture that was saved from being staid by a coat of bright white paint my grandmother had insisted upon as a new bride.

Some might have said such refinishing of antiques was a travesty, but I liked the more casual, lived-in look of the place.

"Is it gonna be weird sleeping in here? Wasn't this your grandparents' bedroom?"

"It was, but Granddaddy didn't stay in this room after Grandma died. It hurt too much to be here without her. I still need to go through and pack up and donate their things to make room in the closets."

He stood just inside the doorway, scanning the space. "Where do you want me?"

Over me. Under me. Inside me.

Heat moved into my cheeks as I imagined the myriad ways we could take each other in this room. In this house.

God, is the air conditioner broken?

Every inch of my skin felt as if it were on fire, urging me to strip down to nothing. To strip *him* down to nothing.

For a moment, I pictured myself walking over and nudging the duffel bag off his shoulder, then taking his hand and backing toward the big king-size bed that had fresh sheets I'd thought to put on last night. Not with this in mind, but...

Sawyer jerked his head back toward the hall. "I thought I saw a bedroom across the way."

Right. Because he has no intention of sleeping with me.

And that was for the best, really. Because I didn't share my bed for a reason. Even now, I was often plagued with nightmares, and I didn't really want to give him more explanations about that.

Clearing my throat, I struggled to tamp down the lust. "Yeah, it's one of the guest rooms."

"Cool, I'm gonna go get unpacked."

"I'm gonna go have a bath." At least in the privacy of a locked bathroom, I could do something about this need thrumming through me.

If I hoped that would make him picture me naked and ask to join me, I was sorely disappointed.

He just smiled an almost brotherly sort of smile. "You deserve a good long soak. Enjoy." He turned toward the hall and started to walk away.

"Sawyer?"

"Yeah?" The eyes he turned back to me were expectant.

Please stay. The words hovered on the tip of my tongue, a desire driven by so many reasons. But what came out instead was, "Thank you for doing this."

For long moments, he stared at me with stormy gray eyes. "I'd do anything for you, Wren. Sleep well."

I stood there for a long time after he shut the door and walked away, clutching a hand over the heart that already felt a little bruised.

If you'll do anything for me, can't you find it in yourself to want me?

CHAPTER 14

SAWYER

"You sure you don't want me to stay with you?"

Willa shook her head, her hand automatically reaching down to stroke Roy's ears. "I'll be okay. They need to see me standing on my own. I learned enough from observing my entire family growing up to know that."

I still didn't like it, but I absolutely saw her point. It would be important to her that no one see me and assume I was somehow pulling strings as the man in the relationship. Not that I'd ever do that, but I understood her sensitivity on that point because of her parents' marriage. She was here at the main ferry company offices to reassure leadership and staff. She didn't need me for that.

"Okay. I'm gonna swing by the hardware store and pick up a few things."

"Sounds good. I shouldn't be more than an hour."

Aware of the avid gazes of the ferry company staff inside, I skimmed my fingers over her cheek to tuck a lock of hair behind her ear. I told myself it was for their benefit that I bent to brush my lips over hers. But that little catch of her breath? That was purely for me. And I was probably going to hell because, damn it, I wanted my wife in every way it was possible to want a woman.

"Text me if you get through early."

"Uh-huh."

I shouldn't have enjoyed that dazed look in her eyes so damned much. Not when I had no intention of following through on this unexpectedly mutual attraction.

Opening the door, I nudged her inside, toward a smiling Winslow Hobbs, who'd been manager since before I joined the Navy. Roy obediently stuck to her like glue. I watched for a moment as she shook Winslow's hand and followed him toward the offices in the back. She had this. Given I had plenty of time to kill, I elected to walk to the hardware store. I didn't have so many things to get that carrying a couple bags would be a big deal. Maybe a walk in the bright summer morning would clear my head.

Between being in a new place and a way too vivid imagination offering mental images of Willa naked in that bathtub, with a secretive smile and an invitation to join her, I hadn't been able to sleep for shit last night. It had taken everything I had to walk away from her with that picture in my head. Even if she was attracted—and it seemed like she was—we hadn't even dated. We'd gone from friends—long-distance ones at that—to married in the blink of an eye. She'd had major losses, major changes, and she was vulnerable. I was meant to keep her safe, not take advantage. So, I'd wandered the house, exploring the place I'd be calling home for at least the next several months and noting an assortment of small repairs that needed to be taken care of.

Hence, the trip to the hardware store. It was something I could do to contribute. Given Willa's status and my own current unemployment, that was important to me. While our friends had been wildly enthusiastic about our marriage, that wouldn't be the case for everyone on Hatterwick. Plenty of folks would remember me as the son of the town drunk. The trash from the wrong side of the island who wasn't remotely good enough for the likes of Willa. There was still a part of me that agreed.

"Sawyer Malone!"

I jerked my head toward the unmistakable summons and held in a scowl. Speaking of not good enough. Miles Busby was crossing the street, headed straight for me. Eldest kid of another prominent family on Hatterwick, he'd been a couple years ahead of me in school and stratospheres above me in social standing. I'd been one of his favorite targets. He'd stopped physically bullying me once Ford and Rios had completed our quartet, but the snide remarks designed to undermine my self-confidence had continued all the way until I'd left to join the Navy. He'd been a shit all his life, even before his little sister Gwen disappeared. His family's tragedy hadn't done a damned thing to improve his attitude.

He was all smiles as he intercepted me, and that just put me on edge. What did this fucker want?

"I understand felicitations are in order."

"Excuse me?"

The smile got a little wider, as if he thought I didn't under-stand what 'felicitations' meant. "On your wedding, of course. My sincerest congratulations to you and Willa."

Ah. So the island grapevine was doing its job. Everybody knew—or would, by the end of the day. But that didn't explain why he was talking to me about it. Miles had never said a sincere thing in his life, and there wasn't a chance in hell he thought this marriage was a good thing.

"Thanks."

I don't know what he expected, but when I said nothing else, the faint, uncomfortable pause gave me an unreasonable sense of satisfaction.

"Right, well, as a descendant of one of the original founding families, Willa will be expected to have a role in celebrating the traditional events around Founder's Day, like the parade and the ceremonial wreath laying."

Willa would hate all of that. She loathed being the center of attention.

"Why exactly is this your concern?"

Busby adopted a faux-innocent expression. "Oh, didn't you know? I'm the mayor of Sutter's Ferry now."

Just fucking perfect. This man had no business at all being in a position of power, no matter how small.

"I'd love to get together with you and your lovely bride to discuss the schedule of events and opportunities for her to participate and connect more deeply with the town's history and community this year. It's so important for Willa to be part of these traditions, now that she's back and has taken on leadership of the Sutter legacy."

Right. As if she hadn't been back already contributing to the town for the past ten years. He didn't give a damn about her until she was in a position to do something for him, and now he thought he could get to her through me? Was this what it was going to be like now? People who used to treat me like a piece of shit on the bottom of their shoe were now going to try to ingratiate themselves with me to access my wife?

I doubted Willa would want anything to do with any of this, but it was her decision how she wanted to navigate her family legacy, so I wouldn't cut it off unless she wanted me to.

"I'll be sure to mention it to my wife." That was as much as I'd promise him. I wouldn't speak for her without knowing where she stood.

"Wonderful. I look forward to seeing you both."

Sure you do.

Humming a noncommittal note, I continued on my way. I'd have to be mindful of how I behaved toward people, now that Willa was linked to me. Not that I routinely went around being an asshole, but anything I said or did would reflect on her. I didn't want her impacted by my losing my temper or sticking my foot in it with somebody. I guess that meant that, for a while at least, I was also partly responsible for upholding the Sutter legacy. The weight of that felt odd on my shoulders. I wasn't accustomed to living up to something. It made me wonder how Willa had survived the expectations of not one, but two different family names.

At the hardware store, I collected more congratulations, along with the light bulbs, faucet seals, and WD-40 I'd come for. There were even a few "Thank you for your service" remarks thrown in that I didn't know what to do with, and at least one overheard, "I can't believe she married *him*," that was more in line with what I'd expected. All in all, I just felt... weird. I'd been confused enough about my place here before I'd added Willa into the mix. Now I wondered what the long-term consequences of our marriage would be. Would I become the de facto bad guy once we split? That was how divorce worked, right? People took sides, whether they knew the whys or not. I didn't relish the thought, but I was no stranger to judgment. Better I be the target than Willa.

The idea of it left me with a bad taste in my mouth. I didn't want to think about the end of things. And that was just bone stupid on my part. I'd known what this was going into it. Just because she was temptation personified didn't change all the reasons we couldn't work for real. I was effectively her bodyguard, and I'd do well to remember that, for her sake as well as my own.

At least a half dozen more people stopped to congratulate me on my way back to the ferry offices, slowing me enough that I spotted Willa waiting just outside the doors by the time I got loose. She wasn't alone. Some middle-aged guy in a suit was stepping closer to her than he had any business being. I picked up my pace just as Roy neatly inserted himself between them, conveniently expanding her personal space bubble by swinging that massive head toward the guy's crotch.

Good boy.

"—Anthony Strand of Albemarle Development Group. I had intended to wait to approach you, but here you are. It's kismet. I'd like to set up a meeting."

I recognized that slick salesman's smile. Judging by the frown Willa shot him, so did she.

"About what?" Her hand automatically reached for mine as I joined them, but Strand paid no attention to me.

"About investment opportunities, Miss Sutter. The development of your property."

Well, that clinched it. He wasn't a local. Didn't know about our marriage, and didn't know a damned thing about Willa as a person.

I watched the shutters come down. Her shoulders straightened and her jaw firmed.

Stubborn streak activated. I'd seen this look off and on her whole life. Willa didn't dig in about much, but when she did, nothing could budge her.

"I have zero interest in selling or developing anything. And even if I did, it's all going to be in probate for a while."

Strand's smile turned a little brittle around the edges. "I understand it's too soon for you to have decided anything. My apologies for jumping the gun, as it were. Maybe you'll change your mind." He extended a business card that she pointedly didn't take.

Nothing in his expression outwardly changed, but something in his scent or posture must have. Roy rose from his seated position, stepping toward Strand with a low growl. Willa didn't correct him.

Evidently recognizing he'd get no further, he withdrew the card and took a cautious step back. "Another time then. Good day, Miss Sutter."

We both watched him stride away.

"I'll sell that land when hell freezes over," Willa muttered.

I drew her in, rubbing at the tension that had lodged in her nape and shoulders. "What would you like to do with the land? I mean, not that you have to do anything with it. I know you said you'd like it to stay pristine."

"Actually, I'd really like to create a protected wildlife sanctuary for the horses. It was something I wanted to talk to Granddaddy about for the last year, but there just wasn't a good opportunity with Grandma's failing health and then his own grief. But I guess there's not really anything stopping me from pursuing that now. At least once things are settled around my parents."

At the reminder, her shoulders tensed up again. We were still waiting for the other shoe to drop in terms of whatever legal attacks they were planning to make. Better to get her focused on the future, on the potential there. I brushed a kiss to her temple. "I think that's a great plan for it. And very you." Easing back, I studied her face. "How did the meeting go?"

She looped her arms around my waist and smiled up at me, those changeable hazel eyes brightening like sunlight glinting off water. "How 'bout I tell you over lunch? Then we can swing by Mr. O'Shea's office to tell him officially about us, even though he's probably already heard."

"Sounds like a plan."

CHAPTER 15

WILLA

I hesitated outside the door of the island clinic. Making the appointment had been an impulse. Part hope, part practicality. I knew this marriage with Sawyer was supposed to be public-facing only, but in the event that he changed his mind, I figured it was better to be ready. And maybe a more optimistic part of me was hoping I'd manifest that mind change by coming here today.

Committed, I tugged open the door and stepped inside. Since it was a medical clinic, I was sans Roy. Sawyer had taken him for a jog down on the beach, and I really hoped that didn't backfire before I met them at the cottage for some more packing.

Nina Lambert looked up from the front desk and grinned. "Willa! You're looking fabulous. That newlywed life treating you well?"

Heat flooded my cheeks at her implication. But—well—that was exactly what I wanted, wasn't it? The notion of sex with Sawyer had been occupying a significant portion of my waking and sleeping thoughts since the moment he'd first kissed me. It was a nice departure from the nightmares that still plagued me more often than not.

"It's good."

Nina's dark brown eyes danced, but I didn't feel like it was at my expense. "You got one of the good ones there. You know your man changed my flat tire when he was back in high school?"

"Oh?"

Her firm nod made the beads on her headful of braids jangle a little. "Sure did. I was stuck out on the ocean road with my Nico in the backseat—he was only two then. Didn't even have a jack in that old car. Sawyer came along and took care of the whole thing."

"He's always been good about stuff like that."

"Glad to see him back on-island and to know the two of you are happy." She thrust a clipboard at me. "Here. Fill out this paperwork and sign here, here, and initial here. We'll call you back in just a few. And I was so sorry about your granddaddy. He'll be missed."

"Thank you."

It only took a few minutes to dispense with the paperwork. Fifteen minutes later, I'd been weighed and had my blood pressure checked.

"Little on the high side," Kristie Turner announced as she peeled off the cuff.

I surreptitiously wiped my hands on my shorts. "I have some medical anxiety." That was putting it mildly. After my experience off-island, I barely took more than a Tylenol these days, and I avoided medical settings like the plague. On the rare occasions I needed something, I favored online providers. Professionals who couldn't physically touch me. But this was Gabi. I could endure all this with her.

"We'll check you again before you leave."

She led me to a patient room. "Dr. Carrera will be with you shortly."

I took one look at the paper-covered exam table and veered to take the visitor's chair. The less I felt like an actual patient today, the better.

Gabi didn't keep me waiting long. She came through the door with a burst of energy. "Girl, I know we've both had a lot going on, but this was not where I thought we'd be seeing each other next."

I laughed, some of the tension draining. "It seemed the most efficient place for a catch up."

"We don't need to talk about the epic crash and burn of the situationship I was in most of the way through residency. I'm single now. There, you're caught up on me."

So that was what had put that sadness in her eyes when she'd first come back to the island. I was willing to bet that had been why she'd been able to come back early. Before I could ask her more questions, she barreled on ahead.

"*I* want to know exactly how it is you just *married* the guy you've been crushing on since basically sixth grade?"

For about five seconds, I considered telling her the truth. But no doubt these walls had ears, and Florence had warned me it was imperative for everyone to believe this marriage was real. That meant the fewer people in the circle of truth, the better. But Gabi knew me really well. She'd been one of the few friends to have a front-row seat to all those years of pining when we were younger. I'd have a higher bar to keep her from asking questions.

"So... I haven't been completely honest."

Gabi grabbed the rolling stool and plopped down. "Spill."

"Sawyer and I have always been friends. You know that. But things were different after I drowned. I mean, it's easy to love your hero, you know? He risked his life to save mine. Literally breathed me back to life. I don't know if that's when things changed for him. He still thought of me as too young, and there was Jace, who would have had Opinions."

She snorted. "Oh, I'm sure. Your brother's never been short on those."

"We stayed in touch when he left for the Navy. Even though he wasn't here, we got closer in a lot of ways, talking about fears and dreams."

"When did things change?"

"Oh, not for years. I didn't even realize things had changed for him for a long time." This was getting into the story we'd decided on together. There was enough plausibility and distance that no one would be able to disprove it. "About three years ago, we met in Raleigh while he was on leave. It was a quick couple of days before he had to get back. We were just going to hang out because we wanted to see each other. But then..." I trailed off, knowing Gabi's romantic heart would fill in the gaps.

"Then he realized you were a sexy AF, grown-ass woman, and he couldn't keep his hands off you?"

If only.

"Something like that."

Gabi clapped her hands, her eyes sparkling. "I love that for you. But why keep it a secret?"

"Because of Jace. Not that we need his permission, but we weren't sure how he'd react." I paused as it occurred to me we were going to have to tell my brother we'd gotten married. I really *didn't* know how he'd take that news. But that was a problem that could wait a while. One thing at a time.

"So you two have had a secret relationship for the past three years? God, it must have been so hard having him deployed and in harm's way."

This, at least, wasn't a lie. "It wasn't great. I'd still like to slap him upside the back of the head for not telling me about his shoulder injury. But he didn't want to worry me, and he thought to surprise me when he came home for good."

"Mission accomplished there. So, how did he propose? Was it super romantic, like making passionate love to you and then declaring he couldn't wait another day to call you his own?"

Oh, the fantasies *that* scenario incited in my brain.

The story we'd settled on wasn't nearly so sexy.

"It was a lot quieter and more practical than that. We were up on the north end of the island, watching the horses and catching up. This was right after he got back, before the funeral." *Before the reading of the will.* That had seemed an imperative detail to throw in there. "Between his injuries and the fact that Granddaddy had just died, we were both keenly feeling the fact that life is short. With him actually home and out of the Navy, we didn't want to wait anymore. You know me. I have zero interest in a big splashy wedding with all those people and eyes and whatever, so we decided to elope. Since that takes a lot less planning, here we are." I took a breath. "Which brings me to why I'm here today... for some of that planning we didn't do in advance."

"Ah. Birth control. That I can help you with. Though I also love the idea of little Sawyers and Willas running around filling that big ol' house with joy."

I could see it. Filling Sutter House with family as it was meant to be. But that was a fantasy predicated on a lot of lies. Sawyer wouldn't be making a real life with me. As soon as the threat to me was definitively over, we'd divorce and get on with our real lives. If the mere thought of that made me queasy, I blamed it on the fact that I hadn't had anything but coffee this morning.

Forcing a smile I didn't feel, I lifted a brow. "I've been married for all of two days. Maybe let us get used to things before you give us the two-point-five kids to go with the dog."

"Spoilsport. But fine. I suppose you two deserve plenty of

time to make up for all those years of long distance." She waggled her eyebrows and grinned.

Please, God, yes.

"Now, I'm gonna need you to pee in a cup."

CHAPTER 16

SAWHYER

"I think this is the last of it." I slid the box into a hole between a bookcase and a chest of drawers in the back of my truck.

Willa stepped on the tire and pushed herself up so she could lean in to attach one of the bungee straps. "Aren't you glad I'm not one of those women with eleven-thousand pairs of shoes?"

I took the other end and stretched it across the load, securing it to the next hook. "I'm grateful you're exactly who you are, every single day."

"I want to gag a little because you two are so cute, but I'm too pleased you're happy to give into it." The side-eye Bree shot me made me question how pleased she really was.

Through the whole process of packing Willa's stuff and hauling it up to Sutter House, she'd been giving me looks that suggested she didn't completely trust me. But she hadn't said a word and hadn't pushed. Maybe this was carryover from her fallout with Ford years ago. Or maybe she was reserving judgment. That was fair enough. She was one of Willa's best friends, and she had to be feeling some shit over the fact that she hadn't known about us.

Willa leapt down, brushing her hands off on her shorts. "Well, I guess this is it."

"Good thing, too. They've issued a hurricane watch for that storm off the coast. Either way, we'll be getting a shit-ton of rain in a few days." Once we got all her stuff stowed away, we'd be working on prepping the house to deal with that.

Bree's hard shell cracked, and she pulled Willa in for a huge hug. "I'm gonna miss you like crazy."

"It's not like you're not going to see me on the regular. I'll be coming by the brewery all the time."

"Yeah, but it won't be the same as coming home to have you here." She wiped at something that might have been a tear. "I'm even going to miss that big lug of a dog. Maybe I'll think about getting my own."

"You should totally do that. There's a mutt at the shelter who would be perfect for you. I'm pretty sure he's part Aussie Shepherd. Smart as a whip. He's very trainable and super chill inside."

Bree laughed and let her go. "I'll think about it. Do you need help unloading on the other side?"

"No, we've got it. Honestly, the fact that we've gotten everything in two loads really highlights how little stuff I have."

Because she cared more about experiences than possessions. It was just one of the things I'd always admired about her. "You ready to get rolling?"

"The sooner we go, the sooner we're done."

"And the sooner you two can get back to the boning you'd rather be doing," Bree added.

"Bree!" Willa's face had turned the color of a grape tomato.

"What? You're newlyweds. It's expected."

Good thing there was a truck between me and the two

women to hide my dick's reaction to that. "Right. Let's go, Wren."

With one last hug, Willa climbed into her Jeep, and we started our caravan out to Sutter House. I spent the whole time mentally reciting naval regulations to kill the semi-permanent woody I'd had basically since the moment I said, 'I do.' It didn't work.

What did was the sight of the unfamiliar vehicle waiting in the drive when we got home.

Who the hell was this?

The guy leaning against the bumper of the gray sedan straightened as we slid out of our respective vehicles. "Willa Sutter?"

She frowned. "Yes?"

The guy moved toward her, and I hustled to intercept. Roy was corralled in the house to maximize hauling space, so I was on full guard-dog duty.

"I have a delivery for you."

Her frown deepened. "What kind of delivery?"

I made it to her side just as he offered her a large manilla envelope. I had a real bad feeling about that envelope, but Willa took it.

"You've been served."

"Son of a bitch." They'd tracked her down here? At home?

The guy's eyes widened, and he lifted his hands, backing away. "Just doing my job, man. Sorry about whatever this is."

I scowled after him until he'd made it back into his car and drove off. She already had the contents pulled out by the time I turned. Over her shoulder, I read the top of the document. *Petition for the Adjudication of Incompetence.*

The papers shook in her hand, but her voice was steady. "Well, we knew it was coming. I guess now we call Mr. O'Shea."

I held her hand as she did that right from the middle of the driveway.

"It's here. No, I haven't read it yet. Uh-huh. Uh-huh. Okay, we'll see you then. Thanks, Mr. O'Shea." She hung up. "He's going to come out at the end of the day, as soon as he's done with appointments, so we can talk about all this."

I stroked a thumb along the skittering pulse in her wrist. "Are you okay?"

She huffed a humorless laugh. "No, not really."

I couldn't fathom what she was going through right now. What she must be feeling. What she might be remembering. Because I couldn't do anything else, I wrapped her tight in my arms. "I won't let them get to you."

On a sigh, she burrowed in. "I know. It's just dragging up a lot of shit."

"Do you want to talk about it?" As soon as the words were out of my mouth, I wished I could take them back. "You don't have to. You don't owe me an explanation." My curiosity about what she'd been through had more to do with exactly how many lifetimes in hell her parents had earned.

For a long moment, she stayed quiet. "I don't know specifically what they're claiming, but I suppose you should know at least the basics of what they have to work from. Let's get Roy and go for a walk. I need to move. The stuff can wait to be unloaded."

The moment the door opened, Roy bounded out, dancing around her, his whip of a pittie tail wagging a hundred miles per hour. He sniffed her from all sides, then engaged velcro mode, sticking right at her hip as she headed for the stairs that led down to the beach. There were no signs of the horses today. Maybe for the best. I didn't know how they'd react to the dog.

We strode partway down the empty beach until Willa dropped down on a rise of sand overlooking the water. Roy stretched out along her left leg. I sat on her right and waited.

"They committed me in the first place on the grounds that I was suicidal."

"What the fuck? You were never suicidal." I paused, realizing I didn't know for certain. "Were you? I didn't think things were that bad." I cursed myself. What did I know about the details of her pain? Maybe it had been that bad.

But Willa only shook her head. "No, but that was the only way they could make sense of me being in the water that night. And since I couldn't remember—still can't remember—how I got there, I didn't have any way to argue. That in and of itself might have been okay. In truth, it should have been maybe a 72-hour hold for evaluation. But what should have been 72 hours turned into nearly two years."

Rage tore through me, every bit as vicious as the storm whose teeth I'd snatched her from. But she didn't need that from me, so I fought it back until I could keep my tone level. "How?"

"I don't know exactly. It started out as treatment for the trauma I'd been through. I had serious holes in my memory, and they were working with me, trying to fill in the gaps. They tried all sorts of things. Hypnosis. EMDR. Virtual reality. Drug therapies."

"They gave you drugs for traumatic amnesia? Is that even a thing?"

"There actually are some used for victims of traumatic brain injuries. Which, technically, I had because of the cerebral hypoxia. We don't know how long I was without oxygen before you revived me."

A lifetime. That's what it had felt like as I'd fought first the sea to get her back and then the fates to give her breath. I had my own lingering trauma around that night. But this wasn't about me.

"Nothing seemed to work, and my parents pushed them to keep trying other things. The treatments got more experimental. When I said I wanted to go home, I was told that it was all for my own good. Really, I think my parents just wanted them to fix me. I'd never been what they wanted me to be, and I was so much worse after drowning."

This had all happened because I hadn't gotten to her fast enough. Because I'd helped her sneak out at all.

Willa's hand closed over my clenched fist. "No. This is not on you. I know you've blamed yourself all these years, but I'm not going to keep telling you if you're going to take this on yourself. This is *not* your fault. If you hadn't helped me sneak out that night, I would have found another way."

I choked down the self-recrimination and loathing. "I'm okay." I wasn't. Not even close. But she'd had to live through this nightmare. I could survive hearing about it. "Keep going."

"My behavior was considered erratic, prospectively dangerous to myself and others. And I suppose it did look like that from the outside. My anxiety was through the roof. I was in this totally unfamiliar place, with unfamiliar people. I kept having PTSD flashbacks. I had a few escape attempts, attacked a few orderlies in the process. That was when they started keeping me drugged for compliance all the time."

I'd already imagined seventeen ways to disable and torture Willa's dad before she continued.

"Eventually, I figured out how to hide my meds under my tongue until I could dispose of them in the toilet. I knew how they expected me to behave, and I mimicked that, analyzing the staff, trying to figure out who was on my side. I managed to convince a nurse who was a new hire to mail a letter to my brother. Jace didn't know any of this was happening. My parents had told him I'd been sent to boarding school. He came to get me immediately, and as he was over eighteen and family, they couldn't stop him from checking me out and spiriting me away before anyone was the wiser. I owe him my life for that. I don't know how much longer I could have lasted in there."

She might as well have stabbed me directly in the heart. The fuckers had kept her caged and drugged for *two years*.

They'd put her through hell for *two years*. I wrapped my arm tighter around her, pulling her close. "I'm so sorry they put you through all that, Wren. If I'd known—"

"If you'd known, there wouldn't have been anything you could've done."

"We'd have found a way to jailbreak you. Somehow."

One corner of her mouth lifted. "I don't doubt y'all would have tried." The faint smile faded. "Did you know I had no idea Gwen was even missing until Jace got me out?"

"Seriously?"

"I went from the beach where you pulled me out to a hospital on the mainland. And from there to the facility where they kept me for two years. I never came back to the island, and I wasn't allowed to talk to anyone from home."

"So the police never questioned you about that night?" In the days and weeks after her disappearance, I thought they'd questioned practically everyone on the island. Certainly everybody who'd been at that party.

"I don't know if they even tried to get to me. It was well documented that my memory was shot, so I wouldn't have been able to give them anything either way."

"It must have been devastating to find out about her like that. To have to deal with it as if it just happened. Because for you it did." Gwen had been one of her closest friends. She and Gwen and Gabi had very much been the Three Musketeers.

"It haunts me that I can't remember. What if I saw something that could've helped with the investigation?" I could see the depths of guilt in her eyes. God knew I understood it.

"You can't give in to that kind of guilt. It'll eat you alive."

She glanced up at me and arched a brow. "Spoken from the voice of experience?"

"Yeah."

With a sigh, she tipped her head to my shoulder. "I did try

to push myself when I came back. To try to remember. It didn't go well."

There was a wealth of pain and trauma in those few words. What additional suffering had she put herself through in the name of trying to find out what had happened to a friend?

We'd never talked about any of this before. There'd always been a huge invisible *Keep Out* sign. I didn't want to traumatize her any further, but since she was opening up a little, I had a few questions.

"What's the last thing you remember from that night?"

"Playing in the surf with the dog. Then it's a big blank until I woke up to you."

"What about the storm rolling in? The party breaking up?"

Willa shook her head. "Nothing."

I thought back, considering. "That was at least half an hour before I went to look for you." What the hell had happened to her in that span?

"I broke your rule."

"What?"

"You told me not to leave the beach without one of y'all."

"You remember that?"

"Everything before is very clear. From you helping me sneak out, to all the ground rules you laid out." She straightened to meet my gaze. "I wouldn't have broken them without a good reason. I wouldn't have gone into the water without a good reason. I just... don't know what that was."

I stroked the hair back from her face. "I believe you."

The list of what teenaged Willa would have considered good reasons was remarkably short. I could only think of two. To help an animal in trouble. Or to help a friend. What if she'd gone into the water after Gwen? What if I'd managed to save Willa and let Gwen die? The thought of it made me physically ill.

Willa reached up to cup my cheek. "I've thought of it, too. It was a fucking miracle you managed to save me. If she was out there, there was absolutely no way you could have gotten to us both. And there's no evidence she was there. It's all pure conjecture because I can't remember, and this is the kind of shit my brain throws out to torture me. So don't you dare take that on, too. You saved my life. Period. You're still saving it."

I hoped that was true. And I hoped for her sake that someday she got answers that would vanquish the thought monsters.

With a twitch of her shoulders, she let her hand fall back to her lap. "Anyway, I don't know how much of this they'll get into with the petition. This is all my perception of what I went through, and no doubt they'll have documented my unstable memory. There's no one to corroborate. It'll be my word against the professional opinions of the doctors there. They'll have case notes. The fact that I left against medical advice. I'm not entirely sure how we combat that."

"They won't have anything current. They won't have the truth. We will." I cupped her cheek. Her eyes were full of remembered pain and fear and a whole host of emotions I couldn't read. "No one is going to get to you. No one is ever going to make you go back to that place or anywhere like it. You will never have to face those people ever again."

I'd do anything to make sure of it.

CHAPTER 17
WILLA

I sat in a patch of sunlight beside a window that opened onto what counted as a green space. A grassy patch with a few spindly trees. Bare of leaves this time of year, nothing disguised the anemic reach of their skeletal branches toward the swatch of open sky above. The trees hadn't quite given up the fight for freedom. I couldn't say the same for most of my companions.

They sat in corners or huddles or shuffled around the common room in the slippers that were as close as we came to real shoes. Everything in here was neutral—white or gray or beige. Lifeless. As if the place itself were sucking the will to live out of all of us.

I didn't know how much longer I could stand this and stay me.

The familiar rattle of the medicine cart pulled my attention from the window. Step. Step. Rattle. Pause. Step. Step. Step. Rattle. Pause.

I kept my head down, hoping the orderly would pass me by. I didn't want the pills that made me feel like a zombie. I'd begun hiding them in my cheek, weaning myself off, but I wasn't sure I could pull that off in here.

Step. Step. Rattle. Pause.

"Time for meds, Wilhelmina."

They never called me Willa here. That was my father's doing. "That's your name. I gave it to you." As if by contributing half my DNA, he had a right to dictate who I was.

I curled in on myself, praying that turtling up would somehow protect me.

"Wilhelminaaaa." The orderly's sing-song voice seemed to echo in the abnormally quiet room. He shook the little paper cup full of pills.

No. I couldn't do this anymore. I wouldn't.

Exploding up from my seat, I struck out at the hand holding the cup, sending the pills flying like so much confetti. Darting past him, I made for the door out of the common room. But it wouldn't budge when I shoved at the bar.

"C'mon. C'mon!" I threw my full weight against it, to no avail.

The orderly was closing in. I bolted to the left, past Mrs. Tate and her endless knitting projects. She lifted rheumy eyes and rose, dragging her partly finished blanket as she began to shuffle after me. Pete and Maisey abandoned their game of checkers as I flew by. Their faces were too pale, too lax. That grayish cast wasn't from months without the sun. They looked... dead. But that didn't stop them from joining Mrs. Tate and the orderly in herding me toward one corner of the room. Suddenly, all the other patients were on their feet, part of the mindless, zombie-like pack.

No. They wouldn't take me! They wouldn't pull me in again.

There were no other doors, so I backed toward the window, frantically searching the furniture for something I could hurl to break the glass.

A splash of crimson drew my attention to another man

shambling in my direction. His mouth hung slack, and his eyes were vacant. Blood trailed down his face and soaked the front of his shirt, dripping onto the floor as he kept coming, coming, coming. One hand reached out to touch me—

"No!"

"Willa!"

Someone I couldn't see wrapped me in restraints, and I fought back, lashing out with everything I had, trying to break free.

"Wren, wake up! It's me. It's Sawyer. Wake up!"

The sound of his voice dragged me out of the dream. Like a swimmer breaking the surface, I gasped in huge lungfuls of air, still sobbing with terror. Roy was bouncing on the bed, barking. And Sawyer... Sawyer was right there, arms wrapped around me.

"I've got you. I've got you. You're safe."

I sagged into him, burying my face against the warmth of his chest and holding on for dear life, because he was real, and I wasn't back inside. There was no room for mortification or regret. I didn't care that he was getting a front-row seat to my brokenness, because he was my safe place.

He rocked me for a long time, until the tears stopped, and my breathing finally leveled out. "That must have been one hell of a nightmare."

"You could say that." On a sigh, I pulled back far enough to scoop a hand through my hair. "I should have expected it after today."

"Your time off-island?"

"With an added zombie chaser. Literally. That was new." I remembered the bloody guy who'd nearly touched me and shuddered.

His wince was sympathetic. "I'm guessing the chances of you going back to sleep are probably close to nil."

I glanced at the clock. 2:24. "Not likely. I can read for a

while. Or stream something on my laptop. That's what I usually do."

"I'll do you one better. Come on. Let's go downstairs." He slid off the bed and held out a hand with a look that was reminiscent of Aladdin offering Jasmine a magic carpet ride. I wanted to follow him anywhere when he looked at me like that.

"You really don't have to stay up with me. I didn't mean to wake you."

"You didn't. My stomach did. I want a snack. I'll fix us something."

Shocked to realize I could actually eat, I put my hand in his.

The house was dark and quiet but for our soft footfalls and the click of Roy's claws on the hardwood as we went down to the kitchen. It struck me that there was nothing creepy about the house. I didn't feel weird being here, despite the incredible age of the place. It just felt... comfortable. I didn't know how much of that was the house and how much was the fact that Sawyer was here with me.

He opened the fridge. "Sit."

Because I didn't want to be as far from him as the breakfast nook, I boosted myself onto the counter opposite the stove and watched him. He pulled out cheese and butter from the fridge, then snagged a loaf of bread from Panadería de la Isla.

"Grilled cheese?" I asked.

"Midnight snack of champions." He set a skillet on the stove and turned on the burner.

I watched him move, admiring the efficiency as he sliced the bread and put together the sandwiches. Only when he laid them into the skillet did I register he wore only a pair of low-slung, cut-off gray sweatpants. The handful of lights he'd switched on highlighted the dip and curve of the muscle he'd packed on during his naval service. He'd tended a little toward skinny growing up, but now all that height had bulked out into a package I couldn't help but admire.

He was walking by to put the cheese and butter back into the fridge when I noticed the ink on his left shoulder.

"You have a tattoo." Instinctively, I reached out to run a finger over the intricate compass with a quartet of swallows. "It's beautiful."

He glanced over his shoulder at me, and I realized he'd stopped with the cheese still in his hands. "All four of us got one right before we shipped out from basic training to our first postings. A reminder we'd always be there for each other."

"I like that." Aware I was practically petting his shoulder like a cat, I dropped my hand.

Sawyer continued on to the fridge, putting the food away. "What about you? Do you have any ink hiding somewhere?" His teasing smile told me he didn't expect the answer to be yes.

"Actually, I do."

"Oh, really?" Looking more than a little intrigued, he flipped the sandwiches.

Because it was the middle of the night and felt like a time for confessions, I slid off the counter and turned my back to him, lifting my hair to reveal the nape of my neck. His finger gently traced the design, and I shivered at the touch.

"A wren," he murmured.

Dropping my hair, I turned to face him. "More specifically, a wren taking flight. I got it after I came back to the island."

"Why a wren?"

"You were always the one who didn't treat me like I was broken. You gave me strength, so it was sort of my way of keeping you with me after you left." After the words were out, I realized they probably revealed more than I'd intended. But I could see that it meant something to him that I'd effectively inked our connection onto my body. Made him a part of me.

He took a step closer, closing the distance between us to mere inches. I had to tip my head back to keep his gaze. The air between us felt electric and raw. Intimate. Testing the moment as much as myself, I laid a hand on his chest, feeling the smooth, warm skin beneath my palm and the thudding heart beneath. When I licked my lips, he tracked the motion. His eyes darkened, his pupils springing wide as they drank me in. One hand curled around my hip, and he began to lower his head... only to jerk to a stop, his nostrils flaring.

"Shit." He leapt toward the stove, shoving the pan off the burner and saving our snack from ruination.

I ached at the loss of the moment. At what might have happened without that interruption. And it *was* an interruption. Whatever had been happening between us was over, as evidenced by Sawyer efficiently plating up the sandwiches and offering one to me. "A little crispy around the edges, but still edible."

"I'm sure it's fine. Thank you."

We kicked back against opposite counters and ate standing up, chasing the food with glasses of milk. I gave Roy the last bite of mine, which he nipped delicately from my fingers and promptly chomped in one bite. I did feel better, and that was more than I'd expected, given my usual response to nightmares.

"I think maybe I could go back to sleep."

"Okay then." He made sure the stove was off and escorted me back upstairs.

At the door to my room, I hesitated. "Sawyer?"

"Yeah?"

"Will you stay with me?" Now that I was up here, I didn't want to risk falling back into the dream.

"Sure."

He followed me inside. We crawled into bed. Maybe it was pushing the envelope, but I reached for Sawyer's arm, tugging it over my waist. He shifted, tucking around me as a proper big spoon. Roy assumed his position on my other side.

Sandwiched between my two protectors, I slid into a blessedly dreamless sleep.

CHAPTER 18

SAWYER

I woke to the scent of vanilla and lavender. Sometime in the night, Willa had shifted positions to face me. She slept like a koala, snuggled close against my chest, her head on my shoulder, an arm and a leg wrapped around me. It was adorable, but for the effect her warm breath against my bare skin had on things south of the border. My dick stood at attention, begging me to work down those bit-of-nothing sleep shorts she wore so we could get up close and personal before the knee that was perilously close to my balls twitched and did some damage.

Sunlight streamed through the sheer curtains, brighter than I would've expected. I lifted my head to check the clock and nearly jolted as a massive black head popped up on Willa's other side. Roy blinked at me with big, golden eyes. I'd have sworn he arched one doggy brow at me, as if to say he wasn't at all sure how he felt about sharing his bed with the likes of me. Or maybe it was jealousy that his mama was wrapped around me instead of him. I couldn't blame him. The warm weight of her felt pretty fucking fantastic.

On the nightstand beyond, I finally spotted the clock.

Nearly 7:30. Later than I'd thought, but God knew, she'd needed the sleep. I wondered how often she had nightmares. I gathered they weren't infrequent, and I hated the idea of her having had to deal with those alone. Staying stuck in the fear because she couldn't wake up or, worse, coming out of it with no one to comfort her. I mean, she had the dog, and I understood he was absolutely an emotional support animal. A damned good one at that. But it wasn't the same as having someone take care of her. I liked being the one to do that. Probably way too much. Same as I liked being in this bed with her, just like this.

Willa stirred against me, and I held my breath as her knee shifted against the erection that hadn't wilted one damned bit. Her palm flexed against my chest, almost like a cat making biscuits, then heavy-lidded eyes met mine and a slow, sleepy smile curved her lips. "Hi."

What would it be like to be greeted by that smile every day?

"Mornin'. Sleep okay?"

"Like the dead. You're apparently good at scaring away nightmares."

I stroked the hair back from her face. "Anytime."

Roy grumbled and head-butted her between the shoulders. With a laugh, she rolled over, removing the threat of her knee from my groin.

"Good morning, sweet boy. Are you ready to go out?"

With a woof, the dog scrambled out of bed. Willa swung her legs out of bed and lifted her arms high in a stretch that pulled her sleep tank tight across her breasts. That had my big boy brain jumping on the campaign for keeping her in this bed.

"I'll let him out and start the coffee."

"I'll be down in a little bit." After I'd done something about this reaction to her.

She snagged a light robe, sliding it on as she strode into the hall after a dancing Roy.

By the time I made it downstairs, I smelled bacon. The dog

was hunched over his bowl, snarfing down his breakfast. Willa herself stood at the counter, cracking eggs into a bowl. I fought the urge to cross the room and slide my arms around her from behind, pressing a kiss to the little tattoo on the back of her neck. In the bright light of day, such things didn't feel quite as possible. Instead, I moved to the coffeepot.

"You had yours yet?"

"Not yet. I wanted to get this started first."

"I'll make it for you. How do you take your coffee these days?"

"A little less sweet than back in high school. Cream, one sugar."

I pulled mugs down from the cabinet and poured, moving over to hand her one of the blue speckled stoneware pieces I recognized as Mimi's work. Those eyes met mine over her shoulder. Paired with that shy smile, it just hit me right in the gut, and I found myself smiling back. Damn it, I liked the domesticity of playing house with her. I liked everything with her, way too damned much.

Lifting my own mug, I kicked back against the counter. "So, what's on deck today?"

"Well, I checked the weather report. That hurricane watch has been amped up to a warning. We've already got a lot of supplies here. Hurricane panels for the windows and the like. But we'll need to take stock and go into town for other supplies. And while we're there, I want to go ahead and stop by City Hall to see what Miles wants."

"Not gonna put it off? As I recall, you never much liked him."

"He's an ass. That opinion hasn't changed since high school. But it's part of the gig as a Sutter. Given the impending hurricane, he's probably going to be pretty busy, which means I should be able to get in and out pretty quickly." She transferred bacon to a plate covered in paper towels, then turned back for the eggs. "My hope is that surprising him will catch him on his back foot, and I'll have the upper hand in the conversation. I'll take whatever advantage I can get."

"Fair enough."

We ate and drank our coffee at the kitchen table, and I did my best not to notice how her robe kept slipping off one shoulder, exposing a tantalizing stretch of creamy skin I wanted to trace with my lips.

"Where are all the hurricane supplies stored?"

"The hurricane panels are in a rack in the shed off the back of the garage. There's a generator out there, too. I can show you after my shower."

Do not picture her naked. Do not.

"I'll just pop on out and take a look while you're upstairs."

"Okay. I won't be long." She shoved back from the table.

"Thanks for breakfast. I'll get the dishes."

There went that smile again. "Thanks for my grilled cheese last night."

As she disappeared upstairs, I made quick work of the dishes, then strolled on out to the garage. The panels were, as she'd said, neatly organized and ready to go. I found the generator and started a mental list of tasks to prep the property in advance of the storm. The ringing of my phone interrupted me. Spotting Dax Gregory on the display, I answered. "Malone."

"My man. How the hell are you? How's the shoulder?"

"It's better. Still a little twingey but getting there. You?"

"Busy. Sorry it took me a few days to get back to you."

"Not a problem." Honestly, this was a faster turnaround than I'd expected.

"Where are you? What have you been doing since you got out?"

"Well, it's funny you should ask that. I'm back on Hatterwick. And... I just got married."

"Holy shit. For real?" His voice shot up at least an octave.

"Yeah."

"When?"

"Uh, about six days ago."

"Hot damn. Who's the lucky lady?"

I paused. No way around this part. "Willa."

"Like... Hollingsworth's little sister?" Dax was quick. It was part of what made him good at his job.

"Yep."

He crowed. "Ooo hoo! And what did Jace say about all this?"

"He doesn't know. The situation is complicated, and that's actually why I wanted to talk to you."

I gave him the rundown, pacing up and down the driveway. "I need you to help create a backdated trail of communications that suggests we were involved over the last three years."

"Sure, I can do that. It'll take me a little time. I've got several things going on." He hadn't specified, but I suspected some of those things involved off-book, black-ops contract work. Dax hadn't sat on his laurels when he got out of the Navy.

"I appreciate whatever you can pull off. What do you need from us?" As he spoke, I switched over to speakerphone and opened the notes app to jot it all down. "Got it."

"So, you're doing this as a favor to protect her. That I get. Makes sense." This time it was he who paused. "Is she aware of how you feel?"

I regretted some of my honesty during that forty-two hours we'd been trapped behind enemy lines. But, well, when you thought you might die, you shared shit.

Automatically, I glanced toward the house, making sure Willa wasn't within earshot. "It hasn't come up, precisely."

"Is this gonna be temporary, or are you going to take the opportunity to woo her for real?"

"Who the hell uses the word 'woo'?" But I couldn't stop myself from thinking about last night in the kitchen. I'd nearly kissed her again. No audience. No performance. Just because

I'd wanted to. I regretted that I hadn't. She'd tattooed something of me on her body. That alone told me this was more than simple attraction on both sides, and I wasn't entirely sure what to do about it. If I should do anything about it.

"That's the word, brother. So are you?"

"It's complicated. So that's to be determined."

"Well, good luck. I'll send you a link for an encrypted upload of the stuff I asked for."

"Thanks, man. I really appreciate it."

"Absolutely. I owe you, so I'll make sure this does the trick. By the time I'm done, nobody but the two of you will know it's not the God's honest truth. I'll be in touch. My congratulations to your bride."

Willa stepped out of the house just as I hung up, looking pretty as a picture in jeans and some lacy summer sweater thing with a wide neck that exposed more of those shoulders that were driving me wild.

Hands and mouth to yourself, Malone.

Shoving my phone into my pocket, I strode to meet her. "I just spoke to my buddy and got the list of things he's gonna need to lay in a backdated electronic trail for us. He offered his congratulations, by the way."

"Oh. Did you tell him why we needed all this?"

"I did."

"And he didn't think we're out of our minds?"

"Dax isn't in the habit of asking those kinds of questions. But he is very, very good at what he does."

"Well, I'll take all the help I can get. I've got a partial list of supplies here."

"I've got one myself for out here."

"Then let's get on into town and get this done. It sounds like we've got a lot of work to do."

CHAPTER 19
WILLA

Sawyer tugged open the door to town hall and gestured me inside. Roy stayed glued to my hip. I hadn't had reason to come here since my grandfather had brought me to meetings with one of the previous mayors when I'd been a child, but I still knew my way. Bypassing the elevator, I took the stairs to the second floor. At the top, Sawyer took my hand, his thumb brushing over the ring on my left hand. It was a reminder that I was his—at least in a sense—and I wasn't walking into this alone. I appreciated the silent support because I wasn't precisely looking forward to this meeting.

I didn't like Miles Busby. I'd never liked Miles, even when he was just my best friend's older brother. He'd always felt like the politician he'd become. The sort of guy who was constantly looking at people to assess what he could get out of them. I fully expected more of the same from him now. Better to get it over with so I didn't have time to work myself into a state over it.

Peggy Garrett sat at the reception desk, the only part of this office that hadn't changed as the mayor did. She'd always had a glass jar full of hard candies to offer when I'd been a kid. I noted it was butterscotch disks today.

"Willa! How lovely to see you! What can I do for you, hon?" She automatically lifted the top off the jar, even as her smile wobbled a little at the sight of Roy.

I gave him a hand signal, and he quietly sat beside me as I pulled out a couple of the candies, passing one to Sawyer. "Hey, Mrs. Garrett. We don't have an appointment, but I understand Miles has been wanting to meet with me about Founders' Day. We were in town and had a little time, so we thought we'd take a chance that he could squeeze us in."

"Oh, I... well, yes, he definitely will want to meet with you. Let me see if he's available."

She picked up the phone and punched a button. A voice said something on the other end. "Yes, sir. I'm aware, but Willa Sutter and her husband are here to see you."

I frowned at that. Sawyer had a name and identity beyond being tied to me. For that matter, why hadn't she assumed I'd taken his name? That was still the norm around the island.

"Mayor Busby will be happy to meet with you. Go right on in."

"Thank you."

We stepped through a wood-paneled door into a space designed to draw attention. An overly ornate antique desk sat in front of a pair of windows hung with lavish drapes. The patterned rug beneath held the kind of aged patina that didn't come without a price. And if I wasn't mistaken, the leather office chair behind the desk was raised as high as it would go, such that anyone who sat in the pair of conference chairs in front of the desk would be forced to look up at its occupant. I wondered if Miles had bankrolled all this himself or if the taxpayers had footed the bill.

The mayor himself looked a little more frazzled than I'd expected, with his tie already loosened and the top button of his collar popped. He faltered as he came around the desk and spotted Roy. "You came with an entourage."

When I only arched a brow and signaled my dog to sit, he seemed to recover himself. "Allow me to offer congratulations on your marriage, and my sympathies for the loss of your grandparents. They'll certainly be missed."

Understanding how the game was played, I took his offered hand. "Thank you on both accounts."

"Sawyer."

My husband was slow to shake his hand, but at least he'd been acknowledged. I'd take the tiny win. "Sawyer mentioned you wanted to see us."

"I did—do. I'm afraid I'll have to be brief, as they've just officially issued a hurricane warning, and as you might imagine, there's a lot to do to make sure that the town is prepared."

"Certainly, I understand. We came into town to get some supplies ourselves."

"Well, have a seat, and I'll tell you what I'm thinking." He circled back around the desk, confirming my original suspicion about the placement of his chair. "Being a Sutter, you know how important Founders' Day is to the locals on the island. Celebrating where we came from, all the things we've survived. Life on the Outer Banks is challenging, and this festival is a reminder of why we love it, why we stay. In the past, your grandparents have always held a prominent role in the festivities. As heir to their legacy, I knew you'd want to step into their shoes."

'Want' was a strong word, but I was obligated, if not to him, then to the trust my grandparents had placed in me by leaving me everything. "What did you have in mind?"

He rattled on about the parade and the wreath laying at the tombs of our ancestors, recruiting me as judge for the assorted competitions of the day, and then he finally dropped it. "I was thinking it would be a terribly inspiring gesture if you sponsored the annual fireworks display."

"Sponsor, as in pay for," I clarified.

Miles spread his hands. "The town budget is strapped after the funds we're putting into the Fourth of July, and of course, there's no telling what repairs might be necessary in the wake of this hurricane. Fireworks would be such a sign of hope that even though we've lost your grandparents, things will go on."

He wanted money. I'd assumed it would come down to that. I'd had one meeting with my grandparents' accountant to get the broad strokes of what I'd be inheriting, but with the threat of my parents looming, I hadn't done more than that. I hadn't fully absorbed all the rules around the trust dedicated to funding things for the town, so it was possible such a thing could come out of that budget, but I was far more inclined to spend the money on something that would last and improve life on Hatterwick for everyone who lived here, not waste it on some meaningless display.

"Well, certainly I'll take that under advisement as an idea, but I think it will probably have to wait until next year. The estate itself is still in probate, so I'm not going to have the flexibility to do that at this time. But I understand my role here." That role being the controller of the purse strings. Miles believed he'd be able to manipulate me more easily than he had my grandfather. He'd have another think coming about that.

The mayor eased back in his chair, steepling his fingers like the villain in a bad TV movie. "Of course, I understand. Inheritance is so complicated, isn't it? What are your plans for the estate, after everything is free and clear? You know there are multiple development opportunities available for forward thinkers such as yourself."

Flattery will get you nowhere.

I would never understand how Gwen and this pretentious

prick had come from the same parents. "I appreciate that, but I'm not interested. The maritime forest on Hatterwick is rare as an ecosystem. I intend to do whatever is necessary to protect it, including seeking designation as a formal wildlife sanctuary." Of course, such a project was likely years off, but he didn't need to know that.

Rendering the glib-tongued Miles Busby speechless was probably way more gratifying than it should have been. I knew the sanctuary wasn't at all what he'd want for the island. He was all about development and tourist dollars and didn't understand people who weren't.

Having found out what I'd come for, I rose. "We'll get out of your way. We've got hurricane prep to do, and I know you do as well."

"Yes, right. Thank you for stopping by. I'll be in touch about Founder's Day meetings, once those are scheduled."

"Sounds good." As I turned toward the door, my gaze caught on a collection of photos atop the credenza. There were pictures of Miles with his wife and two kids, looking like an ad for a yacht club regatta. But there were also photos of him with his parents, including one of the entire Busby family before Gwen's disappearance, tucked almost in the back. It reminded me that, no matter how much of a douchecanoe I found Miles, he'd suffered a tragedy, too.

"I don't know that I've ever actually seen you alone since I came back to the island to offer my condolences on the loss of your sister. I know the continued lack of answers has to be incredibly hard for your family, and I just want you to know that I miss her every day, too."

I'd made him speechless twice in the span of five minutes. I couldn't interpret the expression that flickered over his face, but eventually he stammered, "Thank you," in a rough voice.

We made our way downstairs and out to the sidewalk.

"Well, I guess that wasn't as painful as it could have been,"

Sawyer muttered. "That was nice, what you said to him about Gwen."

"He's full of himself, but you know there's not a day that goes by he doesn't wonder what happened to her." The same was true of me, though I tried my best not to dwell on it. Pushing too hard about anything from that time never ended well for me.

Sawyer tugged out his keys. "We should get on to the market and pick up supplies before they sell out. It's gonna be crazy today now that the alert's gone out."

"True enough." It was time to look forward to the things I could change.

CHAPTER 20

SAWYER

The village was a madhouse. Tourists scrambled to make the ferry back to the mainland. Service would continue to run as long as it was deemed safe, usually about twenty-four hours after a hurricane warning got called. As I'd determined this morning, Willa and I were already well-stocked out at Sutter House, with hurricane panels for the windows, fuel for the generator, plenty of plastic sheeting, and sandbags. But we joined the throngs of other locals emptying the market's shelves of bottled water and non-perishables, along with extra dog food for Roy. At the hardware store, we stocked up on batteries and duct tape. I rushed us through, feeling Willa's tension ratchet up with all the people pressing too close in the aisles, their own varying degrees of panic fueling her anxiety.

"Let's get home. We've got lots to do." I'd never prepped a house as large as Sutter House for a hurricane before, and already a mile long list was spooling through my head.

As we loaded our purchases into the backseat of the truck, someone called our names.

"Sawyer! Willa! Just the couple I was looking for." Mimi trotted across the parking lot.

I pulled her in for a hug. "Hey. You stocking up for the storm like everybody else?"

"Sure am." She squeezed me tight, then opened her arms to Willa. "Hey, darlin'. It's good to see you again."

"You, too. Do you and Florence have everything you need to ride things out?"

"Supplies, yes. But if y'all can spare the time, we could use a hand getting the last of the hurricane shutters up. Flo thinks we can do it all ourselves, but she's thinking with the brain of someone who isn't vertically challenged. I'm capable of a lot of things, but lengthy reach isn't one of them."

My lips twitched. Mimi was 5'1" on a good day. Mama Flo was nearer to 5'10". Ford's height came from her. "Of course, we'll follow you on out. Are you headed home now?"

"Sure am."

"Meet you there."

The village was so congested it took nearly twenty minutes to make it all the way to the lighthouse. I was glad we'd be able to bypass it on the way back to Sutter House. Mama Flo was at the top of a ladder when we pulled up, a drill in her hand.

I slid out of the truck. "Maybe you ought to let us help with that before you fall and break your neck. Ford would be mighty pissed if you did."

"We prepped for hurricanes out here long before you were big enough to help." In defiance, she drilled in the last screw on the hurricane shutter she was attaching.

"Nobody's questioning your general badassery. You'd yell at me if I was up a ladder by myself with nobody home, too."

She opened her mouth. Closed it again. "Well, you've got me there. I suppose, since you're here, I could use a hand."

Mimi humphed and muttered something that sounded an awful lot like, "Stubborn, pig-headed Amazon."

Willa must've caught it too because she snorted a laugh before covering with a cough. "What can we do?"

Between the four of us, we made quick work of the last of the prep. The lighthouse itself didn't need extra attention, so it was just finishing up all the windows on the cottage and helping them cart the outdoor furniture and grill inside.

When we were through, Mama Flo dusted off her hands. "I have to admit, that went quicker. Y'all come inside for a glass of tea and some cookies."

"Would those be double chocolate chip?" I asked, hopeful.

Mimi grinned. "They would."

"Twist my arm, why don't you?"

The kitchen was a lot darker with the windows shuttered, but no less inviting. The two women bustled about, pouring tea, plating cookies. Because they waved us away, Willa and I sat at the table, taking the window seat. Roy lapped at the bowl of water they brought him, then found a cold spot to stretch out on the slate floor.

Willa propped her chin in her hands. "I'm a little surprised we haven't heard from you since our party. I figured you'd want the update."

"Oh, well, we wanted to let you two settle in," Mama Flo admitted. "Not that the Universe got that message. Married one week. Hurricane the next. But how are things?"

"Well, I got served."

Mama Flo paused, pitcher in hand. "So, they're really going through with it?"

"Looks like. Roland has reported our marriage, and now we're playing a waiting game. He said it could take days or weeks before we hear anything. Not gonna lie, the waiting is killing me. Everything moves so freaking slowly. I just want it settled and done, one way or another."

Because I felt her tense up again, I slid my hand beneath her hair and began to knead at her nape. Her eyes closed, and she sighed, leaning back into the touch. I saw Mimi noticing from where she piled cookies on a platter and chose to ignore the satisfied nod. "My buddy's getting started on backdating things, in case they come after her about the haste of our marriage. Everything's lining up, exactly as we planned."

The ladies joined us at the table, setting glasses of sweet tea in front of us.

Mama Flo sank into a chair on the opposite side. "Good. I don't think anybody here is gonna question it. For what it's worth, marriage looks good on you both."

What the hell did *that* mean?

Willa apparently didn't know what to do with that either. She sipped at her tea. "I'm about ready to get back to work on the Cypress Beach project."

I assumed this was one of the grants she was writing. With everything else going on, her work had been the last thing on either of our minds.

Mama Flo waved a hand. "Honey, it's okay. We have plenty of time. You've got bigger things to worry about just now."

"I know, but things stalled out weeks ago, when Granddaddy died. Life won't stay on hold forever, and either way, I'm ready to get back in the groove. It'll be a good distraction from the rest."

"Fine. But later. After the hurricane goes through, we'll talk and finish making a game plan for tackling what's left."

I picked up a cookie and bit in, closing my eyes as the sweet, buttery taste of it hit my tongue. "Oh my God, this is my childhood, right here."

"You used to work for cookies." Mimi remembered. "It was the only thing you'd let us send home with you for the longest time."

"My pride couldn't hold up to your double chocolate chip cookies. The peanut butter ones, either." I took another bite and chewed. "Not that I didn't notice the stuff you had Ford sneak into the pantry and freezer when he came over. I appreciated it. You're probably half the reason Dad and I ever ate anything resembling a vegetable that wasn't a potato."

Mimi laid a hand over mine. "Your daddy had a big heart, same as you do. It just never recovered from losing your mama and sister."

Uncomfortable with the direction of the conversation, I twitched my shoulders and shoved the last of the cookie into my mouth.

Beneath the table, Willa's hand settled on my thigh and squeezed. "Have you heard anything from Ford?"

"Briefly this morning, actually." Mama Flo refilled her glass. "He's two weeks into a relief aid mission in the Philippines after that recent typhoon, but he still heard about the hurricane warning here and called to check on us."

I paused, another cookie halfway to my mouth. "Did you tell him about us?" I'd considered the ramifications of telling Jace, but I hadn't once thought about what I'd tell my other brothers. What would they think of this lunatic plan I'd agreed to? Would either of them have gone this far to protect Willa under the circumstances? I didn't like the sick feeling that curdled my gut at the thought of one of them being the one to kiss her. To comfort her after a nightmare.

Mine. My wife.

"We thought about it, but ultimately that's y'all's news to share," Mimi declared.

I blinked, and the irrational jealousy slid away again. *Get a friggin' hold of yourself, Malone.*

"Probably for the best," Willa added. "We haven't had the chance to loop Jace in yet, either. I'd rather he didn't hear it from anyone but us."

"Fair point," Mama Flo conceded. "Anyway, he's doing well, and he said to tell y'all hello when next we saw you."

We chatted for another few minutes, until we'd finished our

tea, and I'd grabbed a third cookie. "We should probably get on. Lots to do at home."

Willa's gaze jerked toward me, but I couldn't read the expression in her eyes.

Mimi rose from the table. "Let me pack up some more cookies to send back with y'all. Least we can do for your help."

"I will never say no to your cookies."

After more hugs, a big Tupperware of cookies, and promises to check in soon, Willa and I loaded Roy back into the truck and headed for the north end of the island. Wanting to avoid Sutter's Ferry entirely, I headed east for the coast road that would take us up the Atlantic side. We'd have to cut across on the lone road that snaked through the woods, and it would add another ten minutes to the already nearly twenty minute drive, but at least we'd avoid the crowds.

"We should probably discuss what we're gonna send Dax."

"What *are* we going to send Dax? What does he need us to do?"

"To some extent, he'll layer in some more affectionate language into the existing communication. Love you. Miss you. That kind of thing. But he'll need more. And we'll need to draft some emails and texts from scratch for him to sprinkle through."

She shifted in her seat, as if this were the ancient clunker with the sprung springs I'd driven in high school, instead of a late model Ford. "Is that a thing we really have to discuss? Can't we just write stuff up and send it?"

"Well, for one, the things we write will be feeding off each other. For two, if we get subpoenaed and asked about it, it'd be super weird if we don't remember the things we allegedly said."

"Okay, fair point. Where do we start?"

"We'll have to decide where and how things changed, so he knows when to seed things."

She took a breath. "I kind of already made something up for Gabi."

"Oh?"

"She's my best friend. She knows me really well. I had to give her something when we showed up married."

"Not criticizing your decision, Wren. What did you tell her?"

"About three years ago, we met in Raleigh, while you were on leave, for a quick weekend before you had to get back. We'd just planned to hang out because we wanted to see each other and catch up. But one thing led to another."

I didn't miss the color that bloomed in her cheeks. "Did we go to bed together?"

"I didn't spell it out, but that was the implication."

I could picture it. Finally giving in when we were miles away from home and anyone who knew us. I wouldn't have come up for air for that entire weekend.

And now I was the one squirming in my seat. "Okay, I'll dig back through my records and figure out some dates that will work. You've probably got more flexibility on that than I do, in terms of documentation of where you were when."

She cleared her throat. "Yes."

"Okay, what else?"

"We kept it a secret because of Jace. Because we weren't sure how he'd react."

"Well, that's the God's honest truth. Are we going to tell him the full story when he does find out?"

But Willa didn't answer. Her gaze was fixed out the side window, and that pretty pink had faded from her cheeks.

"Wren? What's wrong?"

"Don't go this way," she whispered.

"What?"

"Not this road. I'm not... I can't..." As her breath went

shorter, Roy strained against his seatbelt to stick his head over the seat, trying to reach her shoulder.

What the hell?

I pulled over, throwing the truck into park, and reached for her. "Baby, what is it?"

"Os...prey Beach. I can't... I've never... been back." She shook under my hands, and I cursed myself eight ways from Sunday as I realized what she meant.

I'd been about to drive right by the site of the bonfire. It had never occurred to me that, in ten years back on the island, she'd never been back.

I pulled her in, pressing a kiss to her temple. "Okay. Okay, I'll find another route. I'm sorry. I didn't think. It's okay."

Keeping my arm around her, I awkwardly shifted the truck back into gear with my left hand and steered us back onto the road, making a U-turn and heading back toward town. I'd take whatever route she needed rather than subjecting her to this.

By the time we reached the road that circled the edge of town, she'd stopped shaking, but her hands were still twisted in knots. "Sorry."

"Don't you dare apologize. This is fine." We still had plenty of time to get everything done. "In sickness and in health, and in taking the longer road home. I've got you, Wren."

Always.

CHAPTER 21

WILLA

Outside, the wind howled, and the rain lashed as the category 3 hurricane battered the island. Sutter House creaked around us, sounding for all the world like the hull of a great ship battling the waves, but our little nest in the dining room was pretty cozy. As the central-most room of the house, it made the safest spot to ride out the storm. Sawyer and I had shoved the table that seated sixteen to the far end of the room and covered the whole thing in a tarp. It resembled an indoor greenhouse with all the potted plants we'd hauled inside. That left just enough room for the queen mattress we'd wrestled downstairs and set in front of the fire-place that opened on the other side to the den. The flue was closed, of course, but an assortment of candles had been set inside, waiting to be lit whenever we lost power. Sawyer had produced a portable power station that would be enough to power our devices, a fan, and the mini-fridge he'd hauled down from Granddaddy's third floor office for at least a day or so. All in all, we were pretty well set.

I was halfway through reviewing my notes on the sustain-able tourism initiative grant I'd set aside after Granddaddy died, when the lights finally winked out. "Well, it held longer than I thought it would."

Sawyer thumbed on the flashlight of his phone and crossed to switch on the battery-powered lanterns set around the room. "Since the storm didn't make it past cat 3, maybe utilities won't be down too long." He grabbed a lantern and brought it over to where I sat in a camp chair, my feet propped on the hearth. "Here, you want to keep working?"

"No, I think I'm probably done for the night."

"In that case, you hungry?"

"I could definitely eat." Now that my attention wasn't absorbed in the work, my stomach decided to make vocal protests at the long stretch since my last snack.

Sawyer chuckled. "Why don't you set up our picnic spot by the fireplace while I pull things together?"

"That I can do."

I put my notes away and moved our chairs to make space for one of the thick comforters. Might as well do this whole indoor picnic thing right. I dragged over a small mountain of pillows so we had something to lean against. Then I carefully lit the candles. All clustered together in the fireplace, they made for a rather romantic ambiance. Not that we were necessarily going for that, but it was hard not to focus on the fact that we were sheltering in place together, all by ourselves. It felt close and intimate. I was achingly aware of the fact that it had been three whole days since he'd kissed me. I'd replayed the other night in the kitchen over and over, wishing he'd just let the damned sandwich burn.

He'd been affectionate since then, touching me often, still sharing my bed. But he hadn't pressed for more. I suspected he wouldn't in private, but not because he wasn't attracted. Those kisses we *had* shared weren't just acting, and sharing a bed had made certain biological facts more than obvious. He enjoyed kissing me. But he'd said he wouldn't do anything I wasn't comfortable with, which meant that if I wanted more, I'd have to be the one to press for it.

Sawyer joined me on the blanket, dropping down with a zippered cooler and one of the big wooden cutting boards from the kitchen. He began pulling things out. Multiple cheeses. Salami. Olives. Roasted red peppers. Apples. A box of fancy crackers. A bottle of wine. The container of cookies Delilah had sent home with us.

"Sawyer Malone, did you really prepare a charcuterie spread for our hurricane party?"

"I mean, it was all stuff in the fridge that would go bad if the power stays off for a while. None of it requires cooking, so..."

"Color me impressed." I couldn't help but wonder if he'd thought to make this a little more romantic himself.

"You want to work on getting that wine open while I start slicing? Corkscrew's in the side pocket of the cooler."

I did as he asked, pouring us each a glass of chilled Lambrusco. "Bubbly. It feels like a celebration."

"Sort of is. It's our one-week anniversary."

Not entirely sure how to take that, I sipped at the wine. "So it is. Nothing has imploded, and no one has come after us to shout 'Liar, liar, pants on fire.'"

He picked up his glass. "Cheers to that."

We clinked glasses and drank.

"Dig in. There's plenty more where this came from."

I piled salami and a slice of sharp cheddar on a cracker with some roasted red pepper and bit in, letting the salt of the meat and the sharp bite of the cheddar meld on my tongue. "Mmm. This definitely beats the last hurricane party I attended."

"Oh, yeah?" Sawyer popped an olive into his mouth and chewed. "What happened at that one?"

I snagged a square of what I thought was gouda to go with a piece of apple. "I was riding things out with Bree and Ed at his place. A bunch of the Brewhouse staff were there, too. Somebody had the bright idea to do karaoke by phone, and it was so bad. Karaoke only works if the singers are good or everyone else is drunk. Bless her heart, Bree has a lot of fine qualities, but being able to stay on key is not one of them."

Sawyer huffed a laugh. "She and Ford were well matched in that. He's totally tone deaf."

Because he'd brought them up, I indulged my curiosity. "Do you know what happened between them that last summer before y'all joined the Navy?"

He stacked pepperoni and cheese on a cracker. "I have my suspicions, but Ford's never talked about it. Shuts down any time anybody brings her up. Why? Do you know?"

I hadn't been the only one to succumb to those strawberry daiquiris, but my allegiance had to be to Bree here. "I know part of it, but it's not mine to tell." I picked up a slice of salami and fed it to a patiently waiting Roy, who'd taken up sentry on one corner of our picnic blanket to hoover up any forgotten leftovers. "Do you think they'll ever make it to being friends again?"

"I don't know. There's a lot of hurt between them. Has to be, to destroy a friendship as long and deep as theirs. I'm not sure what it would take for them to bridge the gap."

We ate and talked of less consequential things as the storm raged around us. When my glass was empty, Sawyer lifted the bottle. "More? It's bubbly, so it won't keep."

"Sure. If you'll help me polish it off."

He split the remaining wine between our glasses and settled back across from me on the blanket, shoving the now empty board aside. The room was warm, but not yet uncomfortably so. The flicker of candlelight and the wine made it feel like a night for confessions and questions.

"What do you want to do with the rest of your life?" When Sawyer went brows up, I hurried to add, "I mean, babysitting me isn't going to be a full-time job. Obviously, you'll want to get back to doing something once I've stopped derailing your life. What might that be?"

He swirled the wine in his glass and took a long sip. "I don't have any idea what I want. The only real constant in my life has been the sea. All those years fishing. Not that I want to go back to that—the Navy, I mean." He dragged a finger around the lip of the glass. "I feel a little lost. I don't know who I am since I was discharged. Now that I'm back on Hatterwick, it's hard not to feel like the son of the town drunk from the wrong side of the island again. A lot of people still see me that way."

Incensed, I set my mostly empty glass on the hearth and sat up fast enough that I startled Roy. He abandoned us for the dog bed in the corner. "I don't. That's not who you are. That's never been who you are."

His lips gave a wry quirk. "It's nice that you think so. But surely you've heard the talk about us."

There'd been talk? "The only talk I've heard has been a hundred percent supportive. Who said something to you?"

"Nobody's said anything *to* me. But there are plenty of folks who think you're slumming it marrying me." He jerked a shoulder in easy acceptance. "They're not entirely wrong."

Furious, I curled my hands to fists. "Fuck them and the rude ass barn they were apparently raised in. They're *not* right." By God, if I did nothing else for this man while we were married, I'd help to banish this demon. "You know who I see when I look at you? Not only my personal hero, who literally brought me back to life. I see an incredible friend. A man who's been willing to not only put his life entirely on hold for me, but inextricably tangled that life up with mine to save me when he didn't have to. I see the guy who steadies me. Who comforts me after my nightmares and holds me to make sure they stay away."

He watched me with unreadable eyes as I edged closer.

Emboldened by the wine, I kept going. "I see the guy I

crushed on from the time I was thirteen. The guy I can't stop thinking about kissing again."

Sawyer's throat worked, and those eyes had gone storm dark in the candlelight. "Willa."

My name was all he said, and I couldn't tell if it was a warning or a plea. I knew what I wanted it to be.

My heart thundered in my chest, as much terror as anticipation. "Can I kiss you, Sawyer?"

"You can do anything you want."

At that incredible, heady invitation, I leaned in and brushed my lips to his. He sighed, as if he'd been holding his breath, waiting just for this. It wasn't for display. Wasn't to prove anything to anyone. It was simply because we wanted. He wanted me, and that was my own personal miracle.

I traced his lips with my tongue, and he groaned, reaching out to drag me against his hard body. Our legs tangled, and I wrapped my arms around him, wanting to get closer. Our hips bumped and shifted, until the bulge in his shorts pressed to the softness between my thighs. I arched against him, wanting so much more. His hands snaked around me, and he rolled so I straddled him.

I broke the kiss only long enough to whimper a little moan as he bucked against me. God, that felt good. Taking his mouth again, I began to rock. His hands skated beneath my shirt, up my back and around to palm my breast. I wanted more of that touch everywhere, with a lot fewer clothes. And he'd *said* anything I wanted... But in a minute. Because the tension coiling at my center was making it hard to think past chasing this high.

His fingers worked down the cup of my bra, and suddenly I felt that delicious, callused touch against my nipple. He gave the slightest pinch and roll, and I detonated, shuddering against him as if I'd been hit by a live wire.

When I managed to pry my eyes open again, I looked down

into his. They'd gone all but black with an unmistakable hunger as he gazed up at me. I wanted everything those eyes promised.

Intent, I leaned down to kiss him again, and something crashed.

We both froze.

"What was that?" I gasped.

"Something hit the house, I think."

We held there, listening for another few minutes.

When I would've picked right back up where we'd left off, Sawyer stroked the hair back from my face in that way he did, and I knew the spell had been broken. Again.

"We should probably stop there."

I wanted to howl in protest, but even in my current state, I could recognize that the last thing we needed was to be bare-assed naked and lost in each other if the roof somehow got ripped off the house.

Still tingling, I slid off him.

"Do you think you can sleep?"

Was he kidding? My body still hummed from his touch, wanting more of it. And now I was wondering if he thought this was some kind of mistake. Sleep was the last thing on my mind.

"I don't know."

He tucked me back against him. "Why don't you give it a try? It's probably going to be a long night."

Okay, he wouldn't cuddle after if he thought it was a mistake. Right?

My gaze slid lower to the tent in his shorts. "What about you?"

"It'll go away, eventually. I have lots of practice when it comes to you."

I let his words sink in, my brain wrapping around them. "Oh."

"Yeah, oh."

Not a mistake, then. Turning my delighted grin into his shoulder, I relaxed against him, laying a hand over his heart. The hammer beat of it belied his exterior calm. His fingers curled around mine, and he brushed a kiss to my brow.

"Goodnight, Wren."

CHAPTER 22

SAWYER

I hadn't expected to sleep. Not with the hurricane, and not with the world's worst case of blue balls. I was never forgetting the sight and sound of Willa lost in pleasure. It had played on repeat in my brain long after she'd slid into dreams. But I woke to silence sometime just after dawn.

The dining room was dark, the candles having guttered out sometime in the night. The lantern batteries had died, but I could hear the quiet whir of the fan and the faint hum of the mini fridge running on the portable power station. Willa wasn't doing her best impression of a koala, and I reached out to find the mattress beside me empty.

I sat up. "Wren?"

No answer.

"Roy?"

There was no telltale scrabble of claws.

Where were they? Were we in the eye, or was it over?

I was dragging on my shoes when one of the dining room doors opened.

"Oh, good. You're awake. The storm passed about half an

hour ago." Willa's voice was a quiet rasp. "I was just taking Roy out to potty."

"How bad is it?"

"We've had worse. I didn't go far. I wanted to wait for you."

I followed her to the front door, noting the sandbags she'd already shifted and the weatherproof tape she'd removed to get the door open. Outside, the sky was a massive expanse of blue, interrupted only by the occasional wisp of cloud. It was as if last night's chaos had scrubbed it clean. But the island itself was another story. Branches and leaf trash were everywhere. The garden we'd put so much effort into reviving had been ripped to shreds. Branches had been snapped off all the trees, some dangling, others having been carried off in the wind. Water stood in low spots that hadn't been there before, because this storm had been big enough to truly change the topography of the land. We'd need to check the dunes on the property. Part of living on the Outer Banks was understanding that we fought a war to keep the land from being reclaimed by the ocean. Sometimes that battle involved making repairs to counter erosion.

A limb had punched through the roof of the garage. "Anything important kept in the top of the garage?"

"I don't know. There's a section of attic space there, but I'm not sure whether it'll be impacted by that hole."

"I'll check that in a bit."

Willa stuck close to me, and Roy close to her, as I worked my way slowly around the perimeter of the house. A handful of the wooden shingles had been ripped off the walls. Debris littered the deck, and some of the railing going down to the beach was gone, along with a few of the steps. But the hurricane panels covering the windows had done their job, and I saw no signs of downed power lines in the immediate vicinity. All in all, it appeared Sutter House had weathered this hurricane as well as it had countless others. There was nothing obvious that I couldn't repair myself.

The garage was a little worse off. There was water inside and more debris, but the limb had missed the attic. Our vehicles were fine. Not that we could get anywhere if we wanted. Part of the road at the base of the driveway had washed out. We'd have to wait for the water to recede before we attempted to get to town, and that would likely be awhile. If the road had washed out at the base of the hill, it probably was through the marshes, as well. I knew from past experience that authorities would prioritize clearing up the town first, so we'd probably be on our own for a few days, depending on what they were dealing with.

My brain spun as I worked through the details. "God willing, we won't have any major utility issues. Do you know if the boat in dry dock is seaworthy?" I'd noted the sailboat when we'd been locking things down, but hadn't spent any time evaluating it.

"It was when Granddaddy put it up last year. After Grandma got sick, he didn't pull it back out. Didn't have the time or the heart."

"We'll keep that in our pocket as an option in case we need to get to town or the mainland before they deal with the roads." It wouldn't be easy to get it to the water from its current location, but if it became necessary, we'd manage.

Willa turned toward the woods, frowning.

"You want to go check on the horses?"

She pulled her lip between her teeth, and for a moment, all I could think of was kissing that little hurt and every other inch of her body. For the thousandth time, I questioned my choice of restraint last night, when it had seemed clear she wanted me as much as I wanted her.

"I know we have plenty to do around here, but if there are a lot of downed trees, it could impact the herd's ability to move around and forage for food. I just want to know they're okay."

I blinked, dragging my brain back to the conversation. Right. A trip into the woods would certainly work off some of this restless energy that we wouldn't be working off in bed. "Let's finish checking the utilities first and pull together supplies. If we're gonna be going for a hike, we ought to go prepared. Boots, day packs, the whole shebang."

Her shy smile bloomed. "Thank you."

No reason for me to admit this was far more self-preservation than accommodating her.

The power was, predictably, still out, and cell towers were down. But water and gas appeared to be fine. I hooked up the generator, and we enjoyed a proper cup of coffee with our breakfast of fruit and cereal bars before packing supplies and setting out in search of the herd. Roy trotted only a few feet ahead, sniffing and returning over and over as he explored the changes.

We elected to follow the road around the perimeter of the woods to see how bad the washout was up to the dunes. There were at least two spots that would be impassable until the water dropped. We had to backtrack a ways to higher ground before we entered the trees. It was a little cooler beneath the canopy. While there was certainly damage and stripped leaves, there was a surprising amount of remaining shade. Neither of us spoke as we picked our way over and around downed trees.

At least one of the live oaks had toppled in the storm. Its roots had been yanked from the earth as easily as I might pull a weed. Only a few of the enormous, twisted branches kept it from fully collapsing on its side.

Willa laid a hand on the trunk, obviously grieving a little for the loss. "This tree was well over a hundred years old."

"It survived a lot. Part of the root ball is still in the ground. It might take a season or two before it fully dies. Maybe we could bring in more dirt or a tree surgeon?"

"That probably isn't the best use of funds, considering the other higher priorities."

"Maybe. But they're your funds to spend as you choose." Or they would be, once all this bullshit with her parents was put to rest.

She bit her lip again. "I suppose it wouldn't hurt to at least consult with someone."

Leaving the tree behind, we forged ahead. Because Willa knew the area best, I let her lead. She didn't speak much, and that was fine. We'd always been easy in silence together. Despite the debris of downed branches and leaf litter, she moved quietly. I wondered if she'd worked on this level of stealth in all her years monitoring the horses or if it was simply natural because most everything she did was unobtrusive. A natural attempt to blend into whatever environment she was in.

"It shouldn't be much farther, assuming they sheltered where I think they did," she murmured. "Roy, stay close and quiet."

Another quarter mile in, the forest gave way to a wide grassy area with a small pond. High ground and trees rose on all sides, making it perhaps the most sheltered spot on the property. And I'd had no idea it was here. Below us, the herd huddled together, their coats flecked with drying mud and sand, tails twitching, clearly tired out from weathering the storm.

"Well, I'll be damned," I breathed.

Across the clearing, the stallion's head came up, his ears twitching in our direction, though we were downwind. He'd probably heard us coming.

Willa did a quick count. "Twenty-seven. I think that's all of them." Though she'd whispered, the stallion took a few steps in our direction, bouncing his head.

I moved closer, pressing my lips to Willa's ear. "I'm not sure we're welcome here."

"It'll be all right. I just need to let him know it's me."

"Willa—"

Signaling Roy to stay, she ignored the warning in my tone and stepped out of the trees, hands lifted in peace. "Hey, Triton. Hey, buddy. I just came to check on everybody."

At the sound of Willa's crooning, multiple heads shifted in her direction. A couple of the mares broke free of the herd and plodded toward her. I braced myself for some kind of action as the stallion—Triton, I assumed—stamped his feet, prowling closer, keeping between Willa and the curious members of his herd.

She held perfectly still. "Hey, pal. Did y'all come through the storm okay? Anybody need medical attention?"

I had no idea what we'd do if she found any injuries. It wasn't as if we could reach the island vet right now. But maybe she just needed something to say.

All attention was on Willa. My muscles tensed as Triton edged in close enough to snuffle her hair. Still, she didn't move. Then the stallion's nose bumped against her shoulder hard enough to knock her back a step.

When I might have bolted toward her, Willa only laughed softly. "All you had to do was ask." Slowly, she extended her hand, holding it aloft for him to sniff.

When he bumped the long stretch of his nose against her palm, she gave him a gentle rub. He pressed harder, so she obliged with a firmer scratch. "Hard to reach spot, huh?"

Triton snorted and leaned into the touch, much as Roy did when she'd found an especially good spot.

Holy shit. Of course, she was a freaking horse whisperer. She'd been in love with these animals from the time she was a toddler.

"You're looking all distinguished now, aren't you? Getting some gray mixed in with the black."

At her words, I realized this was the same stallion who'd been leading the herd since we were kids. While he'd once been coal black, his coat was now more of a pewter gray.

The stallion let Willa scratch for another couple of minutes before bobbing his head and stepping back. The two curious mares came next, and they went through the whole process over again. I didn't step out, and she didn't invite me. The herd was clearly used to her, and I didn't want to unnecessarily stress them and potentially upset this delicate balance.

Once the mares had satisfied their curiosity, Willa slowly circled the entire herd, presumably looking for any obvious injuries. When she made it back around to where I stood, I shook my head. "Damnedest thing I've ever seen. Did you see what you needed to see?"

"Yeah. They're safe here, with plenty of water and grass. Later, we'll probably need to bring in some supplemental food, but I don't think they're stuck. We can head on back."

"I suggest we try a different route. I think if we cut across here, it shouldn't be that far to the beach as the crow flies. It'll be a little longer maybe, but easier going."

"That sounds like a plan."

We were maybe half a mile from the beach where I'd fished her out of the ocean all those years ago, but I didn't mention that. If she didn't realize where we were, hopefully, she wouldn't have the kind of reaction she had in the car the other day.

We worked our way toward the Atlantic side of the island, discussing next steps for back at the house. In all likelihood, it would be a couple of days before we could get out. But we were well stocked, and with the generator, we'd be good for at least a few days.

As the path widened out a little, I took Willa's hand, wanting the connection. "You seem lighter today."

She swung our joined hands companionably between us. "I feel lighter. The house survived, and so did the horses. It feels like maybe the worst is over and this will be the last major excitement for a bit. We could use some dull."

"I'm all for that." I wanted the chance to get back to what was supposed to be our honeymoon period. And if that was because I was starting to consider an actual honeymoon with my wife, well... I was still coming to terms with what that might mean.

Well ahead, I could see the end of the treeline and the hint of beach beyond.

Willa grinned up at me.

"First one to the treeline gets dibs on the first shower." She took off without waiting for my reply.

"Hey!" I bolted after her.

Laughing, she danced and dodged over limbs. With my longer legs, I was closing the distance. Willa glanced back, and I caught the flash of her smile just before her foot snagged on something and she went flying, crashing headlong into the dirt.

"Oh, shit! Are you okay?" I rushed to her.

She shoved up partway, spitting sand out of her mouth. "I —" Abruptly, she froze, then scrambled back on a scream.

"What is it?" Reaching her side, my gaze caught on something white inches away, peeking out of the earth.

There, wedged into the sand, was a human skull with a round hole right between the empty eye sockets.

CHAPTER 23
WILLA

Officer Cory Teague stumbled out of the woods and was promptly sick right at the edge of the beach. At least I wasn't the only one shaken up by our gruesome find. As Sawyer came out after him, I clutched the insulating foil blanket tighter around myself, but it didn't help. I still shook as if we were sitting on a glacier in Antarctica instead of on a North Carolina beach in humid, high summer. Shock was like that. Roy pressed into me, lending warmth as well as comfort, and I clung to him because I was one wrong thought away from descending back into a panic attack.

The faint sound of radio chatter carried on the breeze as Cory reported in, confirming that we had, indeed, found human remains. Chief Carson was no doubt tied up with post-hurricane triage, along with all other emergency personnel on the island, so he'd sent one of his junior officers. He'd probably thought—or hoped, at least—that I'd been hysterical and mistaken. That it was animal bones or a rock or some other benign thing that had been uncovered by the storm. Because we didn't have things like murder on Hatterwick.

But I wasn't mistaken. There wasn't really any other explanation for the round hole just above the empty eye sockets. Not when it appeared the remains had been buried. I suspected I'd be seeing that horrible vision in my nightmares for years to come.

My chest tightened again.

No. Nope. Not going there. Not right now.

Five things I can see. Ocean. Beach. Roy. Sea birds. Driftwood.

Four things I can feel. Sand beneath me. The wind in my hair. Sweat drying on my skin. Blister on my foot.

Three things I can hear. The surf. Gulls. Wind in the trees.

Two things I can smell. Salt and wet earth.

One thing I can taste. Sour in my mouth. I hadn't been sick. Yet. But it had been a near thing.

Sawyer hunkered down before me. "Holding up?"

"I wanna go home," I whispered. Not that I could quite face the lengthy hike back, but anything was better than staying here. Because I knew where we were. We'd come at it from a different direction than I had all those years ago, but this was only a hundred yards or so from where I'd drowned. I hadn't come here in all the years I'd been back on island, and I was barely keeping it together now. The edge of a migraine pressed at my brain, and every instinct I had shouted at me to run.

Sawyer pivoted to sit beside me on the sand, wrapping an arm around my shoulders. "Soon. Cory will need to ask us some questions, I expect."

I leaned into him, wishing for all the world that we'd just gone back the way we'd come.

A few minutes later, Cory made his way over to us. As he'd been only a year ahead of me in school, I couldn't think of him as Officer Teague, despite the uniform. He'd always had something of a baby face, which he'd attempted to offset with a goatee. But I still saw the kid who'd been challenged to eat glue sticks in second grade. He looked about as sick now, his skin pale and drawn beneath the reddish beard.

"Hey there, Willa. I just need to ask you a few questions. You up to that?"

"If it means I can get out of here sooner rather than later."

"I'll make it quick as I can." He pulled out his phone to record the conversation. "This is Officer Cory Teague speaking with Willa Sutter and Sawyer Malone. Can you walk me through how you came to find the... the remains? Where you were. What you were doing out here. How you stumbled upon them."

Focusing on Sawyer's solid presence and Roy's bulk beside me, I took him through it.

"Did you notice any identifiable features or clothing on the remains? Anything that stood out?"

I arched a brow. "Did I notice any identifiable features on the skull I basically fell on? You mean besides the hole that looks like a gunshot wound to the forehead? No. If the—" I swallowed. "If the rest of the skeleton is there, I didn't see. Maybe it's buried beneath the sand."

Cory gulped, and I wondered if he was about to be sick again. I wouldn't blame him.

"Did either of you touch or move the remains at all before calling it in?"

"No."

"Did you notice any other debris, items, or potential evidence around the scene?"

I'd been too busy having a panic attack to notice anything.

Sawyer squeezed me. "No. Nothing. We removed ourselves from the immediate vicinity as soon as we realized what we'd found."

"Do either of you have any idea how long the remains might have been out there? Were they weathered or more recent?"

Did I look like a forensic expert?

"No clue. It's not... fresh," Sawyer said. "In all likelihood, the storm uncovered them."

"Do y'all frequent that area often? Had you noticed any sign of a disturbance on the ground before today?"

"I haven't been to this part of the property in twelve years." I'd done everything in my power to avoid exactly this. Well, not exactly this. I'd never imagined there was a body out here. But I'd given this area a wide berth, attempting to stave off the terror coming near it always incited.

"Did you take any photos or video at the scene before I arrived? I'll need copies of anything you captured."

"No."

"Okay. That's all I've got for now. Chief Carson will probably have some additional questions for you later. Can you think of anything else to add?"

"Is it Gwen?" I knew there was no possible way he could know the answer to that. But I had to ask because the question had been beating against my brain since I'd all but fallen onto the remains.

Cory took a deep breath. "I don't know. According to protocol, the remains will be removed to the medical examiner's office in Elizabeth City on the mainland. Any detailed exam will take time, but they'll probably be able to determine the basics about gender, relative age, and potential race of the deceased. I'm not sure how fast we'll be able to get the remains there, under the circumstances."

Pretty fast, I was willing to bet. Hatterwick had an incredibly low crime rate, at least for anything serious. I suspected Miles would be putting a lot of pressure on Chief Carson to do whatever was possible to expedite things, both from the perspective of being able to reassure the public and because this could possibly provide some closure to a years old mystery.

But if it was Gwen, would it provide closure? Would there

be any evidence of what had happened to her? Anything to suggest how she'd ended up here?

This was so damned close to where I'd been in the water. What if there was something buried deep in my lost memories that might answer some of this? Had what happened to me and what happened to Gwen somehow been connected? It wasn't something I'd allowed myself to consider for years, because even approaching the subject sent me into a blind panic or a migraine. But it was impossible not to wonder now when I knew there were human remains only a few dozen yards inside the treeline.

A shaft of pain shot directly through my eye, and I squeezed them shut.

I needed to stop this line of thought before this migraine struck in earnest. I didn't know it was Gwen. She was just forefront in my mind. The only thing I knew for sure was that someone was dead on my grandparents' property. On *my* property.

What did this even mean for me?

"I think this is enough for now," Sawyer announced. "I'm gonna get her home. It's been... a lot."

"Of course." Cory looked around, as if only just realizing we didn't have a vehicle. "I'd give you a ride back, but I've been ordered to secure the scene."

"We understand. We'll manage. C'mon, Wren." Sawyer climbed to his feet and lifted me to mine.

My legs felt wobbly, as if they were made of rubber.

Sawyer's hands tightened on mine. "Okay?"

Not even a little bit. But I would be. "Just get me out of here."

We both turned at the sound of a motor. Far out on the water, running parallel to the island, a boat was headed in our direction at a rapid clip.

"Do you suppose that's Chief Carson?" God, I really didn't want to endure more questions right now.

Sawyer squinted. "I think it's the Coast Guard."

As the boat neared, I recognized the familiar red-orange color and shape of a Zodiac as it bounced over the waves. It appeared there were two people aboard—the driver and a dark-haired woman who began waving and pointing as soon as she spotted us.

"Is that... Gabi?" Had my best friend commandeered a Coast Guard vessel to come check on me?

The boat turned in our direction, slowing on the approach until it gently beached on the sand. Gabi was over the side in an instant, rushing toward me.

"Oh my God, Willa! We just heard. Are you okay?"

Of course I wasn't okay. I'd just found a body that might be our missing best friend. But I didn't say that.

"I'm not hurt."

As her critical doctor's gaze skimmed over me, my own slid to the driver of the boat as he approached. I couldn't see his eyes behind the mirrored aviator glasses, but he had the same kind of calm, capable demeanor Sawyer projected. He was indeed wearing a Coast Guard uniform beneath his life vest.

"Honey, you have blood on your knees. And if you're wrapped up in that foil blanket and still cold, you're definitely in shock. I want to get you into the clinic."

"No!" The word came out far sharper than I'd intended. But I couldn't take being in a medical facility after all this. I was so very close to breaking. "I just want to go home."

"Willa—"

The new arrival pressed a hand to the small of Gabi's back. "Maybe give her a chance to breathe, Gabs. Reckon she's done had herself a bit of a scare." He offered a half smile. "We'll give y'all a lift somewhere, if you need."

Sawyer took his proffered hand. "That'd be good. My wife's had a hell of a day. Who are you, by the way?"

"Pardon me. Petty Officer First Class Daniel LaRue, U.S.

Coast Guard. At your service." His accent immediately called to mind jazz clubs, beignets, and alligators. The bayou accent was so unexpected, it distracted me for a moment from my own discomfort.

It took some effort to get us all loaded into the boat, Roy included. My limbs didn't much want to cooperate. I clambered gracelessly over the side and would've fallen straight to the floor of the rigid hull of the inflatable boat if not for Daniel catching me. I got fitted with a life jacket and dropped down to huddle at the side. Roy flattened himself next to me.

Gabi sat on my other side, moving in close to take my hands. "I've gotcha. Headache?"

"Migraine," I gritted out.

"We'll get you fixed up as soon as we get back to Sutter House."

Because the light was starting to strobe from the pain, I shut my eyes again and tried to focus on literally anything else. Like the fact that Gabi clearly knew this guy. "New Orleans?"

"Remember that situationship I mentioned?" Gabi murmured.

"Yeah?"

"He's him. I'll explain everything later."

"Holding you to that."

Daniel fired up the motor, putting an end to any easy conversation. The trip to the north end of the island didn't take long. Soon enough, we were easing up to our private dock. Daniel and Sawyer secured the vessel, then helped us out of the boat.

"We'll get those knees cleaned, some meds for your migraine, and I'll finish checking you over. I've got something that will help you sleep if the migraine meds don't do it."

"No!" Instinctively, I backed away from my friend into Sawyer.

His arms came around me. "It's okay. Nobody's gonna sedate you, Wren."

I knew Gabi was staring. This wasn't rational behavior, but I couldn't stop myself. I'd get a little bit of a pass based on current circumstances, but I knew she'd have questions. And at some point, I was going to have to make explanations.

Conversation went on around me as we slowly made our way up to the house.

"—could have been a lot worse. The storm lost a lot of power once it made landfall. There's a lot of cleanup to do, but the degree of objective damage could've been a lot worse."

"—saying power will be restored in a couple days."

"Our generator will hold out that long."

"The roads will take longer."

Everything felt very distant. As if I was observing it all from outside myself. That was good. Better. I didn't feel the pain in my head so keenly this way.

It was Sawyer who cleaned my knees where I'd scraped them up when I'd fallen. Sawyer who cleaned my hands. After that, I sat docile through Gabi's examination, unable to rouse myself to do more than offer one syllable answers.

Dissociation. That's what my psychiatrist had called this. He'd always said it like it was a bad thing. But I needed the distance. Needed that wall between me and everything I was feeling. It was too much. I'd spent the last ten years actively avoiding exactly this. But maybe, if I could keep the wall in place, I could manage to do the hard thing and face the memories that had caused me so much trauma. Maybe somewhere on the other side of them were answers for all of us.

"I don't like this, Sawyer. She's way too shocky."

"She'll be better after she's slept."

I only half listened as she told him what to keep an eye out for. I was too busy reaching for the blissful tendrils of oblivion as my migraine meds began to kick in.

Sawyer was right. Everything would be better on the other side. It had to be.

CHAPTER 24

SAWYER

The police station made me twitchy. I'd never actually been arrested for anything in my youth, but the Wayward Sons had collectively been hauled in on multiple occasions. Rios and I most often because we didn't have fine, upstanding parents to defend us. I knew it chapped Bill Carson's ass that he'd never been able to make anything stick to either of us. The reality was that though we'd flaunted a few rules and raised a little hell, we'd never done anything legitimately wrong. That just flew in the face of how the police chief had always seen us.

But he'd wanted to talk to Willa and me. As it had been three days, we could only presume this had something to do with the preliminary results on the body. Since the water level had dropped and the wash outs had been temporarily repaired, we'd elected to come to him before our meeting with Roland O'Shea. I hoped that wasn't a mistake and that whatever he had to say wasn't going to set off another anxiety attack for Willa.

She'd been fine when she'd woken after the migraine. A little shaky maybe, but given that a body who'd clearly met a violent end had been found on her property, I figured that was normal. There were no more signs of shock or lingering trauma. She hadn't woken with nightmares, and I was finally starting to relax again.

We'd managed to get the house set more or less back to normal, taking down the hurricane panels, cleaning up the debris in the yard, hauling back out all the plants and patio furniture. Electricity and phones were back in service. There were still repairs to be made, and I'd see to those, but I didn't expect to be able to get supplies for that just yet.

"Miss Sutter. Thank you for coming." Bill Carson gestured toward his office with no acknowledgment to me.

I wasn't sure if either were intended slights or not. Willa hadn't taken my name. There hadn't been time, even if that had been her intention. Which, of course, it wasn't. Even if this marriage had been fully real from the get go, I wouldn't have expected that of her. Not when that part of her legacy meant so much to her. But Carson's failure to greet me felt pointed.

Willa tightened her grip on my hand, the only outward sign of her anxiety, and we rose to follow the chief back to his office.

"Have a seat. Can I get you a cup of coffee or something?"

This polite civility was so far from how I'd seen this man behave toward me, toward Rios and Caroline. He'd accused Rios of murder after Gwen disappeared, and when Caroline had been stalked a decade back, he'd acted like she'd brought the whole thing on herself. And here he was offering my wife coffee. I knew it was because she was a Sutter. Because, in Carson's eyes, she mattered in a way the rest of us didn't. Part of me was grateful she wasn't having to bear the brunt of his shit attitude. But I was sorely tempted to push the envelope and ask for coffee myself, to see how far this solicitude would extend. Instead, I kept my mouth shut.

"No, thank you. You said you wanted to see us? Is there news about... about the body?" Willa asked.

Carson leaned a hip against his desk. "Preliminary results

are back from the ME's office. Evidence indicates the remains are of an adult white male. It's not Gwen Busby."

Willa's fingers flexed in mine, and she blinked, clearly trying to absorb the news.

"Then who the hell is it?" I asked.

Carson spared me a glance. "We don't know yet. There's no other documented missing person from the island. The investigation is ongoing, and further forensic analysis will take a lot longer. But I wanted to tell y'all in person, before you heard it through the island grapevine."

Out of courtesy to Willa, or because he wanted to see our reactions? Surely he didn't think we were somehow involved?

Willa remained gracious. "Thank you. Is there any sign of how old the remains are?"

"Not yet. That's one of the details we hope to get from the ME's analysis, so we can narrow down the scope of our search. If either of y'all thinks of anything that might be helpful, or if you find anything else in the course of storm clean up, let me know. Otherwise, I won't keep you."

Willa rose. "I appreciate you telling us. Is this information to be kept confidential for purposes of the investigation?"

"No. At this point, the more people who hear, the better. Maybe somebody will think of something. Thanks for coming in."

Dismissed. I supposed that was a good thing. If he'd believed we had something to do with it, he'd have probably asked more questions.

I stayed quiet until we got back outside. "So... not Gwen. How do you feel?"

She scooped a hand through her hair. "I hardly know. Relieved? Horrified? Both? I was so sure it was her, and now it's not. Some other poor guy was killed and buried on my family's property for God knows how long. It means we still don't have answers about Gwen. I guess a part of me wants to hang onto that. To believe that, somehow, she's still out there. Which is crazy, because if she were still alive, why wouldn't she come home?"

I didn't have any good answers for that. The alternatives I could think of would probably be considered worse than death. If Willa hadn't thought of them, I wasn't about to put those images in her brain. "I don't know. You ready to head over to O'Shea's office, or do you need a bite first? We could swing by the bakery for pastries."

"No, I'd rather get it over with. If he didn't immediately share good news over the phone, I feel like this is going to be more bad news and a strategy meeting."

The moment I clapped eyes on Roland O'Shea, I knew she'd been right.

He waited only long enough for us to settle into chairs on the other side of his desk. "Well, things didn't go precisely as we'd hoped. I reported your marriage to the court, and rather than seeing it as a sign of your stability, your parents are suggesting it as evidence of your impulsivity and poor judgment. They allege you were not fit to consent, and that Sawyer used your fragile emotional state following your grandparents' deaths to manipulate you into matrimony in the name of his own financial gain."

Outraged, Willa shot to her feet. "That's bullshit! All of it!"

I grabbed her hand. "Wren, he knows that." None of this surprised me. John Hollingsworth had never thought much of me.

Willa visibly struggled to rein in her temper. She didn't lose it often, but when she did... She looked back to O'Shea. "I'm sorry. This isn't your fault."

"It's perfectly all right. They're certainly putting you through the wringer with all this. In any event, I'm afraid we're going to have to do a little more to prove the legitimacy of your marriage."

Mama Flo had anticipated this. Thank God Dax was already working his magic on our digital paper trail. I squeezed Willa's hand again, and she lowered back into her chair. "We've got nothing to hide. What all do you need?"

We went over the evidence we could and would voluntarily produce.

"The internet is still spotty since the storm, so it'll take some time to pull together, but we can absolutely do that. What else do you suggest?" Willa asked.

"I also recommend that Sawyer sign a post-nuptial agreement wherein he relinquishes any claim on any of your assets. I would have suggested a pre-nup in the first place had I known your intention to marry."

That was easy. "Done. I don't want any of your family stuff." And that would kill off some of the speculation that I was some kind of gold digger.

"No." There went that stubborn tilt to her chin.

"Why not? This is the easy answer."

"Because I'm not going to dignify this insult to you by having legal paperwork drawn up to that effect. That suggests I don't trust you. This is just one more way my father's trying to take a dig at you, just like he always has."

Her insult on my behalf was sweet but impractical. "Wren, I don't give a rat's ass what your father thinks of me. Let me sign the paperwork. I didn't marry you for your money, so this changes nothing."

The attorney studied her for a long moment, a nostalgic smile tipping the corners of his mouth. "You remind me so much of your mother sometimes."

Willa blinked, taken aback. "Excuse me?"

"The younger her, before she met your father. She could be very stubborn, too."

"You knew my mother back then?"

"Of course. We both grew up here on the island. Went to

school together." A faint trace of something that might have been sadness or disappointment flickered over his features. "She was a very different person before John."

I could only imagine. "Willa's got stubborn genes going back multiple generations, on both sides. But let's talk about this."

We went a few rounds about it, but in the end, I signed the document he'd already prepared.

As we stepped out of the office, O'Shea's secretary hung up the phone. Her eyes gleamed with the kind of excitement that only presaged good gossip.

"That body that was found *isn't* Gwen Busby." Her cheeks colored as her gaze slid to Willa. "Sorry."

Willa just shook her head. "We already knew. We came from the police station."

"Did Chief Carson say who they thought it was?" O'Shea asked.

"Only that it was an adult white male, which doesn't exactly narrow the pool much."

The lawyer shook his head. "It's such a damned shame. I don't know what this world is coming to. But I'm sure the police will get to the bottom of it."

He had more faith in Carson than I did. It wasn't like the guy had all that much experience investigating this sort of crime.

Willa stayed quiet on the drive home. Nancy's announcement about the body had probably gotten her thinking about all that shit again. Not until we carried our couple of bags of groceries into the kitchen did she break her silence.

"Why were you so willing to sign a post-nup?"

She was still upset about that? I set my bag on the counter. "Because I seriously don't care what anyone thinks. I'm 1000% not after your money. Why does it bother you so much?"

Her eyes lit with something that might have been a battle

light. "People have looked down on you all your life for circumstances that were beyond your control. Everything you've ever had, you fought and worked for yourself. You could have become bitter and angry and money hungry. You could have become all the things that they're accusing you of being. But you didn't. You have always been one of the kindest, most honorable men I have ever known, and I resent the hell out of them for trying to diminish you like that."

I stared at her, this kind, big-hearted woman who somehow had so much compassion despite everything she'd been through. She saw injustices and wanted to do something about them. So few people had ever thought me worth that. My brothers. Some of their family. Mostly, I'd learned a long time ago that the opinions of small-minded people didn't matter. But her opinion had always mattered to me. I knew how much she hated conflict, so the fact that she was ready to go to war in my name... well, I didn't know how to describe what that meant to me. But this reaction still felt unnecessary. The thing was signed.

"I appreciate your desire to defend me. Truly, I do. But I still don't understand. Me signing that piece of paper doesn't change anything between us." Yet she was acting as if it did.

"Won't it?" There was an odd blend of challenge and quaver in her tone. "If this is the last attack they can make, doesn't that mean that once it's resolved, I'm safe and you're released from your responsibility here? Is that what you want? For all this to be over?"

Fuck no, that wasn't what I wanted. That had never been what I wanted. But a real marriage wasn't what either of us had signed on for in the beginning. I was a means to an end, not a true match for someone like her. At least one of us needed to remember that before we slid in any deeper. Still, I wouldn't lie to her.

"No. No, I don't want it to be over." Despite the circumstances, these weeks with her had been some of the best of my life. "But that was always the plan, Wren." It was the truth, so why the hell did I feel like Roy had just torn out my guts?

She flinched as if I'd struck her, and I was deathly afraid she was about to cry. I couldn't stand the idea that I'd caused her any kind of pain. But when she looked back at me, it was temper filling her eyes. "Because that's what you actually want? Or is it because you don't think you're good enough? For me? For this? For us?"

The accusation struck me speechless. Because that was exactly what I thought.

She must've seen it in my face because she closed the distance between us, reaching up to cup my cheeks. I couldn't have broken her gentle hold to save my life.

"I wish you could see yourself the way that I see you. The way you helped me see myself through your eyes. We're better together, Sawyer. And maybe I'm just a foolish inexperienced little girl to you—"

I shook my head, curling my fingers into fists to keep from reaching for her. "No, you're not that. You've never been that."

Her throat worked, and her fingers against my cheeks trembled, but she didn't look away. "I know this was supposed to be temporary. I know it wasn't supposed to be real. But it is real for me. A part of me knew it would be when I agreed to this, because I love you. I've always loved you. I know you care for me or you wouldn't have offered yourself up for this lunatic scheme. I think you agreed, not only to protect me, but because it allowed us to both get out of our own way. There's something between us. Always has been. It's shifted and changed over the years, but it's *here*. And I don't want to watch you walk away out of some misguided sense of nobility because you don't think you're worthy. Because you're everything to me."

This was everything I'd never imagined hearing from her. Everything I'd never even let myself dream about. But even as my heart yearned to leap in with both feet, my brain argued with me. She was attracted. We'd been playing at being married for the better part of a month. It wasn't unexpected that she'd slid into that fantasy, too. But that didn't make it real. Not beyond the undeniable chemistry. Because how could someone like her love someone like me?

I opened my mouth.

Willa narrowed her eyes. "I swear to God, if you're about to try to mansplain my own emotions to me, you can stop right there. I'm not going to hear it. I will never again allow anyone to tell me I don't know my own mind. Not even you."

Shit. Was that what I was trying to do? I never wanted to make her feel like I was trying to control or diminish her. I just didn't know how to trust this, because I was too afraid of having the dream of it yanked away from me.

"I'm going to make this really simple for you, Sawyer. I'm not asking for a declaration of forever here. I'm asking you to give us a chance. Do you want me?"

I couldn't give her anything but honesty in this moment. Because this was as raw and vulnerable as we'd ever been. "More than my next breath."

She rose up, pressing her body against mine, lifting her mouth close enough that I felt the warmth of her breath as she spoke. "I'm your wife. So why don't you finally take me?"

CHAPTER 25
WILLA

I couldn't believe I'd just issued that challenge. Couldn't believe I'd spilled out everything I felt like that. I hardly dared breathe, pressing myself close enough that he had to feel my pounding heart and the way I trembled as I waited for him to choose. Because it was a choice. In this moment, he decided whether he wanted this marriage to be real or not.

I knew he cared for me. I knew he was attracted to me. But I was still absolutely terrified he'd choose not. He carried so much guilt and an unworthiness I'd sensed in him all our lives. I hated everyone who'd ever made him feel like less, and I hated even more that even the tiniest part of him believed it. Maybe that was why I'd been so bold. Temper and righteous outrage giving me the courage to speak the truth he needed to hear.

Even if it meant he could shatter me.

"Willa." My name wrenched out of him on a pained groan, and my heart seized.

He was going to say no. He was going to be foolishly noble and find a way to try to gently reject me for my own good. I didn't know how the hell I'd survive it, because it had taken every last shred of courage I possessed to admit how I felt.

Squeezing my eyes shut—because I absolutely couldn't look at him right now—I took a step back. "I'm sorry." I didn't know what the hell I was apologizing for, but I didn't know what else to say. "I—"

He yanked me forward so fast I lost my balance. Then his mouth crashed down on mine, and I lost my breath, because this was different from the other kisses we'd shared. They'd been playful, flirty, sweet. There'd even been that hot, sexy orgasm by the fire during the hurricane. But this kiss held an edge of something that might have been desperation, and I was so here for it. It wasn't a declaration of undying love, but I hadn't asked for that, hadn't expected it. I'd take reciprocated passion and be grateful.

So. Damned. Grateful.

His hands skated down, cupping my backside, pressing me against the bulge in his shorts. I wanted to feel those hands everywhere, and I definitely wanted a chance to explore that bulge for myself. Relieved, aroused, I rocked against him, delighting in the growl that elicited. He set me back just far enough to strip off my shirt, then his own, before we dove at each other again. His fingers were at the clasp of my bra when I heard the rumble—part growl, part confusion.

My lust-addled brain took far too long to understand the sound.

Roy.

I broke the kiss, searching for my dog. He stood at attention a few feet away, my tank top having landed in such a way that it looped over his head. His tail wagged in a jerky, hesitant rhythm, as if he was pretty sure this was a game, but he wasn't quite clear what was happening.

Right, well, he wouldn't know what was happening, would he? It wasn't like I'd ever brought a guy around him.

I laid a hand on Sawyer's chest and stepped back. "Thirty seconds."

Racing across the kitchen, I retrieved one of the chew bones I'd bought. "Here you go, buddy. Here's a nice, tasty bone. You just focus on that, okay?"

I tugged the shirt off his head, and Roy took the bone from me, sending Sawyer a long look before he trotted over to the dog bed in the corner—one of several I'd scattered around the house.

"Now, where were we?" I flicked the clasp of my bra myself and let it slide down my arms, falling to the floor.

Sawyer swore, long and low, his eyes darkening like storm clouds. "Not here."

He scooped me up in seconds, and I yelped, even as I followed his urging to wrap my legs around his waist. "Your shoulder!" It had come a long way, but still wasn't fully healed.

"I promise, I'm feeling no pain."

He hustled us up the stairs, every step a delicious friction against my center that ratcheted up my need. Pausing only long enough to kick the door shut, he carried me straight to the bed we shared and followed me down. Then he simply held there, hovering over me, staring with hungry eyes.

When he said nothing, just continued to drink me in, anxiety began to curl in my gut, souring the lovely buzz of arousal.

"Please don't change your mind."

"Never. I'm just slowing things down a bit."

I wasn't exactly keen on slowing down. I was too afraid he'd come to his senses and think to ask about the one thing I didn't want to admit, because it might make him stop.

I opened my mouth to protest, but he curled his tongue around one nipple and words evaporated into a long, "Oooh."

"So sweet," he murmured. "I knew you'd be sweet."

Suddenly very on board with slow, I threaded my fingers through his hair and cradled his head, keeping him close.

His smile brushed against my bare skin. "You like that?"

"More, please."

"So polite. Such a good girl."

Why on earth was hearing that such a thrill?

He settled in, making himself more comfortable as he cupped the other breast, rolling the nipple between his fingers.

Every squeeze, every suckle, caused a corresponding pull low in my belly. I shifted my hips, seeking relief for the building ache. "Sawyer."

"Mmm?" The question vibrated against my skin, causing my nipple to bud even tighter.

"I need you to touch me."

"I am touching you."

"Everywhere."

He paused, his eyes glittering as they stared down at me. "That's a lot of territory, Wren. You're going to have to be more specific."

Damn him, he was going to make me say it?

Of course he was. This man was never going to make assumptions where I was concerned. Not with something like this. He would never push for anything I didn't want to give.

Well, I was a grown-ass woman. If I could admit I loved him, I could ask for this. Probably.

"I need you to touch my clit." The words came out in a rush, barely above a whisper, but he heard them.

His eyes went impossibly darker. "Fuck. I never in my life thought I'd hear you say that."

I bit my lip. "Too much?"

"Nothing you could want will ever be too much. I just never thought I'd be here with you." His big hands stroked along my ribs. "I've wanted you for so damned long." The admission seemed to pain him. Or maybe that was the erection straining his shorts.

But his confession distracted me from the mortification burning in my cheeks. "Really? How long?"

"Far enough back that if I'd acted on it, I'd have earned a one-way ticket straight to hell, courtesy of your brother."

Talk about a mood killer. "Let's not bring him into this."

"Fair enough." He reached for the button of my shorts. "My wife needs to be touched."

I shivered. It wasn't the first time he'd called me his wife, but it was the first time like *this*, when he was on the verge of making me his wife for real. "God, I love that."

He lowered the zipper and began working down the shorts and underwear. "What?"

"You calling me your wife."

"What do you like about it?"

I struggled to consider the question as the cool air kissed my bare skin. "I... it makes me feel claimed."

So did the look in his eyes as he stared up the length of my naked body, fingers stroking my calves. "Do you want to be claimed, Willa?"

I fought not to curl in or try to cover myself. I wanted this. I wanted him. I'd imagined this countless times before. I just hadn't thought he'd be quite so... talky. "Yes."

"How?"

Were we really having this conversation? I was used to Sawyer recognizing and anticipating my needs without my ever having to say a word. This was new, so I struggled with what to say.

He lost a little of that hungry look, his expression shifting into one of concern. "Is this too much? If it's not working for you, or it's making you anxious—"

I swallowed hard. "No. I was just trying to decide whether I wanted your fingers or your mouth first." Oh my God. Did I really just blurt that out?

He blinked. "And what did you decide?"

"I'm greedy. I want both."

Sawyer's grin spread slow and wicked. "There's my good girl. She knows what she wants."

Well, my very vivid imagination had a lot of ideas and even more fantasies. We'd see if I liked them all in actual practice. "She would very much like more action and less talking, please."

He was still chuckling as he settled between my legs. Whatever trepidation I felt at being completely exposed took a backseat to sensation as he began to trail little nibbling kisses from my knee up the inside of my thigh. Closer and closer he inched until the warm puff of his breath caressed my aching center. My body clenched, needing more than this slow tease.

"So pretty and perfect." He pressed a kiss to the curls just above my slit, and my legs began to tremble. "Are you wet for me, Willa?"

This was it. I was going to die of wanting before he ever got down to business. "Why don't you find out?" I challenged.

He huffed another laugh, and our eyes met. "I like you like this."

"Like what?"

"Sassy and spread out for me to feast on."

"There seems to be a distinct lack of feas—oooh, God!"

His tongue dragged through my folds, just barely touching my clit, but it was enough to make me jack-knife on the bed.

"So responsive." The vibration of his growl against my most heated flesh made me whimper. "And all mine."

"Yes," I gasped.

"Let me have all those sweet sounds of pleasure."

Then he truly went to work, and I completely lost my mind.

There was no room for embarrassment, no room for anything but a riot of feeling as he took over every nerve in my body. So many times he drove me up, stopping just short of sending me flying. Then he'd start over again. And again, until I was a trembling mass of need, moaning his name, begging for release. Only then did he slide one finger into the center of the ache he'd created.

It was too much. It wasn't enough.

"Please." I didn't know what to ask for anymore. I'd lost even the barest grasp of words.

Then he slid in a second finger along with the first, pumping slowly in and out, filling me up as his tongue worshiped my clit. I managed to pry my eyes open. I wanted to see what he was doing. Those stormy eyes were fixed on mine, even as his head was buried between my thighs, and at the heat in his gaze, the wave I'd been riding crashed over me, dragging me under a tsunami of pleasure.

CHAPTER 26

SAWYER

Willa spent so much of her life buttoned up, worried about what others thought, that seeing her come apart like this—knowing she trusted me enough to give herself over to the pleasure—made me feel like a god. The fact that she craved me as much as I craved her made it hard to hold back. She'd said she wanted to be claimed, and damn, I wanted to follow through, burying myself in that sweetness between her thighs and losing myself in this fantasy she'd given me. I wanted to possess her in every way a man could possess a woman. Then I wanted to start all over again, lest I wake up and find out it was all a dream.

Shucking my shorts and boxer briefs, I crawled up the bed, kissing and stroking her quivering torso. "Doing okay there, wife?"

She lifted her head just enough to look at me through eyes that were only half-mast. "I'll be better when you're inside me."

Nothing in my life had prepared me for the impact of hearing sweet, shy Willa say such things to me. Rising to my knees, I gave my straining cock a testing stroke, loving how she watched me. "You want this, sweet girl?"

"Every inch."

Fuck. Me. I was the luckiest bastard in the world.

She sat up, shoving me to my back. "Best save your shoulder."

"What shoulder?" But I didn't resist. I'd felt how tight she was. It'd be better if she was in control for this.

She swung one leg over my hips, settling so the tip of my cock just skimmed through her folds. Holy hell, that felt incredible. I'd never been this sensitive, this turned on, in my life.

Realization dawned, and I gripped her thighs. "Wait. We can't do this." At the look of disbelief and hurt on her face, I cursed myself six ways to Sunday. "I don't have any condoms. I wasn't prepared for this."

Willa relaxed. "I was. I started birth control right after our wedding."

There was so much behind that statement. It wasn't just about practicalities. She'd wanted me from the beginning. And because she had, because she'd thought ahead, we could do this. We could be together, exactly like this, with nothing between us.

God, I wanted that. I wanted that more than anything in the world, because I felt like we were already stripping away every barrier that had ever held us apart. But I needed her to be certain. "Are you sure?"

Her mouth curved in a smile as she bent low to kiss me. "I only ever wanted this with you."

There was something in her voice, in her expression, that pinged my internal radar, but she sat back, taking the first bare inch of me inside, and all thought disappeared. She was so tight and hot and perfect. It took every shred of control I had not to just surge up inside her and take her like some mindless beast. Instead, I kneaded her hips as she slowly worked herself lower.

"That's it, sweetheart." I continued to praise her efforts as she rocked, because I'd already figured out that turned her on even more.

When her body relaxed enough that she finally sank down fully, we both sighed. Perfection. This, right here, with her, was perfection. And it was better than any of the countless guilty fantasies I'd entertained over the years. Because it was real. She was here with me. My wife in more than simply name.

I couldn't stop myself from moving then, little thrusts, surging up to meet her. She braced her hands on my chest and rode, her head thrown back, her high, firm breasts bouncing. She was magnificent, and she was mine. We drove each other up and up, giving into the frenzy, until I felt the electric surge of my release working its way down my spine. I fought to hold on long enough for her to come again, because I needed to feel her come apart around me. Reaching between us, I found her clit and rubbed until she detonated. Her body clamped around me, and I roared my release as her orgasm continued to milk mine for what felt like ages.

Eventually, she collapsed over me, still gasping and trembling from aftershocks. I wrapped my arms tight around her, relishing the feel of her sweaty skin pressed against mine. My wife. The woman I loved. The woman who deserved the words I hadn't yet given.

I stroked her back, working up the nerve and the breath to say it, but she spoke first.

"That was so much better than toys."

The words circled around the brain that was just beginning to get enough blood back to fire, and that radar pinged again, stronger this time. Wait. Did she mean...?

I tipped her chin up so she had to look at me. "Willa, was this your first time?"

The lingering pleasure in her eyes faded as the shutters

came down, and I hated the caution in her expression. "Would it bother you if it was?"

Not an outright confirmation, but not a denial either. Her very reluctance was answer enough. I thought of everything I'd nudged her to do, wondering if I'd pushed her too far. I'd assumed she wasn't experienced, but I hadn't expected her to be a virgin. Gently, I cupped her cheeks. "Are you okay?"

"I'm fine." Her shoulders moved in a restless shrug. "And yeah, there was never anyone I trusted enough for this. I always wanted it to be you."

There was so much tangled up in that statement, not the least of which was the implication that her feelings were as long standing as mine. She'd wanted me. She'd chosen me. No one else had ever tasted her. No one else had ever known the feel of her. I couldn't begin to express the sense of primal satisfaction I felt at that. And it just made me want to explore every inch of her all over again.

Willa bit her lip, worry creeping into those pretty eyes. "Is it a problem? I'm sorry I didn't tell you. I was afraid you might stop."

I wasn't sure what I would've done differently had I known, but I didn't think anything but a "No" from her could have made me stop. "No. I just want to make absolutely sure that you're okay. I didn't hurt you, did I?"

"No. I might be a little sore in places I didn't know I could be sore, but that's to be expected."

I stroked the hair back from her face. "I think we should probably adjourn to the bathroom. There's that big ass tub in there with room for two. We can have a bit of a soak. Relax those muscles." And I could worship every other inch of her until she was ready for me again.

She smiled. "That sounds like an excellent plan."

But before we could do more than roll apart, a volley of ferocious barking sounded downstairs.

"What the hell?" Willa muttered.

I found my shorts and dragged them on. "Stay here." Whatever the fuck was happening, I wasn't about to put her in any sort of danger.

Not that Willa listened. She snagged a robe. "He's not going to listen to you."

"Fine, but stay behind me." I grabbed up the first potential weapon I spotted—an iron fire poker beside the bedroom fireplace—and we raced downstairs.

A male voice was speaking to Roy, but clearly not getting anywhere. The dog was snarling and barking loud enough to wake the dead. I wondered if he was blocking the intruder's route of escape.

Tightening my grip on the poker, I swung into the kitchen. "Freeze!"

But it was me who froze as I caught sight of our intruder.

Willa called out, "Roy, hold!" Then she, too, skidded to a halt beside me.

Across the kitchen, Jace stood a few feet from the door, one hand held out to defend against the dog, who'd quieted instantly at his mama's order. My best friend stared at the two of us, then lifted his other hand.

Willa's bra dangled from his fingers.

"You slept with my sister?"

CHAPTER 27
WILLA

In some dim, distant part of my brain, I'd known that my brother would find out about me and Sawyer at some point. But he'd been such a peripheral part of my life for so long, I hadn't truly put that much thought into it. A sad commentary on the state of our relationship, perhaps, but there it was. I certainly hadn't expected him here *now*, when the evidence of what we'd just done was still wet on my thighs. I realized my mistake as I watched Jace zero in on Sawyer, chill fury covering his face.

Sawyer lowered the poker and squared his shoulders. "I'll accept whatever consequence you think is reasonable, but I'm not going to apologize." His chin lifted in a way that practically shouted he was waiting for a punch.

Before testosterone poisoning could prevail, I skirted around him. "Both of you stop it. Nobody's going to hit anybody, because we didn't do anything wrong. I'm a grown-ass adult. My brother has no say in who I choose to take to my bed."

"He's my best friend," Jace gritted out. "There's a code."

I whirled on him. "He's my husband, so that supersedes whatever bullshit bro code thing you have going on."

My brother was a hard man to surprise. Generally, he knew way more about what was happening in any given situation than 98% of everyone else in the room. It was a big part of how he'd done so well doing... whatever the classified stuff was he did for the Navy. But my bald announcement hit him about as effectively as a gut punch.

His jaw dropped open, his eyes going wide. "Your *what?*"

I held up my left hand with Grandma's ring. "You have a lot to catch up on."

"Clearly. How—"

"Nope. I am not having this conversation without pants."

Jace covered his face with both hands and groaned. "Oh God. Please don't put that image in my head."

I snatched my bra from his fingers. "Grow up, Jace. You show up with zero notice, you get what you get. We're going to go get dressed, and we'll be back down in a few minutes. Can I trust you to behave, or do I need to leave Roy on guard duty?"

On a long exhale, he dropped his hands. "I'll behave."

"Stand down, Roy."

My pooch gave me some side-eye at the command, so I paused to scruff his ears. "It's okay, pal."

Roy sat, no longer at full attention, but evidently not willing to trust my word enough to leave Jace to roam freely in the house. Let my brother feel the full power of canine judgment. Served him right.

Sawyer stayed quiet as he followed me back upstairs. I couldn't read the quality of his silence, and it was beginning to unnerve me. Did Jace being here change something for him? Did he regret the lines we'd crossed in that bed? Damn Jace for just showing up.

"Could he have worse timing?" I muttered.

"Oh, I'm pretty sure it would've been a whole lot worse fifteen minutes ago."

For a few moments, I imagined what it would've been like if Jace had caught us in the throes. That was a level of mortification I didn't ever want to experience. "Fair point." I moved into the bathroom. "But seriously, he's completely out of communication for more than a month, and now he just shows up here without so much as a phone call or a text?"

I started to shrug out of my robe and stopped when I caught Sawyer watching me. Being naked with him, being intimate with him, hadn't felt weird. But this? Cleaning up after, while my brother waited downstairs? This felt awkward.

I really wanted a shower, but there wasn't time, so a quick clean-up would have to do. My hands were shaking as I held a washcloth under the faucet, more from agitation than anxiety. Undoubtedly, there'd be confrontation involved in the explanations we were about to give. I hated confrontation. And why wasn't Sawyer *saying* anything? He'd been talky as hell during sex.

Big hands closed over my shoulders. "Wren."

I met his gaze in the mirror, watched as he nudged my hair aside to press a soft kiss to the tattoo on my nape. The gesture was both comforting and arousing. Then he turned me to face him, the ghost of a smile playing around his lips. "It's going to be okay. Obviously, this isn't the ideal way for this to have come out, but he'll understand. We'll make him understand."

I bit my lip. I loved this man. More than anything, I wanted to keep him. But I also understood that his relationship with Jace was essential. Jace was more than his friend. He was family. All the Wayward Sons were. And much as I was ready and willing to defend our marriage, I didn't want to screw that up for him.

His hands skimmed from my shoulders down my arms. "Raincheck on that bath, okay?"

Some knot in my chest loosened. That didn't sound like he planned to walk back on this new physical side of our relationship. I mustered a smile. "Holding you to that, Mr. Malone."

We finished cleaning up and dressing in fresh clothes. Downstairs, Jace sat at the kitchen table, hands laced behind his bowed head. He looked up as we came into the room.

"How the fuck is it that I sent you as my backup, and you ended up married?"

"What do you mean, you sent him?" I frowned and looked at Sawyer.

"I was the one who was stateside when Jace got the news about your grandfather. I was the one who *could* come, though I would have even if he hadn't asked me to check on you. I didn't set out to keep it from you, it just never came up."

Filing that under the heading of *Things To Talk About Later*, I turned to my brother. "Okay, not that I'm not happy that you're safe and in one piece, but what the hell are you doing here? You can't bother to send an email or a text or even a carrier pigeon for like six weeks, and now you just show up without even knocking?"

"First off, I did text. You didn't answer. I went by the cottage. Bree is the one who told me you'd moved up here."

I retrieved my phone from my purse, where I'd left it on the counter. There were, indeed, multiple unread text messages.

"And I did knock, but it's a big house, and the door was unlocked, and I didn't know..." He waved a hand to encompass what we'd obviously been doing.

Okay, so he had tried. That took a little of the wind out of my sails.

"I'm sorry I didn't give more notice." He winced. "Really sorry. But I didn't have a lot of notice myself. I've been traveling for nearly forty-eight hours to get here."

Now that he mentioned it, I could see fatigue etched in the lines of his face. Dark scruff covered his jaw, and there were lines around his blue eyes that hadn't been there the last time I'd seen him. My temper deflated.

"Have you eaten?"

He blinked. "At some point. A while ago." As if to punctuate the point, his stomach gave a massive growl.

"Sit. I'll make dinner. There's a lot we need to tell you." I'd do better keeping my hands busy while I talked.

As I pulled out ingredients and began to chop, measure, and mix, Sawyer got out beers for us all. I spilled out the whole story, telling Jace everything about the inheritance, all the crap Mom and Dad had tried to pull, and all the reasons Sawyer and I had ended up married in a hurry. Mostly Sawyer let me take the lead, only adding in a few details here and there. By the time we'd brought Jace up to date on the latest threat, I was sliding plates of steaming food onto the table.

His response to the whole thing was a lengthy string of creative profanity. "I'm sorry. I'm so fucking sorry for not being there when you needed me. If I'd known—well, I don't think I could've gotten free of this mission regardless, but I had absolutely no idea that they'd resort to such tactics. I thought they'd left all that behind once you were a grown adult."

I lifted a shoulder in a half-shrug that looked a lot more blasé than I felt. "None of us expected Granddaddy and Grandma to leave me basically everything. Sorry about that. It wasn't exactly fair to you."

"It was absolutely fair. My life isn't here. Yours is. You were the one who lived up to the Sutter name. I don't begrudge you any of it, Wills."

I hadn't fully realized the worry I'd carried about exactly that until he absolved me of it. My brother was a better man than I gave him credit for.

"Anyway, I understand the marriage of convenience. It's kind of nuts, but it makes sense. But that's not what this is." He wagged a finger between the two of us. "I mean, I knew she had a crush on you as a kid, but I didn't expect this."

"I've loved her most of my life."

Sawyer had said little during all the explanations, letting me take the lead on how much and what to tell Jace. But at his quiet declaration, my head snapped toward him.

The corner of his mouth tipped up into a half-smile. "You didn't think you were the only one, did you, Wren? Malones fall once, and they fall hard."

He loved me. Not just now, but for years. The same as I had him. Emotion lodged in my chest like a glowing coal, warming me from the inside out.

"But... why didn't you say anything back then?" I sputtered.

"Because you were too young back then. And Jace would've been absolutely right to kick my ass."

I rolled my eyes. "Boys." But I leaned into his touch anyway, relaxing as his lips brushed my temple.

Jace huffed. "This is..."

Scowling, I stabbed at a roasted potato. "If you dare pull some kind of he's-not-good-enough-for-me, big-brother bullshit—"

"Sawyer is one of my best friends. Why the hell would I think he wasn't good enough for you?"

I closed my mouth with a click.

My husband leaned over to rub at my nape, his finger tracing my tattoo, and I loved that reminder of what was effectively our little secret.

"What I was going to say was that if you two are happy together, I'm certainly not going to stand in your way. And, not gonna lie, I'm grateful you've got someone watching out for you. Above and beyond all the reasons you ended up here, you both deserve all the happiness in the world. Don't let Mom and Dad fuck it up."

"Thank you for that. We don't intend to. How long are you here?"

"It's a fast trip. I've only got a couple of days before I have to get back."

"Well then, we'll just have to throw a party before you leave."

CHAPTER 28

SAWYER

J ace dropped into a wingback chair beside the fireplace in the den after we'd finished eating and clearing up the dinner dishes. "There's one thing I don't understand."

Willa snorted as she snuggled up against me on the leather sofa, Roy curling up in the crook of her legs. "Only one? You're doing pretty well, then."

"If Granddaddy and Grandma had left everything to me instead of you, would Dad be pulling this same shit?"

It was a question I hadn't considered, but Willa's answer was instant. "Of course not. They have no grounds for a competency claim against you. You're a decorated naval officer without a history of documented mental illness. They wouldn't have the same... vulnerabilities to exploit with you."

I couldn't stop myself from tightening my arm around her. Jace watched us, his face unreadable. He'd effectively given us his blessing, but what else would he say in front of his sister? Anything less would damage their already shaky relationship, and I knew he didn't want that. He'd said all the right things, but I still wondered if he was really okay with us as an us.

"So let's extrapolate," he continued. "What's the motive? Is this purely a money grab, or is it somehow about you?"

"I think it's both. Your parents were furious when she came back to the island. Her cutting them off and living her own life on her own terms was a big slap in the face. Coming after her like this is a way to slap back, on top of getting their hands on an inheritance they believe is rightfully theirs. Otherwise, they haven't considered her worth the effort." Realizing how that sounded, I winced. "Sorry, Wren."

"You're not wrong. They've more or less left me alone until now. I'm sure that would've stayed true had Granddaddy not forced their hand. But at the end of the day, slapping back at me is secondary to them wanting the land. Well, and no doubt as a reaction to that utterly inflammatory letter he had the lawyer read before the will. The question is, why?"

"None of us are delusional enough to think this is simply about him trying to protect what he perceives as Mom's rightful inheritance. She doesn't love Hatterwick. She hasn't had anything to do with the island for years, which is the very reason the property wasn't left to her. It's no secret Dad always believed that the rest of the island should be developed. As a venture capitalist, that's his bread and butter." Jace drummed his fingers on the arm of the chair, considering. "Will, you might be a little too young to remember, but when we were little, Dad was pushing some kind of resort development on the island, and he needed Granddaddy's backing to get support from key stakeholders here. He didn't get it, so everything fell through. They had a rip-roaring fight about the whole thing."

I frowned, thinking back. "I dimly remember you talking about this. You'd have been, what? Nine or ten?"

"Sounds about right."

Willa's gaze turned speculative as she stroked Roy's ears. "You think Dad wants to push through some updated version of that?"

"I wouldn't put it past him. A tiger doesn't change his stripes."

"Then to continue the argument, if the estate had been left to you, he'd have considered you worth negotiating with. Both because you're a man and because he sees you as more of an equal. As a woman, I'm not worth his time. I was supposed to be a pretty social climber, like he turned mom into. Except I couldn't even get that right because of my social anxiety. I've been a lifelong disappointment."

It physically hurt me to hear how easily she said it. My dad hadn't been perfect, but I'd known he loved me. How could her parents not understand what a gift she was?

Jace winced. "That's harsh, Wills."

"But true. You know it is. Neither of them ever had any interest in getting to know who I actually am. They were only upset I wasn't who they wanted me to be. And while Dad has never actually known me, he understands me well enough to know that I wouldn't agree to anything he wants to do with this land. I will always choose preservation over development."

"You're like Granddaddy in that. Yet another reason you were the right person to leave it to."

Her lips curved. "Thanks, Jace. I appreciate that. I haven't really made any major decisions yet. No sense in lining people up to do anything until I know for sure it's not going to be yanked away from me."

"Seems like they're running out of options to try."

"God willing," I muttered. I needed this attack on her to be over, not only because I hated seeing her hurt, but because I wanted the time and space for us to figure out what a real marriage between us could look like.

"Amen." Willa squeezed my thigh. "On that note, I'm exhausted. I think I'm headed up to bed."

As she rose, I searched her face. She'd had a lot to process today. Would she be more prone to nightmares from the stress?

She skimmed her fingers through my hair and pressed a kiss to my brow. "I'm fine. Go ahead and visit."

I curled my hand around her wrist and turned to press a kiss to the fluttering pulse there. "I won't be too long."

"C'mon, Roy."

The dog's nails clicked on the hardwood as he followed her out of the room. Then I was alone to face the real confrontation we'd been putting off with polite conversation and conjecture.

Jace rose and crossed to the cabinet that served as a bar. He lifted the decanter of golden liquid in question. I didn't know if it was whiskey, Scotch, or bourbon and didn't much care. After what I'd come from, I seldom indulged in more than a beer. But this conversation felt like it could take a little liquid courage.

"Sure."

He brought me one of the lowball glasses. "How is she really doing?"

I accepted the glass and took a small sip. The smooth warmth of top-shelf alcohol slid down my throat. "Honestly, better than I expected, given how much shit this is bringing up for her. She survived facing down your folks twice in person, and while I think she has a healthy fear of what's underneath all the legal machinations, I think they've pissed her off more than anything else. She's more resilient than I think she's been given credit for."

"I have zero doubt that you're part of the reason for that." Instead of resuming his seat in the wingback chair, he dropped down to the hearth, balancing his forearms on his knees. "I need you to know that I'm grateful you're standing by her. That you're being there for her in a way that I never have been and never could be."

None of this was what I'd been expecting. Frowning, I swirled the liquid in my glass. "So, you're really okay with this? With us?"

"More than, brother. I trust you with her. More importantly, she trusts you, and she trusts almost nobody. With good reason."

The tension that had been lodged in my gut since I'd burst into the kitchen to find him hours before finally loosened. Here was the true blessing I'd needed. If Jace believed I was good enough for Willa, and she herself thought so, who was I to argue?

"How much has she told you about her time off-island?"

That prompted me to tip my own glass back for a deeper swallow. "Enough. I've spent a considerable amount of time in the past few weeks imagining creative ways to kill your parents. Your dad, in particular."

"Get in line." He shook his head, grief and guilt carving lines around his mouth and eyes. "I should've gotten to her sooner. I should have asked questions and pushed when I didn't hear from her. Mom and Dad told me she was at boarding school, and I just thought she was pissed that I'd left for college and essentially abandoned her. I never in a million years dreamed that they'd do what they did. If she hadn't gotten that letter out, I don't know what might have happened."

Remembering the exhaustion in Willa's voice as she'd told me her harrowing tale, I could well imagine the worst. We could all be grateful she'd managed to get that letter out.

"Don't beat yourself up, man. Nobody imagines their parents would do something like that. Nobody would imagine they'd do exactly what they're trying to do to her now."

"After what they pulled on her before, I shouldn't be surprised, but I am. That's on me for letting my guard down and assuming everything was fine while I'm off serving Uncle Sam. But it does seem like O'Shea's got a handle on everything. That he's managed to shut everything down."

"So far. I'm less worried about that than I am about the body we found." We'd given Jace the overview at dinner, but otherwise steered clear of the topic.

"Is Willa having a hard time with it?"

"Had a total breakdown when we found it, which seemed perfectly reasonable considering she basically landed on the thing. But the body was found less than fifty yards from where I pulled her out of the water."

Jace paused, his glass dangling from his fingers. "You think this might have something to do with how she got there?"

I glanced up toward the ceiling, as if that would tell me Willa was safely ensconced in our room. The sound of clanking pipes told me she was in the bathroom. Maybe getting that bath, finally. Assured she wasn't lurking outside the room, eavesdropping, I admitted what had been circling around my brain. "I don't know. Maybe. I attributed the panic attack to finding the body, but what if it had something to do with where we were? Did you know she's never been back to Osprey Beach or that side of the island in all the years she's been back here?"

"No. Really?"

"I started to drive home that way one day, and it almost set her off. In some ways, she's so incredibly strong. In others, she's fragile. And I don't know how much of it is leftover trauma from what she went through, and how much is added trauma from her time off-island. That hospital fucked with her head, man. In ways I don't think we fully understand."

His expression hardened. "They said it was for her own good. That the facility specialized in retrieving lost memories. Best I can tell, they just traumatized her further." He dropped his head. "I didn't do right by her. I should've protected her."

"We can both beat ourselves up for the things we should've done. But none of that helps now. All we can do is protect her. And I will, man. I'll do anything I have to in order to keep her safe."

"I appreciate that more than I can say."

I drained the last of my glass. "We can debate theories some other time. I'm headed up to bed, too." I paused as I shoved to my feet. "I have no idea where you're sleeping. We didn't have a room made up for you, since we didn't know you were coming."

"It's fine. I know where the linens are, and I'll take the room I've always had when I was here. Which is far, far down the hall from yours. On the opposite side. Just so you know."

At his meaningful look, I laughed. "Good to know."

Still chuckling, I climbed the stairs to go join my wife.

CHAPTER 29

WILLA

I checked over the contents of the cooler for the third time. Sawyer's arms slid around my waist from behind, and he settled his chin on my shoulder. "I promise, we've got everything."

"I just want to make sure we didn't forget anything." More, I needed something to *do* while we waited for our friends to arrive. This was our first official party as a married couple—a *really* married couple—and I was excited. This was something normal. I was desperate for some normal.

Sawyer turned me in his arms, his fingers sliding beneath the fall of my hair to rub tiny circles on my nape. "Are you up to this party tonight?"

In truth, my skin felt stretched too tight over my body, and a jittery energy pulsed inside me as I waited for the other shoe to drop. All the legal attacks had amplified my normal anxiety until I was looking for threats from every corner. I'd been even more on edge since we'd found the body—which I figured was a perfectly reasonable anxiety as opposed to my often unreasonable personal anxiety. But I didn't want anyone to know how rattled I was. I didn't want to *be* rattled. I wanted to enjoy the opportunity to truly be newlyweds and figure out what that would look like for our future. Right now, that meant a cookout with the friends who were more family to us than our own blood.

"I'm okay. Promise. I just want this party to go well. It's Jace's last night in town, so tonight is for celebrating."

"That eager to get rid of me, baby sis?"

I shot my brother an impish grin as he wandered into the kitchen. "I mean, you're putting a serious crimp in my love life."

He squeezed his eyes shut and dropped the bag of chips he'd been about to open. "Oh, oh, no. Don't put that image in my head."

"But your overreactions are so much fun."

"Who knew you'd choose *now* to turn into an annoying little sister?"

The sibling banter wasn't normal for us. Never had been. But it felt good to poke at him, especially as I knew he actually was happy for us. Something he'd gone out of his way to tell each of us independently this weekend. With everything else that had been going on, I hadn't been consciously worried about Jace and his opinion, but I couldn't deny that having his support meant a lot.

We were still sniping at each other when the short caravan of vehicles pulled into the circular drive. Gabi led the procession, a colorful fabric tote bag over one shoulder. "I come with s'mores fixin's!"

"Including peanut butter cups?"

"Well, obviously. They make for a superior s'more."

A tall, rangy figure slid out of the passenger seat. "Also Nutella,"

"Nutella?" I considered the addition and the man himself. Gabi had said Daniel was her former situationship. Maybe that was back on if she'd brought him.

"Trust me, it's fabulous." She gave me a tight hug, then scanned my face. "You look better."

"Rest helped." Or maybe that was just the effects of the recent orgasms. I certainly wasn't complaining. "Petty Officer LaRue."

He grinned. "I'm off duty. It's just Daniel. Thanks for havin' me."

Sawyer offered a hand. "Good to see you again, under better circumstances."

"Jace Hollingsworth, get over here and give me a hug!" This order came from Caroline, who carried some kind of casserole dish she passed off to Hoyt before squeezing my brother to within an inch of his life.

"Good to see you, too, Caro."

"How long are you here for?" she demanded.

"I've got to go back tomorrow."

She screwed up her face. "Well, then I guess we'd best make tonight count. I brought the fixings for elotes."

"Hell, yeah." He turned to Hoyt for a back-thumping half-hug that managed not to upend the casserole dish.

As Jace and Daniel were introduced, the sound of more than one more car door opening pulled my attention back to where Bree had brought up the rear. I gasped as a furry bundle leapt out of the backseat, wriggling with joy.

"You got a dog!" Stifling my own squee, I held out a hand, signaling for Roy to hold, though his butt was wagging ninety to nothing as he eyed the new arrival.

It wasn't the Aussie Shepherd mix I'd suggested to her. I didn't recognize this one, which was another sign of how cloistered I'd been the past month. In the normal course of things, I was down helping out at the shelter every week or two, working on obedience training or otherwise exercising the dogs.

"I blame this entirely on you. The house was too quiet with you gone. This little girl is a little over a year old, already house trained, and with some basic leash manners." Belying her new mom's words, the dog strained against the lead, making a beeline toward me, her own thick tail swishing.

Roy whined.

"I know. Wait to be introduced. Sit."

My boy plopped his butt down, but his tail didn't slow.

The dog, who appeared to be some combination of shepherd and lab, was on the small side, maybe forty-five or fifty pounds, with fur a mottle of browns and golds and black tips on her floppy ears.

"Keeley, sit," Bree ordered.

The dog didn't sit, still straining forward, fairly vibrating with curiosity. I dropped down to her level and offered my hand for a sniff. She licked my knuckles and wagged harder. I scruffed her ears and rose a little, gently pressing back until her butt hit the ground.

"Good girl. Good sit. Keeley, huh?" I noted the blingy rhinestone collar.

"Also your fault," Bree declared. "You're the one who made me watch *Ted Lasso* like twenty times through."

"Because it's basically the world's most perfect show."

"We should totally have a watch party," Gabi announced.

"I'm in." I was always in for *Ted Lasso*. "Roy, come."

My dog trotted over, vibrating with joy as he and Keeley sniffed each other from head to tail. Both of them wagged madly before dropping low in play bows.

"Awww, I think it's love," Gabi crooned. "Please tell me he has his own AFC Richmond jersey. Because that's a photo op that shouldn't be missed."

"Well, now you've given me goals. That would be adorable."

"Are we gonna plan a canine fashion show, or are we gonna get started on food?" Hoyt asked. "Because I'm starving."

"Far be it for us to allow you to wither away," I teased.

He patted his flat stomach. "This firefighter requires a lot of fuel, man."

"Let's get everything loaded up to carry down to the beach? The boys have already hauled the picnic table and extra camp chairs down, and the wood's been laid for a bonfire. We can let the dogs go play."

It took a couple of trips up and down the steps that led to the beach before we finally got everything, but eventually the fire was lit, seats were claimed, and we were all digging into the cowboy caviar and guacamole.

Jace kicked back, a beer in hand. "Well, nothing about where I've been and what I've been doing can be talked about, because it's all classified, so everybody update me on y'all. Gabi, I understand you're back on-island. Congratulations, Dr. Carrera."

"Thank you! I loved New Orleans, but it's good to be home."

Caroline draped an arm around her sister's shoulders. "Now that she's getting settled, I had planned to hook her up with a nice island boy so she stays put." Her gaze slid to Daniel in a mix of challenge and speculation. "Are you planning on becoming an island boy, Daniel?"

Gabi rolled her eyes. "Caro."

If Daniel was bothered by the question, he didn't show it. "Well, here's the thing, cher. Your sister and me dated near the whole time she was in residency. Right 'round when she was finishing up, I got offered a promotion with a transfer clear across the country. I let ambition cloud my thinkin', and I chose wrong. Which I figured out 'bout two minutes after I got to Seattle. Took me a few months to rectify the situation and finagle a postin' at Nag's Head to try and win her back again."

"And how's that working out for you?" Bree drawled.

Daniel grinned. "Favorably, so far. She ain't kicked me to the curb, which was more than I expected when I got here."

Gabi leveled a long, heated look in his direction. "Yeah,

well, being locked down together for the hurricane gave us a chance to clear some things up."

"Is that what they're calling it these days?" Bree asked.

Gabi promptly hurled a chip at her head, which Keeley snatched right out of the air.

Hoyt scooped more guac onto a paper plate and studied the other man. "You make her happy, we won't have a problem. You hurt her, she's got me and four other brothers who will make sure nobody finds your body."

We all froze.

Hoyt winced. "Sorry about that. Epically inappropriate, under the circumstances."

Daniel lifted his beer. "Message received, either way."

Forcing a bright smile, I said, "How about we make a rule that there will be no other discussion of unpleasantness tonight?"

Echoes of agreement went around the group, and I settled a little.

"We have a long overdue girls' night we need to plan." Guilt slithered through me as I realized how much time had passed since we'd run into each other at the bakery. "I'm sorry I haven't reached out about that like I promised. I've kind of had a lot going on."

"Girl, it's no problem." Gabi leaned over to replenish her collection of chips. "I hit the ground running at the clinic, so it's not like I've had a ton of extra time, either. Let's get something on the calendar."

I was aware of Gabi watching me as she, Bree, and I tossed around dates. No doubt she hadn't forgotten my behavior the other day. The memory of it made me ill at ease. Gabi wouldn't push for answers yet. Not in front of all these people. But I could tell she was worried about me. I appreciated it. I just wished it didn't mean I had to open up about the most painful part of my past.

After we'd settled on some plans for the next week, Caroline began prepping the corn for roasting over the fire. "How's everything going with the inheritance, Willa? What are your plans for the property, once everything is out of probate? There's been lots of talk in town, lots of questions, but nobody seems to know."

I hadn't talked about this with anybody but Sawyer. Relaxing back into the curve of his arm, I admitted, "Honestly, I'd like to turn it into a wildlife sanctuary."

"Really?" Caroline looked intrigued. "I mean, not that it's a bad idea, but why?"

I took a breath. "Well, the horses saved me, so it seems only fair I do what I can to protect them."

"Saved you how?" Hoyt asked.

I'd never told anyone this story.

"When I was little—maybe six or so?—Jace and his friends had gone tromping into the woods on some adventure or other. I got mad they left me behind, so I followed. I guess technically I got lost, but I wasn't worried about that since the island just isn't that big. But it was high summer and in the course of all my tromping, I stumbled on a few of the horses grazing. It was the closest I'd ever been to them, and I was fascinated. I wanted to get closer, to try to pet them, even though I'd been warned they were wild animals. I was so focused on the horses that I didn't look where I was stepping, and I startled a copperhead. I was only inches away from stepping right on it. But before it could strike, Triton—he's the stallion that's been leading the herd for years now—came barreling out of the trees and trampled it. Without trampling me."

Jace had gone a little pale. "Holy shit. You never told me that."

I jerked my shoulders. "I didn't want to get into trouble. After the snake, he sort of herded me back toward where y'all had gotten off to, and that was the end of it."

He scrubbed a hand down his face. "If anything had happened to you, Mom and Dad would've murdered me."

"It was fine. I was more careful after that."

"After that?" My brother's voice rose half an octave.

"I made friends with them."

"She's a freaking horse whisperer." Sawyer looked over at me, awe in his eyes. "One of the most incredible things I've ever seen."

"I see them on their terms. Which is mostly from a distance. But we understand each other. Because of that, it's always been important to me to make sure the horses are protected. And beyond all of that, it's a unique ecological system that's worth preserving."

"Oh, that makes a lot of sense," Caroline beamed. "Totally fits you."

"How would that work?" Gabi asked.

"Well, it's an incredibly long-term project. Like... years long. The property has to be surveyed and assessed to document existing habitats, species, resources, geographical features and such, to establish a baseline." Warming to my subject, I continued. "Then a habitat management plan has to be developed, any habitat enhancements done, boundaries delineated... and that's all on top of writing up management policies, establishing oversight of the sanctuary, and getting actual legal designation as a sanctuary." I ticked each point off on my fingers. "Plus fundraising. So much fundraising. Just thinking of the peopling involved in that part makes me tired."

Bree popped open a fresh beer. "There's going to be some folks who are hacked off about that. Plenty of people want to see this property developed."

I shrugged. "I'm no stranger to people being upset with me." That had been all my youth with my parents. The idea of dealing with a grumpy public was easier to handle with Sawyer by my side. Even now, he was reaching up, lightly rubbing at my shoulders. "I'll just have to contribute to the island in other ways, like I have been all along. Which, unfortunately, includes Founder's Day."

Jace dipped up more guac. "How'd you get roped into that?"

I flung out my arms wide and made a mocking bow. "I am the last Sutter on-island. Thus is my honor. Our esteemed mayor made a lot of noise about my role as a descendant of one of the original founding families and the importance of participation. Miles has always been about looks. You know that."

"Do you actually want to do it?"

"I mean, no. All of it sounds like the third circle of my own personal hell. But he's not wrong. And maybe this will help mitigate the news that I have no intention of developing the property."

It was a moot point to get into any of it until the lawsuit was settled. But the rest of them didn't need to know about that.

Determined to change the subject, I reached for the roasting sticks. "Who's ready for hot dogs?"

CHAPTER 30

SAWYER

"I hate to leave good company, but this baby means I turn into a pumpkin when the sun sets." Caroline rubbed at the belly bump that I'd swear was bigger than when we'd seen her on moving day when we'd dropped some furniture off at Beachcomber Bargains for consignment.

Did pregnancy work that way? I had no idea. I hadn't been around but for the occasional short visit while she'd incubated Aubrey and Logan, and I'd only been six during my mother's last pregnancy. After what had happened to her, I steered clear of pregnant women. But I wondered about it now. What would it be like to be there, day to day, to see all those changes? Was that something I wanted? Did Willa? We certainly hadn't discussed it. But if we were serious about making a real go of this marriage, it was bound to come up, eventually. Was I willing to take that risk with her life?

"When are you due?" Jace's question jerked me back from the precipice of a mental rabbit hole I wasn't prepared to explore.

"November 23rd," Hoyt announced. "Just in time to make room for turkey and all the trimmings for Thanksgiving."

"You better believe your mama's making me an entire pan of her sweet potato casserole that's *all mine* since this baby is entirely her fault." When I lifted a brow, she explained, "She was the one who gifted us the tequila."

Against a patter of laughter, we helped gather up their empty dishes and food containers.

Caroline hugged me, then Jace. "Stay safe and come home again soon."

"I'll do my best."

Then they made their way up the stairs to the house.

"And then there were six," Bree intoned. "Anybody want another beer?"

More than a little unsettled by the direction of my thoughts, I lifted a hand. "I'm for that. This latest test batch is excellent."

"Pretty sure I'm putting it on the menu. Gotta think of a good name first, though."

Willa dug around in one of the totes. "I'm going to go romp with the pups to let them run off some energy before we lose the last of the light, and then I'm straight up making another s'more. I'll concede Nutella isn't bad, but I'm still a Reese's girl." She came up with a yellow tennis ball. At the sight of it, Roy leapt up, turning circles in ecstasy. His obvious joy brought a light to her eyes.

"Let me know when you're nearly done. I'll have a marsh-mallow toasted and waiting for you."

"That's a deal." She grinned and swooped in for a fast kiss. "This marriage thing has great perks."

As her brother was right there, I resisted the urge to make reference to any other perks, but I definitely thought about them. From the heat that leapt into her gaze, so did she.

"C'mon pups!"

"Guess we'll see how well you behave." Bree unclipped Keeley's leash, and the smaller dog raced after her new best buddies toward the water.

Willa hurled the ball, laughing as both dogs streaked down the beach. The sound carried to me on the breeze, reminding me so much of that long-ago night, I felt a prickle of déjà vu. This was a much smaller group, and the air didn't carry that electric feeling that presaged a storm. But all of us had been at that bonfire. Was anybody else remembering?

Jace nudged my shoulder. "Hey. You okay? You look like you're thinking deep thoughts."

"I was thinking about the bonfire."

I didn't have to specify which one.

Gabi extended a marshmallow toward the flames of the small one we'd been cooking over. "I guess we haven't all been together like this since that night. Not all of us. Willa didn't come to any that summer before y'all left for the Navy."

I wondered if she'd been to any at all since she'd returned to the island. Or had that been something else she'd avoided? I'd always believed she'd come back to Hatterwick to reclaim the life her parents had ripped away, but I was coming to understand that, in her own way, she was still running from the trauma of that night.

She'd raked me over the coals for the guilt I'd carried all these years, but it was hard not to wonder how things might have been different if I hadn't helped her sneak out for that party. I wanted to believe she wouldn't have drowned, but she'd said she would have found another way. If she had, I wouldn't have even been there, because I'd only come for her. If she'd snuck out on her own, we might have lost her entirely, along with Gwen. We probably wouldn't be here now, and she almost certainly wouldn't be my wife.

My gaze tracked back to where she danced in the waves, the dogs at her heels. "Why did she leave the beach?" I hadn't intended to bring it up, but the question just spilled out.

Everyone's attention zeroed in on me.

"What do you mean?" Jace asked.

"Willa is a rule follower. I gave her ground rules that night, one of which was not to leave without one of us. She wouldn't have done it without a good reason."

Daniel kicked back, crossing his legs at the ankles. "Really? I mean, she would've been... what? Sixteen? Hardly a child. And it's not like this island is big. I expect she could've walked on home if she'd had a mind to."

"Could have, yeah, but wouldn't have," Jace said. "Not by herself. She was... sheltered back then."

"Ain't that all the more reason she might've gone off on her own?" Daniel asked. "A li'l adventure?"

Gabi carefully rotated her marshmallow. "Willa was never the instigator. Unless it was something to do with an animal. Hell, she spent most of the party playing with somebody's dog, like she's doing now."

We all looked out to where she was wrestling with Keeley, her smile so wide we could see it from here.

"So maybe she didn't go off on her own. Maybe she went off with your other friend. The one who went missing."

Gabi shook her head. "My brother was the last person to see Gwen alive. He didn't see Willa with her."

"Is he sure he saw Gwen? Or did he catch sight of a teenage gal with the same coloring and figure, dressed like every other girl at that party probably was, and jumped to conclusions? Musta been dark by then, yeah? Easy to be mistook. Maybe he saw what he 'spected to see. Wouldn't be the first to make that kinda mistake."

I wanted to dismiss the possibility. Rios had been so sure he'd seen her. He'd gone to Carson himself to report it, hoping they'd be able to find something that would help them find her. Instead, Carson had made him a scapegoat, and it had been enough that a huge chunk of the island bought into it, despite the total lack of evidence.

Bree circled a finger around the mouth of her longneck

bottle. "Okay, I'm willing to play. Let's follow that thought through. If Rios was wrong, and Gwen left the party earlier with Willa..."

"You're suggesting that something happened to both of them?" Jace's tone was flat.

Daniel lifted his palms. "Me, I'm just playin' devil's advocate. I'm the outsider who hasn't been influenced by the stories everybody tells about what happened that night."

My fingers tapped restlessly against my own bottle. "The remains were found less than fifty yards from where I pulled her out of the water that night."

Gabi's marshmallow dipped into the flames as her attention swung to me. "You think the two are connected?"

"I don't know. The police haven't said how long they'd been there. They may not even know yet. But this island isn't that big. If speculation places Willa and Gwen out there together... And somehow Willa ends up in the water, Gwen disappears entirely, and some guy ends up with a bullet between the eyes, all in the same relative geographic area?"

Jace's brows drew together. "She had a head wound."

This was the first I'd heard of this. "What?"

"When we got her to the hospital, they just attributed it to her being bashed against the ocean floor or against a piece of driftwood while she was caught in the riptide. But what if it wasn't that? What if someone struck her?"

My blood ran cold. I'd imagined countless scenarios, trying to make sense of how Willa had ended up in the water in the middle of that storm. But I'd never imagined this. "You think someone could've attacked them both?"

"I don't know. This is all pure conjecture. But the tides were huge that night. You seeing Willa at all was a goddamned miracle. If somebody threw both of them into the water, that might explain why Gwen's never been found."

The idea of it made me physically ill. That maybe I'd missed seeing her, and she'd died because of it.

Gabi abandoned the charcoaled marshmallow. "If that's the case... then who's the dead guy?"

Daniel slid an arm around her shoulders. "Might could be related. Might not. Don't matter which. Either way, there'da been somebody else there that night. It's not likely either of the girls or the dead guy pulled the trigger."

And if somebody else had been there, chances were, they were still walking around free, with no one the wiser.

I didn't like the line of thought. I didn't like it at all.

Realizing I no longer heard Willa laughing, I searched her out again. She stood shin-deep in the water, stock still, the ball clutched between three fingers. Even from here, I could see the odd, vacant expression on her face. As I watched, the color drained out of her cheeks.

"Something's wrong." I was out of my seat, running toward her before the ball in her hand dropped straight into the water.

She swayed, and I just made it to her before she toppled forward, sinking to her knees.

"Willa, what's wrong?" I gripped her arms, holding her up.

Jace was right there. "Wills? Willa?"

Her eyes didn't focus on either of us, instead seeming to stare at something over our shoulders. I glanced back and saw nothing on that stretch of beach. Her face twisted in absolute terror, and somehow I understood that she wasn't actually here. That scared the shit out of me. I'd seen that kind of expression on the faces of men I'd met at Walter Reed, who'd been in the midst of PTSD flashbacks.

"Wren, baby, can you hear me? Wren?"

At the sound of my voice, her fingers dug into my forearms, gripping tight. "Don't let go. Don't let go. Don't let go."

I held on tighter. "Never. I'm here. I'm right here."

Her breath went short and ragged, and she started to tremble. Roy barked, leaning against us both in the water. Keeley got in on the action from the other side. Nothing seemed to stem the rising tide of panic that had her in its grip.

"Get her out of the water," Gabi ordered.

I scooped her up, and she cried out, her face twisting in pain. Shit, had something stung her? Whimpering, she curled into me as I hurried back to the beach.

"Willa, what's going on?" Gabi reached for one of her wrists, but Willa only clung tighter to me, so Gabi slid two fingers against her throat. "Jesus, her pulse is racing."

Tremors wracked her body.

Gabi whipped the phone from her pocket and turned on the flashlight. "This is going to suck for a second, but I need to check your eyes, hon." She pried each of Willa's eyes open. "Massively dilated."

Willa turned her head away, whimpering.

"Get her back to the house. I can look her over better there."

Back inside, I tried to settle her on the sofa in the den, but she wouldn't let me go, so I just sat down myself. While Jace paced, Gabi checked her over more thoroughly, finding no signs of a jellyfish sting or any other external trigger for what was happening. The shaking had stopped, but I didn't think it was over. Willa lay limp in my arms, but for the death grip she had on my shirt.

Gabi stroked the hair back from her face. "Willa, honey, does your head hurt?"

Not even a flicker of a response. Willa just continued to stare off into space, her gaze unfocused.

I'd seen her have a panic attack before, but it had been nothing like this. Whatever this was scared the shit out of me. I tightened my hold on her. "Wren, you're scaring me, baby."

With a little whimper, she turned her head into my shoulder, toward the sound of my voice.

"She'll respond to you. Keep talking," Gabi ordered.

"Do you have a headache, sweetheart?"

I felt the barest of nods against my chest.

"Do you want your migraine meds?"

Another nod.

"I'll get it. Where are they?" Jace asked.

"Drawer to the left of the fridge."

He was back in less than a minute. Gabi took the box from him and pressed the injection pen to Willa's leg. She didn't even flinch.

I kept up a running litany of reassurances, since the sound of my voice seemed to help, and we waited. Within ten minutes, her eyes drifted shut and the last of the tension drained from her body. She was sleeping.

With a shuddering breath, Gabi dropped onto the edge of the coffee table. "She should rest now."

Daniel straightened from where he'd apparently been leaning against the wall. I hadn't even realized he was in the room. "Bree, you wanna lend me a hand gettin' the food together and makin' sure that fire's good and out?"

Obviously anxious herself, Bree stood. "Yeah. I can do that."

Gabi waited until we all heard the kitchen door shut behind them. "Okay, what the actual fuck was that?"

Jace and I exchanged a look. This wasn't ours to tell.

Gabi scowled. "Stonewall me all you want, but I'm not leaving until I get answers. If that means I need to sit here until she sleeps this off to get it direct from the horse's mouth, I will. But something is wrong with my friend, and I'm going to help."

I didn't want to betray Willa's trust. She was so very private about what had happened to her off-island. But maybe it was time we opened the circle of trust a little and let in some friends who could help.

"It has to be her choice. But we've got plenty of space. You might as well stay the night."

CHAPTER 31
WILLA

I woke to the distant sound of surf. For long moments I lay where I was, listening to the rhythmic ebb and flow. My limbs felt heavy, as if I were waking from a long sickness. It took way too much effort to pry open my eyes. Sunlight streamed in through the bedroom window, and the curtains billowed in the breeze. Something shifted around my legs—Roy, lifting his head. At least some of that sense of heaviness was him, curled up in the crook of my knees. With his heavy bulk lifted, the blood began to flow back into my legs.

When he realized I was awake, he scrambled over and began to lick my face.

With the rasp of a laugh, I half-heartedly fended him off. "Hey, bud. Hey, pal. Good morning." My voice sounded like sandpaper.

Something creaked behind me, and I rolled over, expecting to see Sawyer. But it was Gabi rising from a chair by the bed. What was she doing here?

She poured water from a pitcher on the nightstand and extended a glass. "Here. Sip slowly."

I shoved myself up enough to take it, grateful when the cool liquid slid down my parched throat. Roy glued himself to my side, his tail thumping so hard it shook the bed.

As I drank, Gabi searched my face. "Are you back with us?"

My thoughts seemed to struggle through a layer of cotton. "What happened?"

She dragged the chair closer and sat back down. "What's the last thing you remember?"

I tried to think. "I... was playing with the dogs."

Gabi's dark eyes sharpened. "Is that really it?"

I sensed an urgency here that I couldn't explain, so I tried harder to push through the fog. A low-level unease slithered through me. "I... had a panic attack." A bad one, judging from the way my friend stared at me.

"That wasn't a panic attack. I'm pretty sure it was a full-on PTSD flashback. You were effectively non-responsive to everyone except for Sawyer."

He'd been there. Holding onto me. Keeping me from being swept away completely. He'd stayed. I remembered him wrapped around me after. Where was he now?

Gabi reached out to take my hand. "What the hell is going on, Willa? I'm worried about you."

Before I could even begin to pull together an explanation, the door opened.

"You're awake." The relief in Sawyer's voice was a balm. He crossed to sit beside me on the bed, taking my face between his hands and pressing a kiss to my temple. "How're you feeling?"

"Fuzzy." It was the only thing I knew for certain.

"Are you hungry?"

At the question, my stomach rumbled. "Starving."

"I'll make you some lunch."

"Lunch? What time is it?"

"Nearly noon. You've been asleep for fifteen hours. I expect you'll want a shower and a change of clothes."

I realized I still wore what I'd had on yesterday. My skin felt tight and itchy, as if the saltwater had dried on it. Maybe it had. I couldn't quite remember how I'd gotten back to the house.

"Do you need a hand?"

"I can help her," Gabi put in.

"No, I'm not an invalid. I can shower on my own. I'm just... tired." Which was absurd, really, given how long I'd slept. But whatever had happened last night had clearly taken a lot out of me.

"Okay." Sawyer kissed me again, a gentle brush of his lips to my cheek. "We'll all be downstairs."

"We? Who all is here?"

"Jace is still here. Bree, Gabi, and Daniel stayed the night. They were worried about you."

Of course they were, because apparently I'd totally lost it in front of all our friends. They'd be wanting explanations, and I didn't know how I could get out of it. Not without leaning into the idea that I was fragile and couldn't handle anything else. I'd worked too hard to prove I was stronger. I wouldn't undermine that simply because I was ashamed of my trauma.

I took my time in the shower, letting the spray wash away the lingering mental fog, along with all traces of sand and salt. Then I dragged on yoga pants and a comfortable T-shirt and made my way down to the kitchen.

"Hey. You're up." Bree crossed over and wrapped me in a tight hug. "You doing okay?"

"Better."

As soon as she stepped back, Jace pulled me in. "Good to see you up and around."

"Shouldn't you have left already?" His original plan had involved heading out early this morning.

"I didn't want to go until I knew you were okay."

"But won't you get into trouble if you're late?"

"I've got a buddy, owes me a favor," Daniel explained.

"We're gonna take him by helo to the airport. That'll save him the ferry ride and the drive."

"As long as I'm gone in the next hour, I'm fine."

"C'mon. Sit. Eat." Sawyer extracted me from my brother's hug and nudged me toward the table, passing a huge mug of coffee.

I inhaled deeply, feeling more of my synapses come online with the rich scent of roasted beans. A moment later, he slid a plate with two grilled cheeses in front of me. The sight made me remember that night in the kitchen, and I smiled.

Roy and Keeley stretched out under the table. Everyone chatted easily about nothing much while I worked my way through the first sandwich. Feeling a bit steadier with food, I began pinching off pieces of the second. "I guess I owe y'all an explanation."

"Yeah." Gabi dropped into a chair beside me. "You don't get to scare us all to death and pretend it didn't happen."

Daniel lifted his palms. "Hey now, you don't know me from Adam's house cat. You don't owe me nothin' at all. I can take myself on outside, find somethin' to get into, and come back 'round for Jace and Gabi later if that suits you better."

I glanced at my friend. If she trusted him, I supposed I could, too. "No, that's okay." I swallowed down the bite of grilled cheese, feeling it stick in my throat. I chased it down with more water and took a deep breath. "For the two years I was off-island, I was institutionalized."

I kept the explanation as brief as I could, focusing on the sandwich instead of looking at any of their faces. It wasn't as much as I'd told Sawyer. I didn't think I could bare my soul to that degree. But it was as much a reason as I could manage for my seemingly irrational behavior.

"It didn't seem to matter what treatment they tried, I've never gotten any more clarity on what happened that night. And any time I've come anywhere close to it, I... well, you saw.

Usually I can head it off before it gets too bad, but it came on too fast last night."

"Lot of similarities." Sawyer's fingers stroked along the tension in my nape. "Beach bonfire. Some of the same people. Playing with a dog, just like you did back then. Maybe it started to trigger a memory."

"I..." I tried to reach for last night, but my brain seemed to bounce off it as if I'd hit a rubber wall. "I don't know. Maybe."

Jace's jaw was set like granite. "Exactly what kind of treatments were you put through?"

"A lot of medications. Hypnosis. Electroshock therapy. Some other stuff. None of it worked. I still can't remember."

Gabi knit her hands together. "I'll admit this isn't my area, but none of this sounds right. I did a rotation in psychiatric, and I never saw anything like this. And there was absolutely zero reason they should've kept you for that long."

"I want to do some digging into that hospital and that doctor," my brother growled.

"To what end?" I didn't want to drag all of this back up again. I'd made my explanation, and now I wanted it all to go away again.

"Because what I saw last night wasn't just a normal panic attack. It wasn't just a PTSD flashback from whatever trauma you experienced. Every time you get anywhere close to whatever happened that night, you have a panic attack or fall into a migraine or get physically ill. Your reactions don't look like normal trauma."

"You're not a psychological professional. Why would you have any idea what 'normal' trauma even looks like?"

"I... there are things I've seen in my work that I can't talk about. But I'm saying that whatever you went through in that hospital was not normal."

I'd known that. Deep down, I'd always known that. I'd known it as it was happening. But in the aftermath, my only motivation had been to get as far away as possible. And I had. I wasn't eager to drag any of this back up again. "Maybe you're right. But this is me. This is my life, for better or worse. What would a potential malpractice suit get me? I'll still be damaged."

Jace's eyes flashed. "You're not damaged."

"I'm not weak. There's a difference."

"If this doctor did this shit to you, God knows what he might have been doing to others since then. Maybe someone *should* dig into it," Bree suggested.

The idea that others would be trapped and effectively tortured the way I was made me physically ill.

"If that's the case, then absolutely, he needs to be stopped. But I don't want anything to do with it. I don't ever want to see him again."

"Nobody's gonna make you, Wren." Sawyer pivoted toward me, caging me into the shelter of his arms. "But you can't just spend the rest of your life running from this. Because you are. You came back here—fought tooth and nail to build something for yourself—but you haven't fully taken back the island. In a sense, you're still trapped by your own fears. I'm not saying those fears aren't a hundred percent justified. But something happened to you. Something's been happening to you since we found that body. And we're all wondering if it could be connected."

"What are you talking about?"

He took a breath. "We found those remains about a mile north of Osprey Beach. Not far from where I pulled you out all those years ago. Is it possible that you left the party that night with Gwen? That something could've happened to both of you? That being in that area started to trigger something?"

I let my mind drift in that direction and hit the blank wall again. "I don't... know. I can't see."

Gabi laid a hand on my shoulder. "I think you should talk to someone."

I jerked away. "Absolutely not." Even the idea of it had the grilled cheese sandwiches threatening to come back up.

"Honey, I get you went through a horrific experience, but not all psychological professionals are like that. And if it can get you some relief—"

"No. I don't want to do anything else to stir up the hornet's nest. I just want to get back to my life. This—all of this—it's too much." I hated admitting it. It felt so much like the weakness I wanted to overcome.

Wary, I glanced up. No one was looking at me like I was crazy. That was something. But I hated the expressions of pity and frustration scattered around the table.

Jace lifted his hands. "Okay. We'll let you be. I'll do my digging and keep you out of it."

"Thank you."

He pushed to his feet. "I've got to get going or I'll miss my flight, and my commanding officer will have my ass."

"Guess we're headed out, too." Daniel rose, and so did Gabi.

Because I didn't know when I'd see him again, I stood to give my brother one last hug.

He squeezed me tight. "I'm sorry I wasn't there for you when I should've been. It won't happen again."

That felt like an impossible promise. And either way, I wasn't his responsibility. But sensing he needed this, I squeezed him back. "Stay safe, hear me?"

"Promise. I hope to make it home for Christmas if I can. It'll be good to have it back on-island."

I instantly flashed back to the best Christmases of our childhood, held right here at Sutter House. "Well, that's absolutely something to look forward to."

Gabi hesitated. "We'll see you at girls' night?"

"Absolutely. I need some normal, and that sounds fabulous."

With a flurry of more hugs and goodbyes, they were gone.

Bree gathered up her pooch. "Come on by the Brewhouse when you're ready. I miss seeing your face all the time."

"Thanks, girl. Let's schedule a play date for Keeley and Roy."

"It's a promise."

Then she, too, was gone, and I was alone with my husband for the first time in days. He pulled me into his arms, and I settled against his chest, content to just stay there.

"I know that was hard for you, telling everybody about what happened. How're you doing?"

"I don't know. Maybe there's a part of me that's relieved not to be hiding anymore. But if something did happen back then, if I did see something... I just can't remember. And I'm afraid of what might happen if I push too hard."

"Okay. Then we won't push."

I looked up at him. "That's it?"

He stroked my cheek. "Wren, I only ever want to help. If you're not ready now—hell, even if you're never ready—that's your decision. You've been living with this longer than the rest of us. You know what you can handle. So, yeah. That's it."

"Thank you." I snuggled against him. "I'm sorry I scared you last night."

He drew in a slow breath. "I'll admit, you might've taken a few years off my life."

I stilled, listening to his heart thump beneath my ear. "Do you regret tying yourself to me?"

Sawyer tipped my chin up, so I had to look at him. "No. I love you, Willa. I signed on for better or worse and everything in between." The corner of his mouth curved. "And if you're really feeling better, we can pick back up on some of those plans your brother's arrival interrupted."

The worry that had lodged beneath my breastbone released. "I do seem to recall discussion of time in that big ass tub."

He scooped me up, one arm beneath my knees. "I didn't carry you over the threshold our first night here. Why don't I rectify that situation?"

"Why don't you?"

CHAPTER 32

SAWYER

"A re you sure you don't mind me leaving you on your own tonight?"

I skimmed my hands down Willa's arms, stopping to clasp both her hands. "I'll be absolutely fine. You go and have fun. And if Bree gets a little too free with the bartender pour, call me. I'll come get you."

My wife rose to her toes and gave me a lingering kiss that stirred a whole host of other ideas for the evening. But I knew she needed time with her friends. It was more of the normal she so desperately wanted. So I kept my suggestions to myself as she stepped back.

"Love you."

That would never get old. "I love you, too. Drive safe."

She hefted the canvas bag of snacks. "C'mon, Roy."

The big dog happily followed her out the kitchen door.

Then I was alone in the big house that suddenly felt far too empty. I hadn't been here on my own before. Since I'd come back to Hatterwick, Willa and I had been joined at the hip. I was gradually getting accustomed to the idea that this was my home now, but being here without her felt strange.

It had been two weeks since her panic attack. She'd wanted to get back to normal, and I'd done everything I could to foster that. There'd been no more attacks, no nightmares, no headaches. If I hadn't been there, hadn't seen, I wouldn't have known she'd been struggling. She'd gotten back to her grant writing and even begun attending committee meetings for the upcoming Founders' Day celebration. Her capacity for compartmentalizing was impressive, though I wondered if it was really healthy.

There'd been no further word on who our dead guy was. If the investigation had turned up anything, Carson wasn't sharing. I had to acknowledge that we might never get answers about who it was or what had happened. That uncertainty stuck in my craw and made me restless. If I was honest, that wasn't the only reason. What Jace had said about Willa's reactions not looking like normal trauma had been circling my brain since he'd left. He hadn't spelled out what he meant, and we hadn't had time to discuss it before he'd been forced to return to duty, but that hadn't stopped my own speculation. It didn't take me anywhere good.

Prowling into the kitchen, I grabbed a root beer from the fridge and carried it out to the back deck. What the hell *was* I going to do with myself tonight? I'd updated my resume already and sent out a handful. The storm damage around the house had been repaired. I'd even picked up a handful of other repair jobs around town from folks who'd had damage and didn't need or want to wait on the bigger contractors. A few more were lined up over the next couple of weeks. I didn't mind construction work. Seeing visible results of my labor was satisfying, and I enjoyed working with my hands, feeling useful. It was a good distraction from everything else.

I missed my brothers. It was odd being back on Hatterwick without them. Having Willa in my life as my wife, my partner, my focus, was great. But it wasn't the same.

I considered texting Hoyt to see if he wanted to do something, but if he wasn't on duty at the fire station, he'd no doubt be home with his family. I didn't want to take him away from his pregnant wife.

Maybe Daniel was off duty. Although, if he was, he was probably up on Nag's Head instead if here. That wasn't exactly a hop, skip, and a jump.

Which left me exactly... nowhere.

When my phone rang, I pounced on it. Dax.

"Hey, man."

"I call with good news. Everything has been effectively planted, and there is no reason that anyone would think that you and your lady love have not been actively seeing each other for the last three years. Feel free to start pulling info for the courts."

The courts. Right. Because the lawsuit was still open. Because of the hurricane, Willa and I had gotten extra time to gather all the documentation. Crazy that I'd forgotten for even a moment. But in the grand scheme of things, after finding human remains on the property, everything else had felt relatively quiet.

"That is good news. Thanks, man. And not that I think you have any moral qualms about doing this, but it seems worth mentioning that even though it didn't start how you laid everything in, it is real. For both of us."

"Man, that's awesome!" When I didn't immediately reply, he added, "Why doesn't it sound like it's awesome?"

Dax had a quick and admittedly suspicious mind. And I knew he'd operated in some of the same circles Jace did now, so I took the opportunity and filled him in on everything that had happened since we'd last spoken.

"I just can't shake what Jace said."

"Well, of course not. The implication is that either she saw something that was so traumatic that her brain and body are noping out anytime she gets remotely close to remembering what it was, or someone took what was already a horrible experience and exacerbated it so she *couldn't* remember."

Hearing it laid out so succinctly made some of the itch in my brain go away. "Yeah. Yeah, that's it exactly. And my worry is that, in either of those scenarios, there's another actor out there who was involved that night. Either doing something to her directly, or potentially doing something to this guy who got shot—which maybe Willa saw happen."

"Have the remains been dated to the same time period?"

"No idea. I think forensics is still doing their thing. And either way, we're not law enforcement, so there's no reason the police chief would update us. But I worry that if she did see something that someone wanted to keep secret, what if that someone is still out there and sees her as a threat?"

"Fair concern. But let's think this through. Willa's been out on her own all these years. If somebody meant her actual harm, wouldn't they have already come back to do that?"

Ten years where she was on her own, with no one to protect her. Jesus. And yet, she'd been fine all that time. "In theory. But there's never been any suggestion she was going to remember before."

"Is there a suggestion that she might now?"

"Not really. But ever since we found this body, she's been having pretty extreme reactions to things. That's what made us start thinking about all of this in the first place. It's just got me paranoid about everybody we pass on the island, wondering if they had something to do with what happened to her. Do they have secrets they'd hurt or kill to keep? I can't shake the idea that something bigger is going on here. Jace is planning to look into the doctor and the hospital to see what he can find out. At the very least, it sounds like there's a malpractice suit waiting to happen, but I haven't heard anything from him. Given his deployment status, there's no telling when that might happen."

"You want me to look into it? See what I can find?"

"I'll owe you."

"Consider it a wedding present. Do you know the name of the facility and the doctor?"

Thanks to Jace, I had some of that information without bothering Willa about it. I didn't know how she'd feel about my doing this, so the less I had to involve her, the better. "The doc is Collin Caswell. Not sure about the hospital itself, but it's located in Columbia, South Carolina."

"Okay, I'll see what I can find out. Do some digging into the good doctor to see if I can find a connection to Hatterwick. If nothing else, it might give Jace some additional lines to tug toward supporting that malpractice suit."

"Thanks, Dax. I appreciate it, man."

"Now, you let me do my thing and go enjoy this time with your wife. Be vigilant, but don't let the paranoia take over, okay? We're doing what can be done and taking the steps to establish a threat assessment. I'll let you know what I dig up."

I hung up the phone, feeling a little steadier. Like I'd at least voiced my fears and taken some steps toward either dismissing or validating them. With Dax's go ahead, I went inside to grab the laptop and begin the laborious task of gathering the email trail to prove our relationship. It was something else productive I could do that would, hopefully, finally get rid of this bullshit lawsuit from Willa's parents and allow her to truly move forward with her life.

I wanted that for both of us. I wanted the chance to start figuring out what a life together would really look like.

And as I logged into my email and began pulling the emails Dax had so seamlessly slid into our chain of correspondence, I ignored the voice of disquiet in the back of my brain, saying it was too soon to relax.

CHAPTER 33

WILLA

"And, finally, a big thank you to Anthony Strand of Albemarle Development Group for his generous sponsorship of the Founders' Day fireworks display."

So Miles had finally found someone to foot the bill and have his way. I politely put my hands together to clap along with the rest of the dozen or so committee members. Strand accepted his accolades and thanks with a faux *aw shucks* sort of attitude, but I saw this for what it was—an effort to ingratiate himself with the mayor and all the rest of the founding families of Hatterwick. There was no other reason for him to be here at this committee meeting. He hadn't approached me again about developing my land, but I figured it was only a matter of time.

"Okay, so Founders' Day is less than two weeks away. Does everyone understand their marching orders?" Miles scanned the room, brows arched in question. When no one added anything, he pushed back from the table. "In that case, this meeting is adjourned."

Thank God. I'd hit my quota of people and bullshit all in one fell swoop. I wanted the quiet of home. Sawyer was working across the island today, replacing some beach stairs that had been destroyed in the hurricane. Maybe I'd stop by the market to pick up something special for dinner. He'd done so much taking care of me, I wanted to do the same for him.

"Miss Sutter."

I held in a groan and did my best not to scowl at Anthony Strand. "Can I help you?"

He flashed that smarmy politician smile. "I just wanted to check in and see if you'd reconsidered your stance. I'm in a position to make you a very wealthy woman."

"I already have more than I could ever want, Mr. Strand. And I'm not interested in what you want to do to my island."

His gaze chilled. "You're being short-sighted and naïve."

"If I am, it's my prerogative. I'm not buying what you're selling. Roy."

My faithful pup rose to his feet, silently stepping in front of me.

Again, Strand backed off, this time with no parting civilities. That was fine by me. I didn't have any inclination to talk to him ever again.

Shoving the paperwork into my messenger bag, I untangled Roy's leash from the table leg. Not that he needed it, but the illusion of control made some of the other committee members less nervous about his presence. Most had gotten used to him over the past month, and a couple had even begun bringing dog biscuits.

"Ready for a walk, pal?"

Roy's tail thumped with enthusiasm.

I scruffed his ears. "Such a good boy. Let's go."

We'd only made it down to the lobby of Town Hall before I got hailed again. I closed my eyes and sucked in a fortifying breath before turning to see who wanted something from me now.

Roland O'Shea strode across the room. "Oh good. I caught

you. I thought you might still be here." He took one look at my face, and his face twisted into a wry smile. "Miles has been droning on again."

I winced. "Is it that obvious?"

"You aren't the only one who's been roped into committee meetings. I just wanted to give you the update on things."

"Walk with me a bit? Roy needs to go out."

"Sure." We left the building, making our way down the block to a grassy area where my pup could relieve himself.

"I got all the documentation you and Sawyer pulled together delivered to the court yesterday. The judge will need time to sift through it, but I have every reason to expect this will be the end of things. Anything else from your parents will likely get seen as a nuisance suit."

The idea that it could finally, truly be over made me giddy. I was eager to get back to being a newlywed. Turned out, I really loved being a newlywed, and I wanted to focus on building this new life with Sawyer. But I knew better than to count my chickens before they hatched.

I blew out a breath. "I confess, I'll believe it when I see it. That's no shade on you, I just... My dad doesn't give up easily."

"True enough. It's unprofessional of me to admit, but I'll take great pleasure in thwarting him."

I went brows up. "Oh?"

He rolled his eyes in a self-deprecatory fashion and sighed. "I had a thing for your mother, way back in the era of the dinosaurs. Your dad came in and swept her off her feet. I eventually met my Sheila when I was in law school at Georgetown, so it was all for the best, but I still kind of resent him for that. If you'll forgive me for saying so, he's a smug SOB."

I laughed. "You're not wrong. I admit, seeing him knocked down a few pegs is satisfying for me, too. And really, I can't thank you enough for all your hard work on all of this. Everything my grandparents have entrusted to me is really overwhelming, and I couldn't have made it through this transition without you."

"Henry and Vivian were dear friends for a long time. It's my honor to continue to serve the next generation of the Sutter family."

"Thank you. That means a lot."

"Well, I won't keep you. I'm sure you've got things to do. That new husband to get back to."

"Miss Sutter."

We both turned at the hail to see Chief Carson hustling across the street. I instantly tensed. Roy pressed closer, and I appreciated that Mr. O'Shea didn't abandon me.

Carson nodded at him in acknowledgment, then focused back on me. "I wanted to let you know that the remains on your property have been identified."

My stomach twisted. We'd already known it wasn't Gwen, but what if it was someone else I knew? "And?"

"Chief!" Miles inserted himself into our little group. "Did I just hear you say the body's been identified?"

He nodded. "I was coming to find you next. It's Joe Anderson."

I blinked, sifting back through my memories. The name meant nothing to me. "Who was he?"

"You don't recognize the name?"

"Should I?"

Miles frowned. "Wasn't he a fisherman or something?"

"Maybe a picture will help." Carson pulled out his phone and swiped at the screen before handing the device over to me.

The man on the screen looked vaguely familiar. He was, perhaps, in his mid-twenties, with shaggy brown hair and a scraggly goatee. Nondescript brown eyes stared out of a narrow face. But still, nothing really pinged. Shaking my head, I handed back the phone. "I mean, he looks vaguely familiar, but if he's a local, I don't know him."

"Miles is right. He was a fisherman, who probably worked with your husband, back in the day."

"Back in the day? Sawyer hasn't worked commercial fishing in more than ten years. Is this photo that old?"

"Older. According to his old boss, Anderson was a seasonal worker, and not all that reliable. So when he didn't show for work, they didn't think anything of it. They just thought he'd skipped town and blown things off. He had no family to speak of, so nobody reported him missing."

"That's so sad. How long ago was this?"

Carson's gaze stayed steady on mine. "Twelve years. He was last seen a few days before Gwen disappeared."

Chill bumps rose along my arms.

When Miles spoke, his voice was tight. "Do you think it's connected?"

"We don't know. We're digging into Anderson's life as much as we can, trying to piece together a better picture of who he was and what he was into." The chief looked back at me. "Think back really hard. Can you ever remember seeing this guy around your grandparents' place? Maybe he did odd jobs or something."

Roland edged closer to me. "Are you suggesting that Henry or Vivian Sutter had something to do with this man's murder?" He'd lost the easygoing, avuncular tone, and I could tell even the implication pissed him off.

"No. We're just trying to come up with a reason he might've been on the property."

"Chief Carson, the remains weren't found anywhere near the house. The woods aren't fenced off. And I don't remember anything from back that far. Particularly around the time of Gwen's disappearance. I never got those memories back after I drowned. Even before that, I never had anything to do with my grandparents' or my parents' business dealings. I have no clue how this guy might have known my family at all. But if he disappeared that close to when Gwen did, could his murder have something to do with her disappearance?"

"It has to," Miles insisted. "What are the chances that something like a murder and a disappearance would happen at the same time in a place this small and *not* be connected?"

Carson grimaced. "We don't know. At this point, there's so little forensic evidence left. The only thing we know for sure was that he was shot. We don't have the bullet. We don't have anything. It's possible that, after all this time, we may never know. But we're going to keep looking. I just wanted you both to be aware of what's going on, and to let you know that we'll have a team out on your property doing a more thorough search for additional evidence."

"Of course. Yes. Whatever y'all need to do, I'm happy to cooperate."

"Good. I'll be in touch." He started to turn away.

"Chief Carson?"

"Yeah?"

"Could you text me that picture?" Maybe if I looked at it some more, eventually I'd figure out why his face looked so familiar.

"Sure."

Once he'd confirmed the image had sent, he and Miles walked away, continuing to talk in low voices.

I blew out a breath.

"You okay?"

"Yeah, I think so. I'm just creeped out. Hatterwick has always felt so safe. It's hard knowing a guy was killed on my property at all. Worse, that it was right around the same time my friend disappeared. I hope it means they'll find some new threads to follow in terms of her disappearance. We could all use some answers."

"From your mouth to God's ear, Willa."

"I've gotta go. Groceries, then home to get back to work."

"I'll keep you posted. As soon as I hear anything, you'll be the first to know."

"Thanks, Mr. O'Shea."

He smiled at me. "At this stage, Willa, I think you can call me Roland."

"I appreciate that."

We went our separate ways. But all through my trip to the island market, my brain continued to spin on Joe Anderson. Where had I seen his face before? Maybe I'd seen him when I'd been a kid, but I didn't think it was that. The memory, such as it was, felt more recent. It wasn't until I'd loaded the groceries in my Jeep and sat in the driver's seat, staring at his photo, that it finally hit me.

"Holy shit."

CHAPTER 34

SAWYER

I got home later than I'd planned, but it had been worth it to see a project all the way to finished. Especially as it had resulted in my picking up another job for next week. Carpentry was something I'd learned growing up, out of necessity. When you couldn't afford to buy new, you learned how to fix things. Commercial fishing had been my summer job for years, but construction had been how I'd filled in during the school year. I'd picked up after-school jobs on various construction crews as soon as anybody'd been willing to let me swing a hammer. Paddy Floyd had broken some rules by allowing me on to his crew at fourteen and paying me off-book. But that income had helped keep a roof over my head during stretches when my dad hadn't been able to function.

I wasn't keen on the idea of working for someone else, but the idea of getting my contractor's license, and maybe doing for others what Paddy had done for me, had been circling around in my head. It was a way I could give back to the community. Maybe all my time with Willa was rubbing off on me, or maybe it just felt like a way to slowly overwrite the long-held perceptions other locals held about me. The rumblings about me and

Willa had died down in the past several weeks. Or at least, folks had been more careful not to voice their opinions in earshot of me. But I was past giving a damn what any of them thought. Willa and I knew our marriage was real, and that was the only thing that mattered.

Sliding out of my truck, I carefully knocked sand off my boots before heading toward the house. I wanted to kiss my wife, then grab a shower and a root beer. Or maybe a root beer in the shower. Then maybe we could watch a movie we'd already seen with dinner and make out on the sofa. If making out turned to more, well, we were newlyweds. Pleased with the idea of that itinerary, I let myself inside.

Something simmering on the stove scented the kitchen with tomatoes and spices. Taco soup maybe? Already salivating, I toed off my boots and went in search of Willa. Had she finished for the day, or just started supper and gone back to work? I found her in the den, hunched over her laptop. Roy curled up beside her with a Nylabone.

"Hey, beautiful."

"Hey." She looked up, and the expression on her face had the smile fading from mine.

"What is it? What's wrong?" Her cheeks were too pale, and her mouth was pinched. Had she had another panic attack? I closed the distance between us, kneeling beside her.

"The police have identified the body."

Oh God. I hadn't gone through the village before I came home, so I hadn't heard anything myself. "Who is it?"

"A guy named Joe Anderson."

Did I know a Joe Anderson? I tried to think.

"Here." Willa turned the laptop in my direction and pointed to a picture.

I noted multiple tabs open to what appeared to be social media and a lot of Google searches. The guy on the screen looked familiar. "I used to work with him. Back in high school when I was fishing in the summers. He came on as a seasonal worker, I think. I haven't seen him in years. I guess this is why."

She knit her hands together. "The last time anyone saw him was the week before Gwen disappeared."

Untangling her fingers, I laced them with mine. "Is that what's got you upset? You think he had something to do with what happened to Gwen?"

Her throat worked as she swallowed, and her eyes took on a haunted edge. "I don't know. But tell me why he's showing up in my nightmares."

Her words sent a shiver down my spine. "What are you talking about?"

"You remember, a couple months ago, that night I woke up screaming and said that I'd been back in the hospital being chased by zombies?"

She hadn't said a whole lot about that nightmare, but that piece had stuck. "Yeah. Hard to forget."

"He was one of the zombies. He was shuffling along with the pack of them, blood trailing down from his head, dripping onto the rest of his clothes." Her fingers tightened on mine. "Why did I dream of this man bleeding from the head two months ago, before we ever found the remains? Sawyer, what if I saw him murdered? What if that's something locked away in my head?"

The idea of that was utterly terrifying on multiple fronts. If she saw a man be killed right in front of her, that very well might be traumatic enough to cause the kinds of reactions she had. But more, if she'd seen the murder, then presumably she might have seen who'd pulled the trigger, and that person might believe she was a threat.

Willa took a deep breath. "I think I have to try. I think I have to push in a way I never have before."

"No. Not only because it will hurt you, but because if any word leaks out that you're starting to remember what happened that night, if whoever killed this man is still around, they could perceive you as a threat and come after you." And how could I protect her when I had no idea what direction the danger might come from?

"They could come after me anyway, whether I remember or not. I don't know why they haven't before now."

"Either because they're no longer on-island at all, or because they're close enough to know you've never remembered. Plus, there was no body, until recently. No one even knew Joe Anderson was missing until we stumbled on his remains. If his killer is still here, he's gotta be sweating bullets, wondering if he's gonna get caught. That makes whoever it is dangerous. We don't need to do anything to draw attention to you."

"I get that. But you were right in what you said when Jace was here. A part of me is still running. I haven't completely taken back my island. There are whole chunks I avoid. I've done everything possible to stop myself from reacting. To not put myself in a position to get triggered. Because once I go down that rabbit hole, I can't stop myself. And it usually involves pain and sickness and general horribleness."

She tightened her hold on my hands. "This last time—yes, it was bad—but you kept me grounded. I knew you were there. Part of me did, anyway. I knew I was safe with you, even though I couldn't stop all the reactions that were happening. And I think... if I hadn't fought it so hard, if maybe I'd leaned into the fragments and flashes I was seeing instead of focusing on the terror, maybe I would've seen more."

I didn't like this. Any of it. "What are you saying?"

She framed my face in her hands and pressed her brow to mine. "I think I have to try to face this. I think I have to try to remember. And I want to do it with you there. To see if I can push through. If I know who killed this guy, or if this had something to do with what happened to Gwen, I owe it to her to try.

And God, I owe it to myself. I've been living with this hole in my memories for years. And I've tried to tell myself that it's okay that I can't remember. But I don't feel complete. I'm so aware, all the time, that there's a piece missing. If I can do this, if I can get answers, I have to take the risk."

I hated everything about this. I didn't want her to do anything that would put her in danger or in pain. But she wasn't wrong. If whoever was out there thought she was a material witness and believed she could remember, then she'd be inherently in danger for the rest of her life, whether she ever remembered or not.

Better that she try to excavate those memories on purpose, to potentially identify the killer, so that the police could do their job and get them off the street.

I eased back to look into her face. "I don't like it, but I get it. And I'll support you. We need to talk about this and make a careful plan for how to approach it in a controlled manner, so that you're as safe as you can be."

"I can agree to that." She straightened. "I think we have to call the others."

CHAPTER 35
WILLA

I t took nearly a week for everything to come together. Because I wanted to mimic the circumstances of the night everything went wrong as much as possible, we waited for the weather to cooperate. The storm off the coast wasn't anything worrisome. Certainly not a hurricane. It might not even make it close to land before we were through with all of this. But it would add to the ambiance and hopefully be another weight on the side of remembering.

"Okay, Daniel's in place and has the bonfire started. Bree's in-bound with dinner. It's time." Sawyer smoothed his hands down my arms. "You ready?"

I took a breath. "As I'll ever be."

Gabi extended a hand with two little orange pills in her palm. "Remember, the propranolol will help control your heart rate and the shaking and sweating. You'll be a little tired, but it won't sedate you or affect your memory."

That had been Gabi's genius idea. Use chemistry to circumvent the physiological aspects of the panic attack. I'd been nervous. Since my time at the hospital, the only prescription meds I'd taken were antibiotics. But we'd done a test run earlier in the week, which had allowed Sawyer to drive me all the way to the edge of Osprey Beach. I'd still been ill at ease, but I hadn't lost control. It had felt... miraculous.

I swallowed down the pills with most of a glass of water.

"It'll take about an hour for it to reach peak efficacy, so that gives us time to get out there, have some food, play with the dogs."

That was another element of the plan. While we wanted to duplicate the bonfire, we also didn't want to draw attention to ourselves. If anybody was watching, this would just look like a group of friends hanging out at the beach, as so many people did. It wouldn't be until after that I'd really begin pushing things. Assuming I lasted that long.

Wiping my sweaty palms on my shorts, I nodded. "Let's do it."

Gabi squeezed me in a hug. "I know this is hard for you, and I'm proud you're being brave. But remember to be kind to yourself. If it doesn't go how you want, we can try something else."

"Thanks." I really hoped we didn't have to try something else. I hoped that coming at the trigger so directly would pop open my faulty memory like a key in a lock. That was probably far too simplistic an aspiration, but I held onto it, nonetheless.

"I'll meet y'all out there."

Sawyer waited until Gabi had gotten into her car and headed down the drive to pull me in. "I'm gonna be right there the whole time. If you want to pull the plug at any point, you say so. You'll get no arguments from any of us."

I leaned into him, soaking in his warmth and strength. "I want to think I wouldn't pull the plug. That I'll be strong enough to face whatever needs facing. For Gwen, for myself, I'm going to try. And I need you to let me, even if it gets hard. No matter how I react, whatever happened... already happened. It can't truly hurt me anymore. I might not remember that in the moment, so I need you to."

"I suspect it's gonna be a rough night for us both."

"It'll be better because you're with me. I love you, Sawyer."

"I love you, too, Wren. Let's do this thing."

We piled into his truck for the drive down the west side of the island, to where that night had begun. I made the concession of riding up front with him instead of behind the seat under a blanket. Instead, Roy was in the back seat, buckled into his seatbelt, tongue lolling in excitement over going for a ride.

The house I'd grown up in had been sold years ago, my parents cutting any ties to the island other than my grandparents. After some storm damage, the new owners had expanded the porch and changed the color to a pink that bore a little too much resemblance to flamingos for my taste. But I could still see the window I'd slipped out of and where the vine-covered trellis I'd climbed down had once been. Sawyer had been waiting two houses down, in that old rattle-trap truck of his, lights off. We paused there in the dying light of sunset.

"I always used to think of you as Rapunzel sneaking out of your tower," he murmured.

My lips curved. "I confess, I kinda had some Romeo and Juliet fantasies going on, wishing you'd climb up the trellis to my room."

"Not sure it would have held me, even back then. And I'm damned sure Jace wouldn't have been as supportive then as he is now."

"My fantasies about you were a lot more chaste back then."

He cut me a glance. "Are you having delightfully sexy thoughts about me, wife?"

I tangled my fingers with his. "Let's just say that I might have a few roleplay scenarios in mind for after we get through all this."

"Something to look forward to." Pressing a kiss to the back of my hand, he pulled away from the curb.

From there, the drive to Osprey Beach only took about

fifteen minutes. He drove the same route he had that night, weaving through residential streets that gave way to the trees, past the park and beyond to the crushed-shell back road that wound its way to the Atlantic side of Hatterwick. He parked beneath the same trees, though the area was more overgrown than it had been then. We slipped out of the truck into the hush of greenery, but even from here, the ocean called. I curled my hand around his, and we followed, Roy dashing a few feet ahead.

It felt different approaching this together. As we walked, I scanned the beach, remembering. "There were so many people here that night. It seemed like more than all of Sutter's Ferry High."

"It probably was. There were already summer people on-island at that point. You didn't go through the crowd."

"No, I edged around them." Too overwhelmed to dive straight into the deep end, cutting through the crowd.

We followed the skirting path I'd taken.

"I thought for sure you'd decide you wanted to go in ten minutes."

"I considered it. Then I found Gabi and Gwen and made friends with the dog. Looking back, I don't even know whose dog it was. I didn't recognize her."

"She looked a lot like Keeley. Some kind of shepherd mix."

As if we'd summoned her, Keeley spotted Roy from across the beach and made a beeline in our direction. Roy whined and danced, looking back at me for permission.

"Go see your buddy."

With a joyful bark, he took off, a streak of black in the dark-ening night. Sawyer and I continued at a more sedate pace toward the waiting fire. It was much smaller than the one from back then, but it still gave the ambiance. Daniel, Gabi, and Bree waited at a nearby picnic table. Low strains of music carried on the breeze.

"Doing okay?" Sawyer asked.

"So far, so good. I'm anxious, but it's more anticipatory than active, if that makes sense."

"Absolutely."

We weren't the only people on the beach, despite the distant clouds. Had any of them been here that night? Did any of them know how momentous it was that I was even standing here? Was someone out there, even now, watching me, waiting to see what I'd do?

I tried not to think about that as we roasted our hot dogs and talked. Maybe I didn't talk much, but that wasn't unusual at social gatherings. I let everyone else carry the conversation as I soaked up the atmosphere and waited for some kind of sign that this was working. With nary a flicker, I grabbed a ball and moved to the edge of the water with the dogs, falling into the easy, familiar rhythm of fetch. I could still hear music from the little Bluetooth speaker Bree had brought. Sawyer was at the picnic table, watching me. All of them were, though they tried not to be obvious about it. I didn't blame them. After what had happened last time, no doubt everyone was braced for me to lose my shit.

By the time full dark had fallen, I hadn't remembered anything. I didn't have any clear memory of leaving the beach with or without Gwen, but objectively, I knew I had at some point. How else would I have been so far north when Sawyer found me? So I trotted back to the group at the table, draping my arms flirtatiously around his shoulders.

"Time for a post-dinner walk."

At their expectant looks, I shook my head.

"We'll be back," Sawyer announced.

Hand in hand, we trudged down the beach, keeping close to the waterline, where the sand was firmer. Despite the medication, I could feel my body trying to react. The edge of a headache was working its way up my temples. Though I had no clear memory, I tried to focus on those physical sensations, using them as a compass and turning toward them. I pulled us away from the water and into the woods.

"Do you remember coming this way?"

"No." But something in my gut told me to keep going.

The canopy of trees blocked out the waning moon, so we were making our way by cell phone flashlights.

"Is this a good idea? I have a better light in my truck."

"I wouldn't have had a better light back then. Just something like this."

Thunder rumbled in the distance. I knew somewhere behind us, Gabi, Daniel, and Bree were following. I could just barely hear the signs of their passage, and only because I knew following us was the plan. If someone had followed me that night, would I have noticed? The wind from the incoming storm would've blocked out any obvious sounds of movement beyond our own. Someone could've gotten the drop on me. On us? To what end? I didn't know.

We walked and walked, until I caught a hint of movement ahead. Shining the light, I saw the fluttering remains of crime scene tape. We'd made it all the way to where I'd stumbled upon Joe Anderson's remains. And there'd been nothing.

I'd faced my fear directly, and it wasn't some magic key that unlocked everything and brought those missing memories instantly into focus. As ever, my mind was a blank wall.

The headache was stronger now, but not unmanageable. Turning away from the crime scene, I pushed my way out of the woods and back onto the beach. The storm was nearly on us now, with clouds building above the island. The tide was rougher. I could almost feel the roll of it beneath my feet and swayed.

Sawyer's arm came around me in an instant. "Okay?"

"Yeah. Yeah, I'm... fine. I mean, not fine. I can still feel something. But I still can't remember anything. There's no flashback. No hallucination."

His gaze turned out toward the ocean, where the swells already pulsed with the energy of the oncoming storm, but it was nothing to the crash and snarl of wind and water from that night.

"I was just about to turn back, to try searching somewhere else, when I heard you. At least, I thought it was you." Sawyer's voice was low enough I barely heard it over the wind.

"I heard something and turned around just fast enough to see you going under." His shoulders went rigid, and his throat worked. "It was a fucking miracle I even spotted you. No one should've been on the water in that storm, let alone *in* it. Especially not here, with the riptides."

"I knew about those riptides. I wouldn't have just... jumped in on a whim." I'd always known that, even when the popular theory that I'd gone in to rescue a dog had taken root. I stared out at the frothing waves. "I don't know how I got there. And I don't know how you managed to get me out."

His voice went to gravel. "I almost didn't. I took a monumental gamble, calculating what I knew of the tides and swimming toward where I thought you'd be, rather than where you went under." He squeezed his eyes shut, and I wondered what he saw. What he remembered.

"You were so pale, so still, when I dragged you out. And I couldn't find a pulse. You were dead." He whispered the words, but the truth of them hit me like a shout.

I turned into him, tightening my arms around his waist. "But you saved me. I'm right here because you didn't give up on me."

"I've never been more scared in my entire life than when I started CPR. I don't even remember all the deals I made with the Almighty if only you'd live. Then you started coughing."

He pulled me closer and buried his face in my hair, and I

finally did have a memory of him doing exactly this that night. I
held on tighter, understanding that, in this moment, I was the
one grounding him.

"I didn't want to let you go."

"You don't have to. Not ever again. I'm right here." I stroked
his back. "I'm sorry. I'm sorry you had to go through that. Then
and now. I didn't know what I was asking of you, coming back
here like this."

We stood like that for a long time as the wind kicked up
around us, a preview of the storm to come, until a voice
called out.

"Not to break up whatever li'l moment y'all are having, but
this rain's about to cut loose, and I expect we ought to get back
to clean up our stuff."

Daniel.

He and the girls emerged from the trees.

"Any luck?" Bree called.

My shoulders slumped as I was forced to admit the truth.
"Nothing. I think we've gotta call this a bust."

CHAPTER 36
SAWYER

B ack at Sutter House, our group sprawled around the den. I dropped onto one end of the sofa and hauled Willa into my lap, as much to comfort myself as her. I hadn't anticipated how much *I'd* remember from that night, and I was still a little shaken by revisiting my own trauma.

The memory had been so clear. That bone-freezing terror of seeing her slip below the surface and not come back up. The burn of salt in my eyes and lungs as waves crashed over my head, stealing my breath. And still I'd used every shred of energy I'd had to dive again and again, even knowing too much time had passed. By the time my hand had brushed fabric, I was certain I'd be pulling back her corpse. I hadn't been wrong. But neither had I been able to admit defeat. I hadn't been able to let her go then, and I certainly wouldn't start now.

I needed to feel her. To be absolutely certain she was here—warm and alive and mine. Had we been alone, I'd have taken her straight up to our room to affirm that in far more intimate ways but, given all our guests, I had to settle for this. For now.

Willa cuddled against me. Disappointment rolled off her in waves. I didn't blame her. I knew how much strength and courage it had taken for her to face this. To get nothing out of it had to be a crushing blow. I hadn't realized how much hope I'd put into getting some kind of answers tonight myself, so I'd know who the threat was and how best to protect her. For the moment, we were batting zero.

"I'm sorry to have wasted all y'all's time. I really thought I'd get... something."

Gabi sat forward in her chair. "Okay, maybe you didn't remember things. Yet. But you also didn't give in to a panic attack. That's huge."

Willa managed a wry smile. "That was certainly better than the alternative. So thank you for that."

"Of course. How's the headache?"

Her look to Gabi was sharp. "I didn't say I had one."

"You didn't have to. Doctor, remember?" Gabi just arched a brow in question.

At length, Willa relaxed again. "It's fading. Didn't hit full-blown migraine territory. So that was better, too."

"Don't you be thinkin' tonight was a waste just 'cause you didn't latch onto nothin' yet. Somethin' could still shake loose in your dreams or when you least expect it." Daniel crossed his legs at his ankles. "Be patient, cher. Those memories gonna come up when they good and ready and not before. You only just started really workin' on it."

"I hate the idea of that. I hate not knowing when something might trigger me. The whole point of tonight was to do this in a controlled fashion to avoid that." When Gabi opened her mouth to speak, Willa cut her off. "I don't want to be on any kind of medication all the time. I'll admit this was... okay. But I'm not gonna take anything permanently unless I absolutely have to."

"Okay, so the direct approach didn't work. Let's brainstorm," Bree suggested. "What else can we try that allows you a little more control over the when and where?"

"Maybe looking through old diaries or journals from back then? Put yourself back in the headspace of when you were sixteen."

"I don't have any. I never went back to my parents' house after Jace sprung me from the hospital. I walked away with literally nothing rather than risk falling under their control again."

Nothing. She'd brought nothing at all. It was another piece I hadn't quite put together. I don't know what I'd thought. Maybe that Jace had gone back to retrieve her things before bringing her back to Hatterwick. Maybe that was part of why she clung so hard to the pieces of her past her grandparents had given back.

"I can probably lay hands on mine somewhere. I think they're probably in a box in the attic at Caroline's. If you want to read through them, I'll see if I find them."

Willa huffed a laugh. "So I can get the play-by-play of how you were crushing on... let me think. Who was it that year? Rand McFarland?"

Daniel straightened. "Who's Rand McFarland?"

Gabi rolled her eyes. "He was my lab partner in chemistry. Total Peter Parker type. For about five minutes, I was convinced we were meant to be. I only realized later that he was flirting with me so I'd help him pass."

"It was a very intense five minutes, as I recall."

"Well, he did have really great dimples," Gabi admitted.

"Better than these?" Daniel smiled and pointed to the indentions in his own cheeks.

She pretended to consider. "Mmm. I think his were deeper."

"Well, cher, it's not the size of the dimples, it's how you use them."

Gabi's grin turned wicked. "And you use yours so well."

As everyone else burst into laughter, I lifted a hand. "On

behalf of all of your honorary brothers, I have to say—keep that to yourself. I don't need those mental images."

But the moment of humor lightened the general mood of the group in a way we'd desperately needed.

"Right. We'll save Sawyer's sensibilities and get back to the matter at hand." Gabi winked at me. "Pictures from back then might help, too."

"I've got some of those," Bree added. "They're at Pop's. I haven't looked at them in forever, but the man never throws anything away."

That was probably a blessing. A couple of years after that summer was when she'd had her falling out with Ford. With her temper, I wouldn't have been shocked if she'd ritually burned anything that referenced him. Ed would've realized and done what he could to keep her from that kind of regret.

"You might also make a playlist of the music that was popular at the time," Daniel suggested. "Never know what might jog your memory."

We continued to toss around ideas, but we were pretty limited in what we could manage on our own. What we really needed was a psychological professional with a specialty in handling traumatic memory. But I didn't think Willa would go for that, even now. Not after her prior experience. So I kept my mouth shut on that subject.

"I appreciate all the suggestions. At this point, anything else has to wait. Founders' Day is this weekend, and I'm tied up with that. Bree, you will be too, with all the extra people in town for the celebration."

"True enough. There's gonna be a lot of people on-island. The Brewhouse will be slammed."

Founders' Day was a big deal on Hatterwick. It often served as a sort of homecoming celebration, where former locals who'd moved off-island came back to visit. Given our supposition that Willa might have been left alone because whoever had killed Joe Anderson simply wasn't here, I worried that the festival might bring him back. Was the killer a local? There was no way to know, but I was uncomfortable with Willa being out and about among a bunch of strangers.

"Are you sure you have to do this? Is it going to be too much for you being around all those people?" Maybe it was a dick move to bring up her normal social anxiety when that wasn't my real concern. But if her mind hadn't gone down the same paranoid path as mine, I didn't want to add to her worries.

Willa shrugged. "I'm the last Sutter. This is part of my role here. For the most part, I'm okay with it. Committee meetings suck, but it's been fine. And once this is over, I'll be done for several months, until it's time to do it all over again. I don't want to tarnish my family legacy by bailing just because I hate peopling. I'll do what I need to do. It'll be fine."

"Those are more people than Roy will be able to handle," I pointed out. "And Miles has already made it clear that it's *just* you, so I won't be with you for everything." I didn't like that, either.

Gabi straightened. "I know you don't want to take anything regularly, but you could try another beta blocker or something like a Xanax simply for the situational anxiety around having to interact with all those people. It might help keep you leveled out during those stretches when none of us or Roy can be with you."

When Willa didn't immediately reject the idea, I considered it progress. "I'll think about it."

Everyone took that as their cue to leave. There were hand-shakes and hugs and the scruffing of dog ears all around. Then, at last, my wife and I were alone.

I pulled her into me. "How're you feeling?"

Her hands skimmed across my chest. "I was going to ask you the same question. Tonight was hard on you. I'm sorry for it."

"I'm a big boy. I can handle it."

Her eyes sparked with heat. "I was thinking you could handle me."

The urge to claim her, to sink into the warm, willing heat of that body I loved, came roaring back. "Are you up for that?"

She rose to her toes, pressing close so her breasts were flattened against my chest. "I'm up for anything you want to do to me, Sawyer. Take me however you need."

I wouldn't turn her down. I needed this woman like I needed to breathe. Scooping her up, I carried her upstairs to our bed. But as I stripped her down and worshipped her in all the ways I'd imagined, I couldn't quite shake the sense that there was a storm on the horizon other than the literal one outside that was already passing.

CHAPTER 37
WILLA

Sutter's Ferry was under siege. At least, that was what it felt like to me. The central portion of the village had been blocked off all the way to the marina. A stage was set up at one end of Main Street, with a chalkboard announcing the different bands who'd be taking it over all day. The streets were lined with booths displaying everything from carved driftwood art to tidy jars from the Golden Dunes Honey Company. Interspersed throughout were tents for local restaurants serving pared down versions of their regular menus. I might have loved it but for all the people.

There were so many.

When I'd lived in the village proper with Bree, I'd deliberately pushed my own limits, working in public, or otherwise getting out and about some every day, even during prime tourist season. But since my grandfather had died, and Sawyer and I had moved out to Sutter House, I'd backslid. It had been so easy to stay holed up out there—first because of the stress and strain over the lawsuit and then simply because we were lost in our own little honeymoon world. That would have to change moving forward. I'd have to go back to making an effort.

"Willa! Sawyer!"

I turned toward the familiar voice and spotted Delilah waving from one of the booths. Relieved to see a friendly face, I cut through the crowd in her direction.

"Hey, sugar! How are y'all this morning?"

I accepted her warm hug without reservation. "Making it." It was the best I could offer without lying.

Her dark eyes were knowing. "There are a lot of folks here today."

"I think we have Miles to thank for that."

Our mayor had taken what had once been effectively a party for the locals at the end of the summer season and turned it into an Event with a capital E.

"He did a big push this year around the homecoming theme, reaching out through social media and email to island residents who've moved elsewhere, encouraging them to come back to visit."

There'd always been some who came home around this time. But this year, it felt as if they'd all said 'Yes' to his invitation. Ever since the 5K foot race had finished this morning, more and more people had appeared. I could barely move from booth to booth without someone encroaching on my personal space. Sawyer had done his best to stick close, shielding me with his bigger body, but he could only do so much, and I was very aware of the just-in-case dose of propranolol Gabi had pressed on me.

"Guess that was a success," Delilah said. "I've seen some people today I haven't seen in years."

"How's business?" Sawyer glanced around the tables, which already looked half-empty.

Delilah beamed. "Booming. I've already sold most of my canvases and quite a few prints. And a good portion of the pottery I had prepped is already spoken for. Nothing makes me happier than a reason to get back into the studio."

From the next street over, I could hear the band changing out to something a lot louder and more raucous. So much input and noise. I missed Roy and his big, comforting presence. But he'd have been on high alert with all these people because I was, so it was best that he'd been left at home.

I dragged my attention back to the conversation. "Where's Florence? I expected she'd be here with you." There was no sign of the taller woman.

"Oh, she went to get us some lunch before the big rush."

"That's a good idea. Wren, you wanna get some food before it gets any worse? If we go now, we can probably eat before you're supposed to report for the start of the regatta."

The Founders' Day Regatta was the first of several events I was expected to be present for. Some of it was ceremonial, and some was simply for the photo op. All of it meant I wouldn't have my trusty emotional support husband for most of the afternoon. Being fortified with food would likely help.

"That's probably a good plan."

"Craving anything in particular? I think I saw the booth for Shell Yeah back around the block."

"I'm not fussy. I'll go for anything that's not near the band."

"You got it. See you later, Mimi."

We ended up at the tent for the Shoreline Sandwich Shack, which was offering a limited version of its usual menu. A familiar, tall figure with silver-shot brown hair was waiting in line ahead of us. When he turned, I almost broke from the line and simply walked away to find somewhere else to eat. But this was my island, and I'd made my position clear.

"Miss Sutter. Good to see you."

I forced a polite smile that I knew missed by at least half a mile. "Mr. Strand. Enjoying the festivities?"

"Indeed. It's quite the turnout today."

"So it is."

Sawyer moved closer to me.

"It's an exciting thing, seeing so many people on the island. Everybody wants their piece of Hatterwick. Lots of opportunity for those smart enough to act."

Before I could reply to the veiled insult, Sawyer tightened his arm around my shoulders. "I'm sorry, are you implying that because my wife isn't a money-hungry jackal, willing to sell her soul for a buck, she's somehow stupid?"

I would've laughed, but for the flash of fury that passed over Anthony Strand's face.

"I wouldn't dare. Good day to you." This last came off in a clear tone of *fuck you very much* as he turned his back on us and made his order.

When he had his sandwich in hand, he left the tent entirely.

"Good riddance," Sawyer muttered.

"Much as I appreciate your defense, you probably shouldn't have antagonized him."

"I didn't like how he was speaking to you. You've told him on multiple occasions that you're not interested."

"Yeah. But people like that can't wrap their brains around the idea that not everyone thinks like they do. That not everyone is motivated by money. Which, I recognize, is a thing I can say because of my personal privilege. But despite what I came from, what I've inherited, I know what it is to have nothing. And I'd still make the same choice."

He brushed a kiss to my temple. "And that's just one of the many things I love about you."

We got our sandwiches and found an empty table in the corner to eat. I could still feel the press of people, but at least they weren't bumping into me. Knowing what was coming for the afternoon, I gave in and took the emergency meds. The last thing I wanted was to get caught up in a panic attack when I was nowhere near any of my supports.

Sawyer checked his watch and balled up his sandwich

wrapper. "Probably time to start working our way to the marina."

By the time we got there, I expected some of this feeling of pressure in my chest to have eased. Hand-in-hand, we made our way down the street, past the Brewhouse and on toward Pamlico Sound.

"Willa!"

At the hail, I braced myself for more peopling. But when I turned, I spotted Roland O'Shea pushing through the crowd.

"Hey, Roland."

He was puffing a little by the time he reached us. "I tried to call you."

Every muscle in my body went tense. "I think the cell towers are overwhelmed by all the extra people. Nothing came through. What's wrong?"

He waved a hand. "No, no. Nothing is wrong. I wanted to share the good news. I heard back from the court."

Sawyer pulled me close. "And?"

"Your parents' case has been tossed out by the judge."

I stared at him. "Tossed out? So it's... over?"

Roland beamed. "It is. The estate and everything that goes with it is yours. Or will be, as soon as the probate process is finished in another couple of months. Congratulations, Willa."

"I don't— This is really, real?"

"Really, really," he assured me.

I turned to Sawyer, looking up at him in giddy relief. "It's over."

He grinned at me. "We won. *You* won."

I turned back to the attorney. "I can't thank you enough for all your hard work with all of this. Protecting my inheritance. Protecting *me*."

"Of course. It was my pleasure." He pulled out a handkerchief and mopped his brow. "Don't let me keep you. I know you've got places to be for Founders' Day duties. I'll be seeing you later at the parade."

"Oh, are you helping out there?"

He rolled his eyes. "I got voluntold I'd be helping coordinate getting the floats in order."

I snickered. "Miles is good at voluntelling people all kinds of things. I'll see you there. And thank you again."

With a smile and a wave, Roland disappeared into the crowd.

For a moment, Sawyer and I only stood there, beaming at each other.

"It's really over. We successfully gave a great big double middle finger to my parents. My dad's got to be furious."

"He made a play, and he lost. Because he was wrong on every level. And you, my wife, have a big, bright future to think about."

Biting my lip, I did a quick dancing squee. "Okay, but after today. I've gotta go be responsible."

Down at the marina, I could see Miles and the other founding family representatives waiting out on the pier where we'd be launching the races. "I'm off to be a Sutter."

"You'll shine brilliantly. But if you get overwhelmed, I don't give a shit what Miles wants. I'll come. Just send me a text, and I'll be there."

"Where will you be?"

"Ed and the other Gray Beards are saving me a stool up at the Brewhouse. We were gonna hang out there during the regatta, and then I planned to come find you before the wreath-laying ceremony."

"You might as well just hang out and get comfortable until after the parade is over. I'll just be going from the cemetery back for that, and the float judging after. Then I'll be all yours."

He waggled his brows and slid his hands over my butt. "All mine?"

I wrapped my arm around his shoulders, rising up to touch my lips to his. "Every naked inch."

"I'm holding you to that, wife."

"You better. We have some serious celebrating to do." Kissing him quickly, I slipped past the barricade and went to do my duty.

CHAPTER 38

SAWYER

"You sure you don't want an actual beer, Malone?"

I looked over at Ed Cartwright, where he stood manning the taps at one end of the bar at OBX Brewhouse. Technically, this was entirely Bree's domain now, but he hadn't completely retired. During extra busy times, or simply when he felt like it, he resumed the position he'd occupied for more than thirty years, pulling pints and chatting up customers. As the afternoon had worn on, he'd kept my glass of ginger ale full. But my fingers were, even now, tapping the glass.

"Nah, I'm good."

I wasn't. Even without the kind of social anxiety Willa had, this was too damned many extra people on-island for my taste. There were too many unknown factors, and I didn't like being this far from my wife. Not that I thought anything was likely to happen to her in broad daylight in front of this many people, but the niggle of unease that had been in the back of my brain since her failed attempt to remember at Osprey Beach was burrowing deeper. Maybe I'd have felt better if I'd heard a damned thing from Jace or Dax, but all had been radio silent from that direction.

Cheers carried on the breeze from down by the water. Presumably the winner of the latest race had just crossed the finish line. I knew—because I'd gone to look twice—that Willa was in the thick of it, congratulating the winners and encouraging competitors. I didn't really understand why she needed to be there for all that. But she'd seemed to be holding up okay when I'd checked. So I kept returning to this barstool, occasionally engaging in conversation with Ed and the rest of his cronies, affectionately dubbed the Gray Beards by Bree.

"That there is a man itching to get back to his woman," Wally Briggs announced.

Duck Adams—so named for the unusual waddling gait he'd acquired after his hip replacement—nodded sagely. "Still in that newlywed phase. Can't go too long without gettin' some."

"Eh? Without gettin' what?" Milt Mitchell asked. The man was practically deaf as a post and refused to get a hearing aid.

"Lucky!" Duck shouted.

"Who's lucky?" Milt wanted to know.

Duck rolled his eyes. "Sawyer! Keep up, man."

Wally snagged a mozzarella stick off the plate of appetizers they were all sharing. "Pretty little thing like Willa... can't blame him for that. He's one lucky SOB."

"On account of the fact that I've known Willa since she was knee high to a grasshopper, I gotta ask y'all to stop," Cliff Clark insisted. He'd spent thirty years working as a pilot for the ferry company, so no doubt he still saw her as a little girl.

"What?" Duck protested. "We're just callin' it like it is. The boy's balls are getting bluer by the minute."

Bree came by, a bar towel tossed over her shoulder. "Maybe keep it down, fellas. I don't think Sawyer wants his love life broadcast for the entire bar to hear."

I scrubbed a hand down my face. God save me from nosy

old men. Not that they were entirely wrong, but that wasn't the reason I was about to crawl out of my skin.

When my phone finally vibrated in my pocket, I yanked it out, praying it was Willa texting me to come get her. Instead, it was an unfamiliar number flashing across the screen. I almost sent it to voicemail, in case it was a spam call. But at the last second I hit answer.

"Hello?"

"Sawyer. Thank God. I've been tryin' to get through for nearly an hour."

"Jace. Hang on. Let me get somewhere quieter." I looked around the bar for somewhere that wouldn't be as noisy as the dining room. The bathroom maybe?

Bree tapped me on the shoulder. "Take it back to the office."

"Thanks."

I edged around the end of the bar and pushed through the swinging door, into the kitchen. The staff gave me a curious look, but I just pointed to the phone and shut myself into the little office where Bree managed the books. I could still hear the clatter of dishes and the sizzle of food cooking, but it was a lot quieter than the main bar.

"Okay. Hey. Sorry about that. It's Founder's Day, and the island is nuts."

"Did Busby rope Willa into helping?"

"Oh yeah. She's currently judging the regatta. I'm at the Brewhouse. Do you have news?" Circling around the desk, I took the chair, absently scanning the room. My gaze zeroed in on the wall of photos, which actually included one of Bree with Ford in front of the original tavern from when they'd been about sixteen. Huh. I'd have laid money down that she'd want those all hidden away, if not destroyed. Maybe it was about the tavern itself and not him.

Jace's voice dragged my focus back to the call. "Yeah. Sorry it took so long for me to get back to you. I had to call in a bunch of favors before I found somebody who could dig far enough to get me the information I wanted. I was right. Nicholas Caldwell was military."

"Who the hell is Nicholas Caldwell?"

"The real name of Dr. Collin Caswell. He changed it after he retired from the military."

"Why would he do that?"

"Because of the kinds of missions he ran. The guy's a PsyOps specialist, and he was known for the kind of interrogations we just don't talk about."

My fingers curled into a fist. "What does that mean, exactly?"

"I don't know anything conclusively, but I think he did something to Willa. I think she saw something that night, and somebody had Caswell use his skills to keep her from remembering. Her reactions look far too much like fear-based conditioning."

I didn't want to know how he knew what that looked like. "You're saying she was tortured?"

"In a sense. Yeah."

If Jace was right, that confirmed all my suspicions that someone out there had a secret to protect. Someone who believed Willa was a threat.

"Who?" I demanded.

"I don't know. I don't know if he'd ever even been to Hatterwick. I'm betting he knows somebody who hired him or called in a favor, and they found some way to manipulate my parents into sending her to that particular facility."

"Well, where the hell is the guy now?" I'd find a way to make him tell me who'd hired him.

"Dead. Taken out about five years ago under suspicious circumstances. The official report was a car accident, but the redacted version is that his brake line was cut. He had a head-on collision with an 18-wheeler."

"Shit." Disappointment slid through me that the guy was already dead, and that it had likely been quick. The man had deserved to suffer.

"Guy with his background wouldn't have talked, even if he was still around. I'll keep digging, try to find out if he had some connection to the island."

"Dax is already looking, so maybe touch base with him, if you can."

"I'll do that. In the meantime, stick close to Willa. We don't know who the threat is, and I don't think she needs to be alone right now."

"Understood. I'll do whatever I have to in order to protect her."

"Thank you. And stay safe, brother."

"You, too."

I didn't give a good damn what festivities Miles had roped her into. I wanted to get her home.

On my way out of the kitchen, I snagged Bree. "I'm going to find Willa."

"Everything okay?"

"I don't know that it's not." In quick, quiet tones, I gave her the update. "I'm going to find her. Keep an eye out, would you? And loop in Gabi and Daniel if you see them. I'll try to text them, but the network isn't handling all these extra people well."

"Of course."

I paused just long enough to send the group a message, only to have it bounce back. Looked like, for now, I was on my own.

Stepping out of the bar, I wove my way to the marina, already formulating a reason for security to let me past the barricade. But when I got there, the barricades were gone, and so were the founding family committee members. Where the hell were they?

"Are you looking for your sweet bride?"

I turned toward the voice to find Marsha McCubbins, the town librarian. "Yes, ma'am. I was trying to catch her before the regatta was over. Do you know where she's gotten to?"

"Oh, you missed the end. Stevie Clapham squeaked out a win over Kelvin Armstrong, and he was fit to be tied, I tell you. Anyway, the mayor and the others have gone out to the cemetery for the ceremonial wreath laying."

Damn. I'd missed her. They'd be driven out to the cemetery on the outskirts of town. There was far less pomp and circumstance around the honoring of the actual ancestors who'd founded Hatterwick. Most folks weren't too keen on being present for the laying of the wreaths at those crypts.

I turned toward the north, as if that would somehow grant me x-ray vision to see through the wall-to-wall bodies. I was more than a mile from where we'd had to park, and given the crowds, it would take me longer to get out there and back than it would to simply wait for her to make it to the staging area for the parade. No matter how much I disliked it, tactically, it made more sense to sit tight.

"Thanks, Mrs. McCubbins. Do you know where they're organizing before the parade?"

As she gave me directions, I forced myself to stay calm.

Nothing had actually changed, other than having my suspicions confirmed.

It would be fine.

CHAPTER 39
WILLA

After the jubilant chaos of the regatta, the relative silence of the Sutter's Ferry cemetery was a welcome reprieve. This late in the day, I could feel the beta blocker starting to wear off, and I regretted not listening to Gabi and keeping a second dose on me, just in case. Exhaustion dragged at me, and I wondered how I was going to get through the parade and the float judging after. I just had to ride on the founders' float and wave a little. I could probably do that without issue. Then maybe I could come up with an excuse to skip the judging. I wouldn't have to fake not feeling well. A low-grade headache was sinking its claws into the base of my skull. I barely heard the commemorative words offered up by the head of the historical society.

Someone edged closer and murmured, "Are you okay?"

I glanced up to find Roland watching me with concern. I hadn't realized he'd joined the delegation for this part of proceedings, but it didn't surprise me. Despite not being from one of the founding families, he'd always taken an active role in the community. It was a big part of why Granddaddy had hired him.

"Just a headache. Today has been a lot," I whispered.

"Yeah, Miles is good at that," he muttered, tugging at his tie. He'd put on a suit jacket for the ceremony, and I was impressed with his dedication to formality. It was too damned hot for that many layers.

I held in a snort of laughter and turned my attention back to the proceedings as each of us representing a founding family walked to our ancestral crypt to leave a wreath. Because our forebears had come from the sea and been sustained by it, each one was created from elements that honored that tradition. Mine was made of a large curve of driftwood, twined with magnolia leaves and Queen Anne's lace, accented with seashells and starfish. At the base was a bow using the same shades of ivory and navy as the ferry company that had kept the island going all these years. I held onto it and waited my turn as the last of the founding families. Some of my compatriots made remarks. I elected to take a moment of silence as I stepped up to the marble tomb and gently laid the wreath in the designated holder.

In general, I didn't just come here. I had no real reason to. As a child, I'd come once a year with my grandparents to do maintenance around the tomb, cleaning up and planting fresh flowers, while they told me stories of my forebears. But I'd never really felt connected. My grandparents' remains weren't interred here. Their ashes had been scattered according to their wishes. But something about today felt different. Maybe it was the weight of the family mantle now resting on my shoulders.

I laid my hand flat against the sun-warmed stone and closed my eyes.

I'll do my best to honor your legacy. To protect what you gave us. To be worthy of the name Sutter.

When I stepped back, Miles launched in with his own over-the-top remarks about looking to the future while honoring the past. I didn't miss the satisfied look he exchanged with Anthony

Strand, who, so far as I was concerned, had no reason to be here. He wasn't from Hatterwick. It had been clear from every interaction with the man that he only saw the island as a payday, one that would destroy everything that made Hatterwick unique. The sooner I could get away from that guy, the better.

As the ceremony wrapped, and the small crowd began to head back to their vehicles, I tried to find some enthusiasm for the remaining events of the day. Or even enough to make myself get back into the bigass Suburban with the other found family members. But that meant more of Miles and his sanctimonious nonsense.

Roland followed my gaze. "You want to ride back with me? You've got the parade next, right? I've got a pass to park near the staging area."

The sense of relief was instant. "That'd be great. Thanks."

I followed him to his sedan, sliding into the front passenger seat. My temples were really starting to throb now. I rubbed at the acupressure point between my thumb and pointer finger, trying to make it abate.

Roland cast me a sidelong glance. "Are you sure you're up to this? You're looking a little pale there. I could run you home right quick and make excuses to Miles and the rest of them."

I forced a wan smile. "I appreciate the offer of an out, but I agreed to do this. I'm going to stick to my commitment. No matter how much I'd rather go crawl into a dark hole and nap. Besides, you absolutely do not have time to drive me all the way to the north end of the island and get back to stage the parade. I think we're already going to be a little late."

As if to punctuate the point, his phone rang. He answered on the car's speakerphone. "This is O'Shea."

"It's Andy. Where are you? The natives are getting restless down here."

"On my way back from the cemetery. I was at the wreath laying."

"Staging was supposed to start ten minutes ago."

"It'll be fine. I'm not that far out."

"I—Somebody grab those banners before they blow away! This was *your* job, O'Shea."

Irritation flickered over Roland's face. "I gave you a copy of the list with the order of the floats for just this eventuality. All you have to do is ensure they're lined up in that order. I'll be there as quick as I can."

"No, no, the high school band goes *after* the Shriners. This is like herding a bunch of feral cats."

"Deal with it, Andy," Roland growled.

Pain exploded in my head, so fast and hard, my vision went white. Nausea roiled in my stomach and my head throbbed from where I'd been struck. I struggled to open my eyes to see who was speaking.

"Deal with it, Anderson."

"Man, I didn't sign on for this. I'm not killin' no girl."

"Then why the fuck didn't you leave her where you found her instead of bringing her here?"

"I thought she'd wake up and follow us."

"So instead you've created a witness and a liability."

I managed to pry my eyes open the barest bit and spotted a tall, wiry man arguing with someone. "Why can't they just take her, too?"

The other man gestured in my direction. "Do you have any idea who this is? No, that wasn't the agreement. You provide the package as ordered. Nothing more, nothing less." I could see only his back. Average build. Dark hair. Voice of authority.

"I'm still not killin' her. I'm no murderer."

"Take care of her, or I'll take care of you."

"No. I'm not—"

In the next second, lightning flashed, and Joe Anderson

slumped to the ground, blood trickling down his face from a round hole just above his vacant eyes.

The scream rose up in my chest, fighting to get out. But I had to hold it in. Had to keep them from knowing I was conscious.

The shooter lowered his gun and spoke to someone else. "Put them both on board. If you're squeamish about getting the job done, then just get out in open water and throw her overboard. The ocean will take care of the rest. I've got to go deal with this bullshit."

Rough hands grabbed me under the arms and began to drag me toward a boat.

"No. No!"

"Willa! Miss Sutter, snap out of it!"

I blinked, and the boat, the night, and the dead man were gone. Instead, I was curled into a ball, pressed against the passenger door of Roland O'Shea's car, my chest heaving with uneven breaths.

Roland stared at me from the driver's seat, concern written all over his face. "Willa? Are you okay?"

Terror still had me in its grip.

Because I'd just had a full-blown flashback to Joe Anderson's murder.

Where someone had been intent on killing me, too.

Roland didn't try to touch me again. "Panic attack?" His voice was gentle.

I managed a small nod, still too shaken to be embarrassed that I'd lost it in front of him. Again.

"Do you want to get out of the car? Do you need some fresh air? Or I can take you straight home?"

I swallowed. "S... Sawyer. F... f... find, Sawyer."

"Okay. We'll find him." Moving slowly, presumably so as not to spook me, he put the car in gear and pulled out onto the road.

I lowered my pounding head to my knees and tried to control my breathing, even as I struggled to hold on to the details that were already trying to fade.

I'd seen Joe Anderson murdered, and from what it sounded like, it had been a case of wrong place, wrong time. They hadn't been meant to take me. They'd been taking someone else. Gwen? I wouldn't have left the party with anyone else. Someone had attacked me. Struck me from behind. Had it all been to take her? Why? Who? The man giving the orders had clearly known who I was and been angry I'd been dragged into whatever was going on. But he hadn't cared enough to see that I lived. What did that mean? Did I know who he was? Had I been interacting with him on Hatterwick all these years, blissfully unaware and protected by my damaged memory?

I didn't know. But clearly things were finally starting to shake loose, and I needed Sawyer to ground me before the next wave hit and I drowned under the weight of my own memories.

CHAPTER 40

SAWYER

T he staging area for the parade was absolute chaos. I couldn't seem to find anyone in charge to ask where the founders' float was supposed to be. Was it meant to be up front? At the end? Hell if I knew. I tried to find Roland, since I remembered he was supposed to be part of the volunteer wrangling crew, but there was no sign of him or of Willa anywhere. She wasn't answering any of my texts—the ones that went through, anyway. I hadn't even been able to get a phone call out since I'd spoken to Jace, and my nerves were humming with anxiety.

Had she been overwhelmed by the crowds and noise and found somewhere quiet to reset? Had something triggered one of her panic attacks? Had someone gotten to her while she was alone? Or had she simply been dragged into yet another endless meeting over Founders' Day bullshit? Any of those scenarios felt possible, especially since I hadn't seen our politically minded mayor.

The parade route itself was less than a mile, so either way, the whole event wouldn't last that long. After that, Willa would be free to do whatever she wanted. But I didn't want to wait that long to find her and confirm she was alright. I needed to lay eyes on her. To reassure myself that she was unharmed. Maybe if I made it back to the Brewhouse or the bakery and got on their Wi-Fi, I could get a call to connect.

"Get those costumes distributed correctly! The pirates go on the pirate ship float, not mingling with the mermaids. And who authorized the flamethrower on the dragon float?! That's a safety hazard. Take it off right now!" The orders came from a harried looking guy who kept glancing at a folded paper in his hand. A checklist maybe?

He was the closest thing I'd seen to someone in charge.

"Hey, man, have you seen Willa Sutter anywhere?"

The man scowled. "Do I look like I'm in charge of her social calendar?"

Tamping down my own irritation, I kept an even tone. "She's supposed to be riding on the founding families float in the parade."

"Dude, I haven't even seen the founding families float yet, let alone the mayor, who's supposed to be at the head of it. In case you didn't notice, I'm dealing with total chaos here."

"What about Roland O'Shea? Have you seen him?"

If possible, the scowl got darker. "He didn't show for his assigned volunteer duties. That's part of why we're in this mess. Said he was on his way back from the cemetery and that whole bullshit wreath laying ceremony. He'll probably insist he couldn't get through traffic as his excuse for bailing." The guy shouted at someone over my shoulder. "The parade steps off in fifteen minutes! I asked for final inspection forty-five minutes ago. Let's move it, people!"

I didn't like that all three of them were missing. It might be nothing. The roads were hella congested with all the people who'd showed up for the festival. It was possible they simply hadn't made it back yet. Or...

That 'or' had me shoving through the crowd back to the

Brewhouse. That was the last place I'd been able to get decent cell service with so many extra people on the island overwhelming the network. I scanned the faces around me as I moved, looking for anyone familiar. Despite the fact that I knew half the people who lived on this island, it seemed like everyone I saw was a stranger. I'd give just about anything to have my brothers as backup just now. But I was in this on my own.

By the time I made it to the Brewhouse, I was practically running. If possible, the dining room was even more full than when I'd left. I wove my way through the tables toward the equally crammed bar.

A hand shot out to grab my arm as I squeezed past. "Sawyer!"

Gabi yanked me into an empty seat. "Hey. Did you find Willa?"

"No. She hasn't made it back from the wreath laying ceremony, and she should have by now."

"Bree filled us in," Daniel said. "You think somethin's gone wrong?"

"I don't know. I hope not. Signal's been shit all day with all these people. I came back here to try to call her on the Wi-Fi."

When my phone vibrated in my pocket, I yanked it out so fast I nearly dropped it. But it wasn't Willa's name on the screen. It was Dax.

Please let this be answers.

"Dax? Can you hear me?"

"Barely. Where the hell are you? Sounds like a rager of a party."

I shoved a finger into my other ear to block out some of the background noise. "I'm at a bar. And there's a parade starting outside any minute. Tell me you've got news."

"I've got better than news. I think I've tracked down the connection between Dr. Caswell and Hatterwick Island."

Every muscle in my body tensed. "What is it?"

"Caswell—or I guess technically Caldwell—attended Georgetown University prior to getting recruited into his elite military unit. I cross-referenced school records with locals from the island and only managed to hit on one overlap—a guy who was at Georgetown at the same time as Caswell."

"Who?"

"An attorney by the name of Roland O'Shea."

My gut clenched. "Roland O'Shea? Are you absolutely sure?"

"Yeah. You know the guy?"

"He's been Willa's family's attorney for decades." He'd been in the middle of their business for years. Privy to all the family secrets. He'd been a trusted confidant. One who'd seemed to be on our side from the beginning when her parents had challenged the inheritance. "Is there any definitive proof he and the doctor knew each other?"

"They were on the rowing team together. Sending you a photo."

The image came through a few moments later. When it finally loaded, I saw Dax had circled two men, with their arms thrown companionably around each other's shoulders. I recognized one as a younger version of O'Shea. I could only presume the other was Caswell.

"I realize it's not precisely a smoking gun," Dax admitted. "There may be some other connection I haven't found yet, but the fact that they were there at the same time and definitely knew each other seems like too big a coincidence to ignore. I figured you'd want a heads up."

And O'Shea was also missing. He'd been at the cemetery with Willa, away from most of the crowds. I had a real bad feeling about this.

"Thanks, man. I've gotta go."

"Did I hear you say Roland O'Shea? The family attorney?" Gabi asked.

"Yeah. Looks like he's connected to the doctor who treated Willa."

"But he's done so much for her since her grandfather died. Do you really think he'd hurt her?"

"I don't know. I hope I'm wrong. But I couldn't find either of them at the staging area. I'd much rather go in with metaphorical guns blazing and have to make some apologies than risk not taking action at all."

"Whatcha need us to do?" Daniel asked.

I tried to think it through. If Willa had remembered something incriminating—or even if O'Shea suspected she might have—where would he take her? His office was in the middle of all the festival chaos. His house was inside the village proper, so I didn't think they'd go there, either. Which left what? Sutter House? No one was up there but Roy. I didn't see him risking a confrontation with a loyal pit bull. He'd want somewhere private. But private for what? To kill her? To scare her? If he'd had something to do with her ending up under Caswell's questionable treatment, maybe he'd lean into those same tactics to traumatize her back into forgetting whatever she might have remembered.

Where better to do that than where it had all begun?

Osprey Beach ought to be deserted, with everyone gathered on the south side of the island for the parade and upcoming fireworks.

It was a stretch. I knew it. And if I was wrong, it could lead to a dangerous waste of precious time. But if I was right...

I turned to Daniel. "Do you have a boat?"

CHAPTER 41

WILLA

My head ached, and I was desperate for a dark, quiet room and the oblivion of sleep. Who knew how long it would take us to find Sawyer in the chaos of the Founders' Day crowd? Then we'd have to make our way back to his truck and drive all the way home. Even thinking of the effort made me want to whimper.

Maybe I could get a text out and tell him to meet us somewhere. Lifting my head, I peered into the floorboard for my purse, but it wasn't there. Had I left it back at the cemetery? I started to ask, then I registered where we were. Roland was driving northwest across the island, in the exact opposite direction from Sutter's Ferry.

"Where are we going? This isn't the way to town."

He flashed a kind smile. "You're still pretty shaken up. I thought it would be beneficial to go somewhere quiet for a little bit, so you have a chance to reset before you have to deal with the rest of the Founders' Day stuff."

"We're gonna miss the parade." We'd already been late.

His shoulders twitched in a dismissive shrug. "Miles will get over it."

On the surface, his logic was sound. It was a kind and accommodating offer. It wasn't as if I wanted to go back for the parade in my current shape. But something didn't feel right. I wondered if it was my own paranoia in the wake of the flashback. Then he took another turn, onto a familiar road leading to the Atlantic side of the island.

"Are you taking me to Osprey Beach?" My voice came out admirably calm, considering that my heart was picking up speed again.

"Yeah, everybody on the island is down in the village, so that'll be nice and quiet for you. Peaceful."

There was nothing wrong with anything he'd said, but my inner alarms were clanging. Maybe it was simply that my beta blocker had worn off. There was nothing to counter my natural reaction to coming here.

You made it through that entire failed memory retrieval attempt. You can make it through this. He's just looking out for you, same as he's done since Granddaddy died.

But there were other places he could have taken me that were closer and still quiet, away from people. Why Osprey Beach?

As we neared the beach, he looked over, his brow furrowed. "Is your headache getting worse?"

I hadn't said anything about having a headache. Of course, I absolutely had one, and maybe that was obvious. But he wasn't a doctor, and somehow, he seemed way too interested in the answer to the question.

The closer we got to the beach, the faster the panic rose. I gripped my fingers together so tight, the knuckles turned bone white. I tried to hold it together. Tried to breathe through the fear. But it was too much.

"Turn around," I whispered.

He cast another worried look from across the car. "Are you okay?"

"No, I can't go here. Please turn around."

He didn't turn around, his focus more on me than the road. "Why? What's wrong?"

"Please." The word came out more as a wheeze now. I pressed a hand to my chest, willing it to loosen.

His face lightened with dawning realization. "I guess it's hard for you to come here after what happened that night."

Fresh on the heels of the flashback, my blood chilled. "What are you talking about?" I struggled to maintain any sort of cool.

"Where you drowned. It was somewhere over this way, wasn't it?"

Something in his gaze was all wrong. His features were set in a mask of concern, but I wasn't buying it. Every inner alarm I had was blaring *not safe*. I had to find a way out of this car.

He kept staring at me, as if he expected to see... something. As I stared back, he finally sighed in obvious disappointment. "It doesn't work anymore. I should have known it would wear off eventually."

I shook my head, not understanding. "What doesn't work anymore?"

His hands tightened on the wheel, the leather beneath his fingers creaking from his grip. "Your conditioning."

"My... what?" What the hell was he talking about?

Roland continued as if I hadn't spoken. "You remember, don't you?"

"Remember what?" But I knew. Because I had remembered —at least part of it. My brain was busy peeling away the years. Roland had been a classmate of my mother's. He wasn't as old as I'd originally thought he was. Twelve years ago, he could've been slimmer, his hair fully dark. It could have been him on the beach that night with the gun.

"I didn't want to do this. I never wanted you to be involved. That idiot Anderson made a mistake." He shook his head. "But

I couldn't risk you sharing what you might have seen or heard. Then you miraculously survived, courtesy of your devoted husband to be. He clearly loved you, even then. Honestly, I was glad you survived. But without any idea what you might remember, steps had to be taken. And it's worked so well all these years because Collin is very good at what he does. Or was."

I struggled to process all the implications of everything he was saying. "You know my psychiatrist?"

"Knew, yes. God rest his soul. We were good friends back at Georgetown. I knew he was exactly the right person to help with my... well, *your* little problem. That's why I made the suggestion to your parents. He was a memory specialist, after all."

Oh my God. This man was the reason I'd been institutionalized for two years. And my doctor had done something to manipulate my memories, conditioning me not to remember.

But Roland assumed that I'd remembered everything. Whether I had or not, he'd revealed enough himself that it made me a threat. No way was he bringing me out here, away from everyone on the island, with any intention of letting me live.

We were nearly to Osprey Beach. No one knew where I was. I had to do... something. But what?

"I was really hoping that this would be a reset. That you would finally go back to the way things were." He looked over at me with an avuncular affection. "I have a terrible soft spot for you, being Vicky's daughter and Henry's granddaughter. You're really special, Willa. I'm sorry about this."

He shifted in his seat as the car slowed, reaching for something inside the suit jacket it was too hot to wear.

Gun.

I didn't stop to think, didn't question. I opened my door and hurled myself out of the car.

I hit the shoulder of the road hard and rolled. The impact drove all the breath from my already struggling lungs, but hearing the screech of tires behind me, I scrambled to my feet and began to run toward the trees, barely registering the pain in my arm from where I'd landed.

"Willa! Don't make this harder on yourself than it has to be!"

I didn't answer, and when next he shouted, he'd lost the kind, gentle tone he'd always used with me.

"Damn it, girl! Come back here."

I flinched as I heard a gunshot, and bark sprayed from a tree not two feet from where I passed. Fresh terror dumped adrenaline into my system, and I ran faster, hurling myself into the trees, dodging and weaving through underbrush. I'd have cover here. I knew this place better than anyone else on the island. The sun was already setting. If I could just stay ahead of him, lose him once it got fully dark, I could get somewhere safe.

But where? There was nothing at this end of the island but Sutter House, and it was miles from here. My only hope was to lose him in the thick of the trees and pray that Sawyer came looking for me before it was too late.

CHAPTER 42

SAWYER

The Zodiac zipped over the waves as Daniel brought us around the south end of Hatterwick, past the lighthouse, then opened the throttle. I kept my weight low, instinctively balancing with the bounce of the boat and willing him to find some extra speed.

Something was wrong. I knew it down to the very marrow of my bones. I just hoped I'd guessed right. If O'Shea hadn't taken her to Osprey Beach, I didn't know where to look next. I didn't think he'd be able to get her off-island without someone seeing. But if he had his own boat, all bets were off. He could get her away, and no one would have any idea where they'd gone. But then what? The moment he showed back up in Sutter's Ferry, there'd be questions. He had a life here. A respected place in the community. He wouldn't want to jeopardize those. So he probably wouldn't take her off-island.

I just had to hope that he chose the same area for all the reasons he must've chosen it years ago. I had no idea what the hell he'd been doing out there. No idea what connection he might have had to Joe Anderson's murder or Gwen Busby's disappearance. But if he'd gone so far as to see Willa effectively tortured and brainwashed to keep from remembering what had happened, chances were that whatever was trapped in her mind was incriminating as hell.

As I tried to wrap my brain around all of it, I began to question and doubt myself. What if I was wrong? What if he was exactly what he appeared to be? What if his connection with Collin Caswell was a total fluke? What if the danger was really from some other quarter, and O'Shea had simply taken Willa home?

The sight of his car right at the edge of Osprey Beach put those doubts to rest. It was parked cattywampus, with the doors hanging open, as if he'd gotten out in a hurry. Like maybe his captive had run.

I waved Daniel toward the beach, and he took us in.

The moment we'd landed, I was over the side, sprinting toward the car. A warning bell dinged, indicating the keys were still in it. Peering inside, I spotted Willa's purse in the backseat.

"She was here." But there was no sign of her now, nor of O'Shea. "I don't think the doors would be open like this if he had her under control. I think she bolted." Which meant she'd gotten away from him, at least for a little while.

Use that big brain of yours, Wren. Stay ahead of him.

"What you want us to do?" Daniel asked.

I tried to put myself in Willa's shoes. If she'd run from him, she'd realized she was in danger. We were right by the woods that had always been her safe place. She'd have gone there. Probably found a place to hide.

I had no idea if O'Shea was armed. It seemed safer to err on the assumption than he was. Daniel could handle himself, but I didn't want Gabi put in harm's way. No way would she stay behind. We were losing the light fast. If Willa was thinking clearly, she might try to double back or lose O'Shea. But if she was riding instinct, I suspected she'd aim for where the horses might be.

"Split up. You two head north by the beach. Aim to cut into the woods where the crime scene tape is. I'll go in from here. Be safe. We don't know if he's armed." And we had absolutely nothing on us.

But I couldn't think about that as I plunged into the woods, praying I'd made the right call.

How much of a lead did they have? Five minutes? Half an hour? My brain was all too happy to offer up a multitude of terrifying things that could happen in that span. I wanted to run. To pour on all the speed until I found them both. But I forced myself to maintain a steady pace, hunting for the trail in the failing light. Racing through here like a bull in a china shop would just announce I was coming. If O'Shea was paying attention, that seemed like a good way to get shot, or worse.

I was on Sutter land by now. There were no formal trails here, only what amounted to game trails worn in by the horses. Would Willa take the path of least resistance? Or would she stay off them in hopes of confusing her pursuer?

Instinct drove me north, toward the deepest part of the woods, and it was finally there that I heard it.

"Willa. Come out now. I know you can hear me."

O'Shea. And he hadn't found her yet.

I crept carefully toward his voice. If I could get the drop on him, I could immobilize him before he could do worse than whatever he'd already done.

"Come now, Willa. You don't want one of these horses you love so much to get hurt on your behalf, do you?"

I'd reached the edge of the clearing. The same one where Willa had brought me after the hurricane. O'Shea stood in the middle, near the pond. The dull gleam of a gun barrel flashed in his hand. With all the limbs down from the storm, there'd be no sneaking up on him. There was simply too much debris to step on or try to dodge. Beyond him, I could see part of the herd, with several of them clustered in the trees. Because I'd seen them with Willa before, I suspected she was in the center, crouched down between equine bodies. They shifted uneasily, focus on O'Shea.

"What did you do with Gwen?"

I closed my eyes at the sound of her voice, both relieved and terrified that she'd revealed herself.

"I did nothing with her. I just saw that she was delivered where she was supposed to be delivered."

Delivered? What the hell did that mean? Had Willa remembered something, or was she guessing?

"Delivered to who? For what?"

"That was never my concern. I just handled logistics. Look, I told you, I never wanted to hurt you. But I've worked too long and too hard for the life I have, to lose it simply because you were in the wrong place at the wrong time."

"Is that supposed to make me feel better? I thought you were a friend. Someone that I could trust."

"Well, I was. So long as you couldn't remember, I was happy to continue on as advisor to you about the family estate, exactly as I have for your grandfather for decades." He paused, his lips curving a little. "And I truly did enjoy going toe-to-toe with your family's lawyers to hand your father his ass. He had a long-standing deal with Anthony Strand, you know. Full development of all this beautiful land. They tried it before, years ago, but of course Henry wouldn't go for it. So John thought he'd simply wait the old man out and pounce when he died. But he didn't count on you. Well done there."

"And what's supposed to happen to the estate if you kill me?"

"Oh, well, I'm not actually sure, since Sawyer signed that post-nup. I don't suppose you've already written up a will? Young people never think to do such things so early in a marriage. I expect it'll be up to the courts to decide whether it goes to your parents or to your brother. But don't worry, I'll do what I can to try to save it from the vultures. I don't want this land developed any more than you do. It's really beautiful here."

He lost the conversational tone. "Now, come out, or I'm shooting this foal here in the front." Pivoting, he took aim at a baby that couldn't be more than a few months old, who huddled around its mother's legs.

Fuck.

I kept edging around the clearing, trying to get behind him and find an angle I could rush him. But there were so many downed trees, I didn't think I could move fast enough to approach undetected.

O'Shea pulled back the hammer on the gun.

"Okay, okay. I'm coming out. Don't shoot." Willa eased out from the middle of the herd, putting herself firmly in front of the baby. "Leave them out of this."

Of course she wouldn't allow one of them to suffer to save herself. Brave, stubborn, infuriating woman. She didn't balk at the gun trained directly on her. At this range, O'Shea couldn't miss hitting something vital.

"Goodbye, Willa. I truly am sorry."

"No!" I exploded out of the trees.

The gun swung in my direction, and I braced for the burn of a bullet.

Something screamed. An unholy shriek of fury that was anything but human. A blur of gray exploded into the clearing, moving almost faster than I could see. O'Shea screamed as the stallion barreled into him. Triton reared with another scream and brought his hooves down, down, down, trampling him until O'Shea had gone silent.

Jesus Christ. There was no question he was dead.

I wanted to run to Willa, but given the enraged animal between us, I stayed exactly where I was, not moving.

Triton tossed his head, pawing at the body, as if to make absolutely sure the threat was dealt with before he turned in the direction of the rest of his herd and Willa. He took a few dancing steps closer, finally settling under her touch.

"I wasn't going to let anything happen to your baby." She pressed her cheek to his. "Thank you for saving me. Thank you for saving him." Looking at me, she held out a hand, wiggling her fingers in a *come here* gesture.

Remembering how she'd approached him, eyes averted, I eased my way toward them until I was close enough to close my fingers around hers. She pulled me in.

"This is Sawyer. He's mine the way they're all yours."

I held perfectly still as the stallion sniffed me, then finally bumped my shoulder.

"That means he wants a scratch," she murmured.

The hand I lifted to Triton's neck shook with adrenaline. "Thank you for protecting her. Again."

The stallion bobbed his head as if to say, "Anytime." Then he called to the rest of his herd and led them away through the trees.

As they disappeared from sight, I pulled Willa into my arms. "Fuck. Are you okay?"

I could feel her shaking against me as her own arms wrapped around me. "Yeah. God. What are you even doing here?"

"I came to find you. Jace finished looking into your doctor off-island. He was former military, with some kind of PsyOps specialty. O'Shea was the connection to the island."

"PsyOps? So that's what he meant about me being conditioned not to remember."

"Did you remember? All that stuff you said about Gwen?"

"Some of it. I—"

Gabi and Daniel emerged from the east side of the clearing. Gabi's eyes were wide, trained on the bloody mess that was Roland O'Shea's body. "Holy shit. What the hell just happened?"

"Karma," Willa said flatly. "And we got another piece of the mystery. Rios wasn't the last person to see Gwen alive. I think I was."

CHAPTER 43
WILLA

"Let me get this straight." Chief Carson stared hard at me from across the table in the interrogation room. "You're telling me that Roland O'Shea, member of the Kiwanis Club, volunteer at the church, and general upstanding member of the Sutter's Ferry community, abducted and tried to kill you?"

Despite the anxiety twisting in my gut, I didn't even flinch. I'd vowed to tell my truth. All of it. "Yes. You should find a bullet lodged in one of the trees not far from where his car was left, from where he shot at me when I managed to escape."

"I'll have my people look for it. And why, exactly, would he do this?"

"Because my memory is a threat."

"Explain."

Once the dam had cracked, I'd been able to remember a little bit more. "Twelve years ago, I left that bonfire with Gwen Busby. We went into the woods to the north of Osprey Beach. I don't know why. I can't remember that part. But while we were there, we were attacked. When I came to, I was on the beach and someone was arguing." I repeated the details I could remember from the flashback.

"When Joe Anderson refused to kill me, Roland shot him."

"You saw that?"

"I saw someone from behind. I didn't know for sure it was Roland until he admitted it himself. Based on what he said tonight, I was never supposed to be there. Gwen was the target. Whose target, or for what, I don't know. But we were both put on a boat. Roland told whoever else was there to take me out to sea and toss me overboard. That was how I ended up in the water that night. I wasn't supposed to survive."

Carson's eyes narrowed. "If all this is true, why didn't you come forward before?"

I'd expected this, so I was ready. "Chief Carson, I literally drowned. My heart stopped. If you'll recall, I was in the hospital for quite some time after Sawyer rescued me. I didn't remember anything at all around that night to begin with. And Roland apparently recommended that my parents send me to a psychiatrist he knew with a specialty in memory recovery."

I told him the rest, about Collin Caswell and my two-year institutionalization, and all the efforts made to ensure I didn't remember a damned thing.

"I didn't remember for years. I couldn't even go near the area without falling into a panic attack or a migraine. But once we found Joe Anderson's remains, I guess that started unlocking things. I started deliberately pushing. It's still not clear, but Roland assumed I'd remembered everything. That all the conditioning I'd been put through had been broken. I guess he started talking because he had no intention of letting me live. But I escaped."

He listened without comment as I went through the last of it, all the way to the point where Triton charged him.

"That animal is a menace."

"No. He was only defending his baby." And me, but I didn't

think I needed to say anything else to challenge his willingness to suspend disbelief. "The horses are wild animals, and so long as they're left alone, they don't cause any problems. Roland was the one waving a gun around, threatening to kill them."

Carson scrubbed a hand down his face, for once looking as old as his almost sixty years. "I don't even know where to start with what to do with all this."

"You start by digging into Roland O'Shea. He was working with someone. He said he was in charge of logistics. He referred to Gwen as a package. She was on that boat, and I think it's not too far out there to assume she left here alive. To where or for what, I don't know." I'd had some time to think about it while the police had secured the scene. "It sounds a hell of a lot like she could have been trafficked. And I know that if that's true, the likelihood of finding her is slim. But you have to try. This is the first lead we've had in years."

I had to clamp down on the sudden surge of grief. If only I'd remembered sooner, when the trail was relatively fresh. Maybe they'd have been able to find something and bring her home.

The chief of police stared at me for a long time, and I was fully aware that the only reason he wasn't investigating me was because I was a Sutter. Well, that and the fact that it was pretty hard to argue with the very clear hoof-shaped wounds all over what remained of Roland's body and the gun with his prints that had been found nearby.

At last, he nodded. "I'll look into it. I don't know what there's left to find after all this time, but I'll sure as shit try. The Busbys deserve that."

At least we could agree on something.

"You're free to go, Miss Sutter. I'm sure I'll be in touch as things move forward, but for now, go on home. You've had... an eventful night."

There was little enough left of it, and all I wanted was to shower and fall face-first into bed.

I stepped out of the interrogation room. Sawyer shot up from the chair where he'd been waiting.

"Are you okay?"

I nodded. "We can go now."

His hand closed around mine, quieting the lingering unease from the prolonged questioning. I'd have more processing to do later, but for now, my brain had hit the point of overload, and I was on autopilot.

When we stepped out of the police station, I saw the sky was already beginning to lighten. It truly had been a long night. We walked through the quiet, empty streets of the village to where we'd left his truck a few blocks away.

"Did he give you any grief?"

"Not as much as I expected. I know he's struggling to believe some of what I told him. But he's promised to look into the boat connection regarding Gwen's disappearance."

"Are you planning to try to dig more, see if you can remember anything else?"

"I don't know yet. Now that we know what was done to me, I probably do need some treatment to work through it. Maybe something else will come of that. Maybe not. But I think I remembered the essentials. For now, that's all I can do."

"It's a lot."

The sun was just peeking over the horizon as we reached the truck. Sawyer pulled me back against him as he leaned against the door, and we both watched as the watercolor wash of sunrise painted the sky.

"Roland is dead, and the threat from your parents to your inheritance is dealt with. It seems like all the threats are over," Sawyer murmured.

"Seems like. I expect it'll take me a while to accept that."

"True enough." He hesitated. "You know, something occurred to me while you were in with Carson. If Roland lied about all this stuff, is it possible he lied about your parents and all the shit they were pulling about the estate? He had the skill to fabricate all of it."

I blinked, taking that in. "I don't know. It would be easy enough to check to see if anything was legitimately filed, but honestly, I don't care. We're estranged for a reason. They kept me locked up rather than listen to me when I said something was wrong. I can't ever forgive them for that. Maybe I'll change my mind someday in the future, but I doubt it."

"Fair enough. What do you want now?"

Sucking in a breath, I turned in his arms and slid my hands up his chest. "Other than a shower and sleeping for the next fifteen hours, I want to put all of this behind me and move forward in this life with you. No threat, no subterfuge. I just want to be in love and have our shot at happily ever after."

His lips curved as he dipped his head down to mine. "I figure it's about damned time."

EPILOGUE
SAWYER

I stepped out of the rain and into OBX Brewhouse, pausing to wipe my wet boots on the mat inside the entryway.

The hostess smiled from her station, where she was wiping down menus. "Hey Sawyer. Willa's in her usual booth."

"Thanks, Carly."

Compared to high tourist season, the bar was mostly empty, though more locals would trickle in now that it was after five. Those who wanted to brave the January cold for a drink or not having to fend for themselves for dinner. I spotted my wife in a booth along the far wall, fingers tapping away on the keys of her laptop, as she often did these days, working on grants or communicating with the team of environmental scientists who were in the process of doing the baseline study for what would ultimately be the wildlife refuge. Roy curled at her feet beneath the table. Beyond them, rain drizzled down the awning windows that were closed for the season, and we were already well on our way toward dark. I looked forward to spring and longer, drier days.

Despite the Airpods signaling Do Not Interrupt to the world at large, she looked up, as if sensing my approach. Those gorgeous hazel eyes brightened, and her smile spread wide. Damn, the sight of that unreserved joy made my heart skip a beat. I didn't think it would ever get old, but I hoped for another fifty or sixty years to test the theory.

"You're back! I wasn't expecting you until the last ferry."

"Got done a little earlier than expected."

She slid out of the booth and straight into my arms, automatically lifting her mouth for a hello kiss I was more than happy to provide. With a contented hum, she eased back, eyes fluttering open again. "Is early good?"

"Turns out early is great and, for once, bureaucracy was on our side." I pulled a folded envelope out of my pocket. "I officially have my contractor's license."

"That's amazing!"

"I've still got a few 'T's to cross and 'I's to dot, but this was the big one." And good thing, too. I already had four people I'd talked to about coming onto my crew who were raring to go.

"Come, sit down. We should celebrate." Willa sat back in the booth, and I slid in right next to her. No reason to be all the way on the opposite side of the table.

She grinned at me and brushed another kiss to my cheek.

"How's your work going today?"

"Going well. I've been here since just after lunch. I managed to get in the zone and almost finished the trolley grant. If we can manage to land it, I think it'll make a big difference to traffic and congestion during high season."

"That'll put you on the mayor's good side."

"It'd be nice if something did. He sure doesn't like my controlling the trust's purse strings." Her focus swung across the restaurant.

Following her gaze, I spotted Drew and Kelly McNamara, Hoyt's younger brother and sister-in-law, and their little girl, Isabelle, who was enthusiastically conducting the music on the sound system with a curly fry. From this angle, I could just see the obvious curve of a baby bump beneath Kelly's sweater.

When Willa just kept quietly watching, lips curved into a faint smile, I finally nudged her shoulder with mine. "What is it?"

"I was just thinking how nice they all look together."

With the chaotic beginning to our marriage, we'd never had a conversation about kids. Not wanting to ruin the easy mood, I tried to keep my tone casual. "Yeah? Is that something you think you want? Kids? Family? The whole shebang?"

Willa went quiet, but I understood this was a reflective silence as she really considered her answer. "I never thought I did. But I didn't think I wanted marriage, either, after the example that was set for me by my parents. I feel like you and I are doing pretty great at that." She squeezed my arm and leaned in for a partial hug. "I think we'd actually make pretty good parents, because we wouldn't make the same mistakes that ours did. Obviously, we'll make our own, but I think we'll do a better job." Her cheeks pinked, and she dropped her gaze to the table briefly before bringing it back to mine. "Is that something you might want?"

I loved this woman so damned much, and she had no idea how much I'd been thinking about exactly this for the past six months. Smiling, I cupped her cheek. "Yeah. With you, anything and everything. Whenever you're ready."

With a little laugh, she tipped her face into my palm. "I don't think I'm quite ready yet. I'd rather be just us for a while. But someday, in the maybe not too long, too distant future." Her eyes sparkled. "After we've had plenty of time to... practice."

Laughing, I took her mouth in another hungry kiss, all too ready to get to that practice.

"Okay, you two. I've got no problem with Willa setting up a

mobile office here, but I draw the line at y'all making it a second bedroom."

My wife eased back, rolling her lips in on themselves to hold in another smile. "Sorry, Bree. We're celebrating."

Bree went brows up. "Oh? There an announcement you want to make?"

"Not *that* kind of announcement." There went those pink cheeks again. Damn, my wife was cute. "Sawyer just got his contractor's license. He's all official."

"No shit? Congratulations, Sawyer." She offered me a fist bump. "You want a celebratory drink?"

"Let's have a couple glasses of whatever y'all's latest creation is."

"You got it."

As she turned to head back to the bar, a motion by the door drew my attention. A teenage girl with a backpack over one shoulder looked around the room. I was shit at judging age. She might've been anywhere from thirteen to sixteen. It was hard to tell, these days. I didn't know her, but there was something about her that seemed oddly familiar. I just couldn't put my finger on what.

She moved toward the bar, and Bree called out, "Can I help you, hon?"

The girl bellied up to the bar, leaning forward on her elbows. "I hope so, I'm looking for somebody."

"You meeting your party here?" Bree made her own quick scan of the room, obviously trying to place her with one of the groups already seated.

"No, not like that. I'm looking for my father. He lives here on the island. I thought, this being such a small place, that maybe someone here would know him."

"We can sure give it our best go. Who's your daddy, hon?"

The girl straightened, cocking her chin in a gesture that had hair rising up along my arms.

"Ford Donoghue."

OH BUDDY, Ford's got some serious 'splainin' to do! His book, *All Along The Watchtower,* releases March 14, 2025 and is already available for preorder. In the meantime, you can get an additional glimpse of Sawyer and Willa's happily ever after (along with cameos from all the Wayward Sons) in their bonus epilogue! Grab your copy here: https://harperjacksonbooks.com/wont-back-down-bonus-epilogue-sign-up/

OTHER BOOKS BY HARPER JACKSON

WAYWARD SONS

- *Smoke on the Water* (prequel)
- *Won't Back Down*
- *All Along The Watchtower* (coming March 2025)

ABOUT THE AUTHOR

Harper Jackson has rescued her co-workers from a hostage situation, battled ninjas, and stopped international espionage —in her head anyway. Now that she's no longer busy devising ways to make staff meetings more entertaining, she's pouring that imagination into tales of breath-stealing, small-town romantic suspense. She believes that peach cobbler with ice cream is the best dessert ever and has a black belt in taekwondo to back it up. She lives in the Deep South with her husband and canine furbabies. Find out more about Harper and her books at https://harperjackson.com or explore the lighter side of her catalog as Kait Nolan at https://kait nolan.com.